FERROMANCER

IRON SOULS: BOOK ONE

BECCA ANDRE

CHAPTER 1

BRIAR STOOD ON THE TILLER deck of her boat, watching the banks of the canal slip past. They were making good time, even with a fully loaded boat, and barring any trouble getting through the last of the locks, they should be home in a few hours.

Lifting a hand to shield her eyes against the glare of the August sun, she squinted at the canal lock in the distance. Lock fifty was the first of the triple locks at Union Mills. The three closely spaced locks would lower them to the level of the Scioto River bottomland for the easy haul to Portsmouth, the southern terminus of the Ohio & Erie Canal.

Unlike the rest of her crew, Briar wasn't all that thrilled about the homecoming. Normally, she could expect a few quiet days relaxing on her docked boat, but that wouldn't be the case this time.

She rubbed a hand across her waistcoat pocket, feeling the folded telegram she had tucked inside. It had been waiting for her at the canal office in Waverly, and she had known before she opened it that it was from her cousin Andrew. Briar might be captain of the boat, but Andrew owned it. He was also her legal guardian and made a point of reminding her often—even if she was twenty-two. But Andrew was a problem for later.

She glanced back at Elijah her steersman. He leaned against the tiller, adjusting for the pull of the mules that walked the towpath two hundred feet ahead of them. On the levels between locks, steering could be a bit dull, but it was necessary. Without someone at the tiller, the boat would follow the mules that pulled it and collide with the bank.

"How's it look?" She waved a hand at the lock ahead of them. Eli's eyesight was better than hers. "Are the gates open?"

Like her, he lifted a hand to shield his eyes and studied the lock in the distance. "Looks like we get to double up," he answered. A boat must have recently exited the lock on their side, which meant the lock could accommodate two boats without draining or refilling. It also meant they wouldn't have to wait.

"Good news." She stepped up onto the deck formed by the roof of the aft cabin. "We're doubling up," she called to Jimmy, her bowsman.

He waved a hand and started across the catwalk that stretched along the center of the boat, connecting the roofs of three cabins and enabling the crew to traverse the boat quickly, especially when the two open cargo holds between the cabins were full.

A few minutes later, they were nearly to the lock. Briar eyed the passing shore and judging their speed adequate, shouted, "Headway!"

Zach, one of her drivers, unhooked the towline from the deadeye, the bolt atop the bow cabin, while his brother Benji moved the mule team to the side of the towpath.

Now it was up to Eli. The boat was only six inches narrower than the fifteen-foot-wide lock. Smashing the wooden vessel into the stone walls would be good for neither.

Briar folded her hands behind her back, not overly concerned. Her crew was good.

Their speed was more than enough to carry them forward into the lock. Eli steered the boat into the narrow confines with only the lightest of brushes of the rub rail against the lock wall.

Jimmy leapt from the boat and deftly looped the bow line around the snubbing post. The boat came to a smooth stop just inches from the miter gates on the other end of the lock. Perfect.

Briar returned to the tiller deck and took a seat on the rail beside Eli. "Does life get any better than this?" She grinned up at him.

"Perhaps, but as this is the only life I've known, I can't say."

Briar nodded in agreement. Having been raised on the canal, she was no judge for any other way of life. But that was fine with her. This was the life she wanted.

Jimmy and Zach left the boat to operate the paddle gear, which would open the wooden panel in the lower part of the gate and allow the water to drain from the lock chamber. The townsfolk who traveled the canals on passenger packets often complained about the delay the locks caused. Didn't they understand that the locks were what held the water in the canal? Without the locks capping each elevation level, the water would drain to the lowest level, leaving this artificial ditch empty and useless.

Eli cleared his throat drawing her attention back to him. "Sometimes, I do wonder what life might be like if the deck beneath my feet wasn't always moving."

"Dull."

"You've never considered—"

"Never. I'll be a boatman until I can no longer walk the deck."

Eli chuckled before growing serious once more. "Things change as you get older."

"Not for me." She squinted against the bright sunlight, gazing at the town in the distance. No, she wanted no part of that.

Locking down through the last of the triple locks, they started across a wide stretch of bottomland carved by both the Scioto and Ohio Rivers here where the two met. With their destination in sight, Jimmy broke into song—much to the rest of the crew's dismay.

Zach winced and moved away. Mute, Zach couldn't voice a complaint, so he beat a hasty retreat to the stable cabin in the center of the boat. Tending the spare mule team would certainly be a welcome respite.

"Someone really oughta tell Jimmy he can't sing," Eli muttered.

"I think he's been told," Briar answered, flinching as Jimmy missed a high note. "He just gets happy and forgets."

Eli shook his head, but like her, he was smiling. Lifting his eyes to the horizon, he pointed ahead of them. "Boat coming up."

Briar followed his gesture and saw that he was right. Another canal boat was moving toward them, heading in the opposite direction.

"They're running light," Eli added.

Benji was already looking back at her from the towpath, and she waved him on. Their loaded boat had the right of way. With only one towpath along the length of the canal, there were well-established rules of right of way. Loaded boats had right of way over empty boats, and if both boats were equal in terms of cargo, then the boat heading upstream was in the right.

"They're not pulling over," Eli said a moment later.

Briar was already observing the same thing. "Certainly they can see that we're loaded." They were hauling timber, the wood stacked several inches above the rooflines of the cabins.

"Lower your towline," a voice shouted from the other boat. "We have the right of it."

Briar exchanged a frown with Eli, then cupped her hands around her mouth. "We're fully loaded," she shouted back. "Let us pass."

"We're headed upstream," came the answer.

"Looks like things are about to get interesting." Briar exchanged a smile with Eli. "See what you'd miss if you became a townie?" She waved to Benji to stop the mules.

Eli chuckled and steered the boat toward the towpath, allowing it to gently bump the soft earthen bank to slow them to a gradual stop.

She watched the other boat do the same, though their steersman wasn't as adept and bumped the shore with considerably more force. An older man moved to the bow of the boat.

"No wonder," Briar grumbled, recognizing the man. "It's Dale Darby."

Eli grunted in understanding.

Briar crossed the catwalk to the bow of her boat and stopped beside Jimmy. With only a few feet now separating the two boats, she could easily converse with the other captain.

"What are you about?" she demanded, now close enough to be heard. "You can see we're running full."

"We're headed upstream." He glared at her, the wrinkles on his weathered face deepening. "Every one knows the upstream boat has right of way."

"Loaded boats take precedence. Are you getting senile, Captain?"

His face turned red, and he turned to the lanky man beside him. "Put the mouthy wench in her place."

"Here we go," Jimmy said, laughing as he left her. He thumped on the roof of the stable as he passed, calling for Zach. Eli had already leapt to shore.

Briar chewed the inside of her cheek in a futile effort to maintain a disapproving frown as the decks of both boats cleared. In a matter of seconds, the canal towpath became the scene of a fistfight to rival any the Guard Lock Tavern could boast. The mule team from each boat watched with indifference, waiting for the question of right of way to be settled.

Briar had no doubt who the victor would be, especially when Eli sent the other boat's champion flying into the canal with a single punch. Eli was an accomplished brawler. It didn't hurt that he was over six and half feet tall and built like an ox.

A smile escaped her lips with the accompanying splash, and she noticed Captain Darby staring at her with a disapproving scowl from the deck of his boat. He had to be over sixty—which was probably why he avoided the fisticuffs with her considerably younger crew.

Darby's daughter-in-law stood behind him, wringing her hands in her apron. She wouldn't be joining the fray. Without a woman in the fight, Briar was relegated to watching as well. A shame.

The contest on the bank was already tapering off. No surprise. Every member of her crew could hold his own, though Eli's large stature tended to deter prolonged engagements. Frequently, he prevented fights altogether.

"Lower your towline, Captain," she called to Darby. "We have the right of way."

A gesture, and Darby's driver, his nose bleeding and lip already swelling, urged their mules into motion, back the way they had come. With the boat moving, Darby's steersman was able to maneuver the boat to the heel path on the other side of the canal. His bowsman hurried to unhook their towline and let it sink to the bottom of the canal so Briar's boat could pass over it.

Her own crew returned to their duties, and soon, they were underway. Briar joined Eli on the tiller deck as their boat drew even with Darby's.

"Ain't fittin'," Darby declared, making no effort to keep his voice low.

"What's that, Captain?" Briar called to him.

His disapproving stare remained on her, and his gaze swept over her trousers. "Back in my day, the sideshows stuck to the show boats."

"Back in your day, you were sweeping out the stables," she told him, knowing her age bothered him far more than her gender. He hadn't become captain of his own boat until he was almost forty. She had been captain since she was twenty.

"Upstart wench."

"Watch your mouth, old man," Eli called to him.

"That'll do." She laid a hand on his thick forearm. "I'll kick his

6

ass myself, if I'm so inclined." She turned away from Darby. "Hop to it, boys. Home awaits."

A small cheer went up, and they picked up speed, leaving a grumbling Darby behind.

"You should have let Eli pound him," Jimmy said, stopping beside her.

"And how would that look? Me, letting Eli beat up that old fool."

Jimmy grinned, the split in his lip gaping open. "I could of done it."

"That wouldn't be much better. Now go tend that lip. If I bring you home looking like that, Mildred is going to pound *me*."

Jimmy grinned again at the mention of his new wife. They had set up housekeeping this past winter, and he could hardly sit still the closer they got to home.

Briar grinned up at Eli. "No, nothing beats this life."

He chuckled at her exuberance. "It's certainly not dull."

THE SUN WAS WELL PAST its zenith when they tied up at the dock in Portsmouth, but there were still plenty of men available to unload the boat and transfer the timber to her cousin's warehouse. At least she wouldn't have to listen to him complain about that.

"Captain?" Eli met her beside the gangplank, a rucksack of dirty laundry over one shoulder. He spent his nights at home with his sister and her family. "You're going home?"

"Unfortunately." She pulled the telegram from her pocket and waved it.

"Did Andrew say why he wanted you home?"

"He's got some kind of business situation to discuss. Why he feels the need to host a dinner party for such a matter is beyond me."

"No offense, Captain, but your cousin likes to put on airs."

"Don't I know it." She tugged her waistcoat straight.

"Shall I walk you to his door?" Eli offered.

Becca Andre

"I can manage. Besides, it's a little early. I thought I'd walk by the train yard and see these new locomotives everyone has been going on about."

"What are you up to Miss Briar?" Eli often dropped the *captain* when the crew wasn't around—or when he was attempting to temper some impulse of hers.

"I just want to see what's so great about them."

"Vandalizing a single locomotive is not going to stop the railroad from poaching our business."

"I'm not vandalizing anything. Where would you get such an idea?"

"Hmm." Eli pursed his lips. "There was that time old man Sweeney's boat sprung six different leaks—"

"His steersman bottomed out on a sandbar outside of Rushtown."

"Or when the Anderson Mill tried to cheat us, and their water wheel came loose from the side of the building."

"A pin worked itself loose, though it sounded to me like they got what they deserved."

Eli was trying not to smile. "How about the hornet's nest in Noah Cooper's outhouse? Or the rat that found its way into Eunice Walker's stew pot?"

"I have no control over nature."

"Uh-huh," Eli said. "I'm fairly certain that Herbert Johnson's fall into that empty lock wasn't an accident."

"Of course it wasn't. You punched him—after he tried to kiss me."

"Oh. Right." Eli shrugged his wide shoulders. "You were still involved."

She rolled her eyes. It would probably surprise him if he knew that was the closest she'd ever come to being kissed. Or maybe it wouldn't surprise him. Eli knew her well.

"I'm not going to vandalize a locomotive," she told him. "As you said, that would be pointless. Besides, I don't know enough about them to damage one properly."

8

Eli sighed.

"Now please, go see your sister," Briar said. "She'll need to get started on those clothes if she's to have them by tomorrow."

"Very well. I guess me and the boys can get you out of jail before we depart."

"Since when do I get caught?"

He gave her a knowing look.

"By someone other than you."

He grunted. "Good point."

She waved him on, and he finally walked away, smiling.

Eli. He was her oldest and best friend. He'd been keeping her out of scrapes since she was a kid. It was a role he fell back into very easily, but she was an adult now. She didn't need a guardian.

Briar stuffed her hand into her pocket to make certain her penknife was still there. Eli was right; it would be futile to vandalize a single locomotive. That didn't mean she had to pass up the opportunity.

The train yards were a busy place, and by the look of things, still expanding. A new warehouse was under construction, and a large stack of cross ties and rails suggested more track was soon to be laid.

Sighing, Briar stuffed her hands deeper into her pockets and gripped the knife for comfort. For years, she'd heard grumblings from her fellow boatmen that the railroad was eating away more and more of their business.

At first, she had shrugged it off. She never had trouble finding work. There seemed to be plenty to go around. But in recent years, the railroad had been expanding at an alarming pace, and she was beginning to notice that some of the more lucrative jobs were drying up. Transporting cargo by train was faster and often cheaper, but that wasn't anything new. What was new was the Martel locomotive. Supposedly, it didn't run on steam.

Briar had only a rudimentary understanding of how a steam engine worked. She couldn't even fathom how something could operate without one. Well, that wasn't true. There was a way, but she wasn't about to attribute the railroad's success to magic.

Not certain if she'd even recognize this new engine if she saw it, she wove her way through the train yard, eyeing the locomotives she found. Evening was approaching, and the activity seemed to be winding down.

Only one train looked ready to go. The boxcars were closed up, and the iron behemoth at the front of the line belched black smoke into the sky. Soot coated most of the locomotive and streaked several of the closest boxcars. Even the nearby warehouses had a light coating of the stuff. Why would anyone choose this over the clean travel along the canal?

Maybe that wasn't completely accurate. The canal itself might not be pristine, but her boat was spotless. She and her crew scrubbed it down each day.

Leaving the locomotive and its busy workmen behind, Briar made her way across the last section of tracks. The sun was dipping toward the horizon. She'd need to hurry so she wouldn't be late, but the lure of a set of tracks that entered a small warehouse drew her attention. Large doors on rollers stood open, and she could see the gleam of what might be a locomotive inside.

The building looked approachable—there were no guards or signs to order her away—so she walked inside. Evening light shone through the open doors, illuminating the front of what was indeed a locomotive. But this one was different. The streamlined exterior looked nothing like the awkward box-shaped monstrosities she had seen outside. There was something strangely attractive about this engine's smooth lines and sleek appearance. She didn't need to note the lack of a smokestack, or read the word *Martel* along the engine's flank to know she had found what she sought.

She gripped the knife, but couldn't bring herself to remove it from her pocket. It was clear to her creative heart that this engine was more than just function. It was art.

"Fool," she told herself. It was a railroad locomotive. This was the enemy.

The sound of voices drew her attention before she could force herself to deface the locomotive in some way. A trio of men was walking toward her building. By their overalls, they appeared to work here.

"...supposed to be locked," a man was saying to his companions.

"I didn't leave it open," another said.

"What's the big secret?" the third man asked.

"You haven't seen Martel's new engine?" The first man glanced back over his shoulder. A quick look around, and he led the other two toward the building.

Briar stepped back behind some crates, not wanting to be caught snooping in a building that was supposed to be locked.

The three men entered the building, the two newcomers voicing their surprise and awe.

"It actually works?" one man asked.

"I hear it runs on that new electricity all the papers have been going on about. It's supposed to work better than steam."

"But it's so delicate and... pretty."

The other men laughed at the description, though Briar found it accurate.

Taking advantage of their distraction, she crept back the way she had come, staying behind the crates. When she ran out of boxes, she crouched behind the last and peered out. The men had moved a little deeper into the building.

She took a deep breath, then sprinted the last ten feet to the open door.

Expecting a shout at any moment, she rounded the door, and keeping close to the wall, slipped around the corner. The building was at the end of the line and apparently meant to be an enclosed space to work on, or perhaps store trains. The back of the structure was bordered by a narrow road with the city streets just beyond.

Crossing the road, Briar ducked into the nearest alley. No shout had come. Stopping, she bent over to grip her knees and regain her composure.

The sound of voices carried to her down the narrow alley. She was no longer concerned about being caught where she shouldn't be, but this wasn't the best part of town. It would be better to cut back across the train yard.

"You don't have the power to kill me," one voice said, making no attempt to speak softly.

Briar was turning away, but hesitated. The speaker didn't sound all that concerned if his life was indeed threatened.

"He's coming for you, you know?" the same man said, his tone smug. "I've already told him you're here. Killing me won't change th—"

Whatever he was about to say cut out in a gurgle.

Briar froze where she stood.

Suddenly, a bright silver-white flash of light lit up the alley that intersected hers.

What the hell? It was far too bright to be the strike of a match or the unshuttering of a lantern. For that matter, it wasn't dark enough for the light to show up that well.

She bounced on the balls of her feet for a couple of heartbeats. Eli liked to remind her that curiosity killed the cat. She liked to point out that a cat had nine lives. Hopefully, she wasn't about to risk one, but she *had* to see what had made that light.

Walking on her toes, she approached the corner where the two alleys met. Her heart beat quicker, but it wasn't in fear. This was like stepping up to the edge of a great height and looking over. Or going toe to toe with a foe twice her size. Eli would have a fit, but the truth was, she lived for moments like this.

Muscles tense, she crouched a little and peeked around the corner.

Whatever had made the light was gone now. A man in a long black cloak had his back to her, squatting beside something on the ground. He shifted a little, and she saw that the *something* was another man.

The cloaked man leaned back, lifting an object in his hands. Was he robbing the fallen man? The item he had taken glinted silver in the evening light.

He rose to his feet, his back still to Briar's position. She couldn't see what he did, but she suspected he might be tucking away what he had stolen. A golden nimbus suddenly shone before him. Was he lighting a pipe?

In the golden glow, Briar had a better view of the man on the ground. His coat and shirt had been pulled open, but where there should be a chest was a gaping hole—as if his heart had been cut out.

CHAPTER 2

BRIAR JERKED BACK AROUND THE corner, pressing her back to the wall and a hand to her mouth. She'd once seen a man killed in a tavern fight, but this was different. What kind of man cut open another after he had killed him? She didn't want to stick around to find out.

Turning, she ran back the way she had come, careful to keep her step light and soundless. She skirted the train yard, running behind a series of warehouses until she reached the houses beyond.

Slowing to a jog, she rounded a corner and collided with someone. Hands seized her shoulders to keep her upright. Imagining that the cloaked man had found her, Briar prepared a scream, then looked up into Eli's frowning face.

"Miss Briar?"

She gripped his arm and after a quick glance over her shoulder, pulled him along with her. "I just saw a man murdered."

"What?" Eli looked back the way she had come. "Were you seen?"

"I don't think so, but I didn't stick around to find out."

"What happened?" Eli asked as they walked, his long stride keeping up with her rapid pace.

"I found the Martel locomotive, but I didn't get a chance to get a look up close because some railroad workers showed up."

"You mean, you didn't get a chance to vandalize it."

"Honestly, I don't know if I could. You should have seen it. I swear it was more art than locomotive."

Eli looked over, his brow raised in amusement. He had never understood her artsy leanings, but he humored her. His expression quickly sobered. "And the murder?"

"I took an alley to avoid being seen and came upon two men, just after the deed was done. I got a good look at the body. It had been cut open."

"It was a knife fight?" Eli asked. "A deep gut shot would lay open a man."

"I didn't witness the killing blow."

"Let me guess. You heard the commotion and snuck closer for a better look."

She decided not to tell him about the light. "I thought it was just an argument."

Eli fell silent, and when she glanced up, she could see the hardening of his jaw. He wasn't happy with her.

"I don't need a lecture," she said, hoping to cut him off before he got started. "What are you doing here, anyway?" She tried to turn the focus on him. "You came looking for me, didn't you?"

"You're a magnet for trouble, Miss Briar."

"Admit it. Your life would be boring without me."

"True." A smile broke through his stony expression, but he quickly sobered. "Shouldn't we report this murder?"

Briar frowned. "I didn't actually witness it. I heard voices, and saw a body and a man in a cloak. That wouldn't be much help." It certainly wouldn't be worth the trouble Andrew would give her for drawing such unsavory attention to the family.

"The murderer is still at large," Eli pointed out.

"Those men knew each other. It was an argument gone wrong. I doubt the cloaked guy is out seeking another victim."

"Unless he saw you."

Briar sighed. "He didn't. Stop worrying about it." She might as well be talking to Big Red, the most stubborn mule on her boat;

telling Eli not to worry was wasted breath. He excelled at seeing mountains where there were only molehills.

They walked in silence, moving away from the banks of the Ohio River, climbing the town's rolling hills. The streets were now cobblestone, and the houses larger. They turned down Andrew's street, and Briar could see the oil lamps glowing to either side of his front door, as well as every window in the house.

A carriage had stopped before the house, and Briar watched a well-dressed man and woman exit the carriage and start up the walk toward the house. This was going to be a miserable evening.

"I guess I'd better use the back door," Briar muttered. Andrew would have a fit if she showed up in her everyday clothes, even though this pair of pants bore no holes.

"I reckon so," Eli agreed and started down the alley between Andrew's house and the one next door.

The stable yard behind the house was a busy place. Briar stepped up on the back stoop, eyeing the commotion. What she wouldn't give for a quiet evening on her boat. A smooth glass of whiskey and her fiddle would have been all the company she needed.

"I'll wait for you here," Eli said, taking a seat on the stone steps.

"This has the look of a long wait."

"You were almost murdered this evening."

"I was not. No one even saw me."

"Are you certain?"

She wasn't, but she didn't want to admit it. "Fine. Suit yourself." She pushed open the door and stepped into the back hall. Eli's sigh followed her inside, making her want to sigh in exasperation. She was already over her brush with death, why wasn't he?

Shaking her head, she toed off her boots and went in search of Molly. Unfortunately, the toe of one sock had a hole large enough to show one big toe, but there was nothing to be done for that now.

She found Molly in the kitchen, deep in conversation with

her housekeeper. But the conversation came to an abrupt end the moment Molly saw her.

"Bridget! Where have you been?" Molly grasped her arm and immediately steered her into the hall. "Mr. Rose has been beside himself with worry."

Briar's annoyance at Molly's use of her given name was momentarily overridden by her amusement at the woman's insistence on calling her husband by his sire name. But then, Molly had a very different upbringing from Briar's. The vexation on her face made their differences clear.

"You haven't bathed or—"

"I bathed this morning," Briar said.

"There's a smear of mud on your cheek."

"It'll wipe off." Briar rubbed her cheek.

"This is a disaster," Molly moaned the words, her smooth forehead wrinkling with dismay. "Dinner will be served in half an hour and you're not dressed." Judging by Molly's elegant gown and how elaborately her light brown hair was styled, Briar knew this would be more than just a matter of changing clothes.

Molly pulled her to the back stairs. "Come on. Time slips past while you argue."

"I can change in minutes."

"This is a very important evening for Mr. Rose," Molly said over her shoulder as she guided Briar up the stairs. "His prospective business partner arrived last night, and will join us shortly."

"What exactly is this new business?"

Molly opened the door to Briar's room. "If you had gotten here sooner, Mr. Rose could have explained it to you. I have no head for such things." She walked to the closet and dug through the sparse collection of dresses hanging inside. Briar tried to spend as little time as possible here. Unfortunately, the canal froze in the winter, forcing her to spend several long months beneath Andrew's roof.

"You must have some idea," Briar said, following her.

"It's a manufacturing job, I understand." Molly selected a gown and turned to face her. "This one, I think." She laid the emerald green gown on the bed. "It goes well with your eyes."

Briar ignored that, her attention on the travel trunk pushed against the far wall. She stepped closer, eyeing the odd silver lock hanging from the hasp. "What's this?" She prayed it wasn't more dresses.

"Oh dear. I forgot to have that sent downstairs. Mr. Martel got in late last night, and Mr. Rose had him installed in this room. He's supposed to take a room downtown tonight."

"Mr. Martel?" Briar asked. No, it couldn't be. "Mr. Martel, the railroad engineer?"

"Yes." Molly's face brightened. "You know him?"

"He's the designer of the new smokeless locomotives."

"Locomotives, that's right." Molly smiled. "That's what Mr. Rose wants to build."

Briar stared at her cousin's wife. Didn't she understand that the railroads could put the canal industry out of business? Especially with these new engines?

"Well, come on." Molly waved a hand at her. "Disrobe."

"I can dress myself."

"Last time I left you to dress for dinner, you climbed out the window."

"Molly."

She crossed her arms. "I'm not leaving until you change. Mr. Rose gave me explicit instructions."

Briar was half tempted to tell her what Andrew could do with his instructions, but stopped herself. Molly was all about proper etiquette and being a good wife. She truly got upset when she failed to live up to those expectations. Molly drove Briar a bit crazy, but the truth was, she genuinely liked the woman. Molly was a good person. How she ended up with Andrew was the part Briar would never understand.

"Please don't make me disappoint him." Molly's brow wrinkled.

"Fine." Briar tried to ignore Molly's grateful smile as she crossed to the bed, unbuttoning her waistcoat. It would have been so much easier if Andrew had married an ass like himself.

"WILL THAT DO, MISS?" THE maid asked, giving Briar a nervous glance in the mirror. After seeing Briar into her gown, Molly had left her with the maid, instructing them both to hurry.

"Yes, yes, that's fine." Briar waved away her concern before she could start back in with her brushes and ribbons. Briar's red hair was now piled atop her head in some intricate fashion with long tendrils left to curl around her face. Briar would be surprised if she lasted the entire dinner before she was pulling it down.

"Will you be needing anything else?" the maid asked, still looking a bit nervous. She must have also fallen prey to Andrew's instructions to make Briar presentable. Poor girl.

"You may go," Briar told her. "I'll be right down."

The girl dropped her an awkward curtsy and hurried from the room, probably to report to Molly that she had finished.

Wasting no time, Briar closed the door behind her. She wanted to nose around inside the travel trunk, but the lock looked daunting. Selecting a couple of hairpins from the vanity table she had just left, she squatted beside the trunk and eyed the lock. This wasn't going to be easy.

It took a few minutes to bend the hairpins, but she soon formed one into a serviceable pick and the other into a makeshift tension wrench. She slid one hand beneath the lock, surprised by its weight and odd warmth. She had been expecting a heavy iron lock, but this seemed to be made of something different.

Sliding the pick into the narrow hole in the lock's face, she felt for the tumblers, just to get an idea of what she was up against. Jimmy had taught her to pick locks last fall when an early freeze had stranded them for almost a week just south of Columbus. She hadn't questioned him on how he had acquired such a skill, and he hadn't asked her why she wanted to learn it.

Now, that skill was going to come in handy. Maybe.

The pin tapped against something in the bowels of the lock. The lock Jimmy had taught her on hadn't felt like this. She pushed a little harder. Were the inner workings laid out differently? What if—

The pick slipped free without warning and bit into the heel of her hand.

"Damn it," she whispered. Blood welled from the minor wound, and she brought it to her mouth, hoping to lick it away before it got on her dress. Molly would have a fit.

She took her hand from her mouth a moment later and was relieved to find the bleeding nearly stopped. A smear of blood marred the pick, and she started to wipe it on her dress, but stopped herself. Life was so much easier on her boat.

She returned her makeshift pick to the lock for another inspection before she inserted the tension wrench. The pick had barely slipped within the hole when the lock suddenly… dissolved.

Briar released the lock with a gasp.

"What the hell," she whispered, watching the lock morph before her eyes. Four legs emerged from the sphere, followed by a head on a long, slender neck. An equally slim tail appeared, and of all the crazy things, a set of silver wings. The body grew more streamlined, formed from overlapping metal plates that fit together with astonishing intricacy.

Briar pulled away so quickly, she landed on her backside.

The creature hanging from the hasp raised its head, regarding her with curiosity. It blinked a set of gunmetal-blue eyes that looked like gems. No, not a creature. A dragon. A little metal dragon. The workmanship would have been a marvel, but the fact that it was moving spoke of something more.

"Dear Lord," Briar whispered. "An automaton." Such creations were the work of a metal mage. A ferromancer. And it was whispered that these mechanical wonders got their animation from a trapped soul.

But how had it come to be here? All the ferromancers and their automatons had been destroyed twenty years ago. Europe's systematic destruction of not only the metal mages, but also their technology, at the hands of the Scourge—an equally suspect organization, had been the stuff of horror stories since she was a child.

The metal dragon dropped to the floor and took a step toward her, its tiny nails clicking against the hardwood.

Briar tensed, not sure what to expect. It was only slightly bigger than her hand, and it moved with such caution that it seemed more fearful of her than she was of it.

It took another step, then leaned toward her, seeming to sniff at her knee.

Slowly, she held out her hand, offering the creature her palm, much the way she would greet a new dog.

The little dragon pulled back, regarding her hand with suspicion before it leaned forward once more, as if sniffing her hand. Its cool nose bumped against her fingers, and she smiled.

"Aren't you cute?" She carefully lifted a finger and rubbed it beneath the chin.

A soft whirring noise came from the creature, the sound not unlike a purr.

"You like that?" she asked.

It rubbed the side of its head against her finger, then climbed over her knee and into her lap. It sought out her other hand and nudged her until she petted it once more.

Briar laughed. "You must have been made from a gentle soul."

The little dragon made another whirring noise, then abruptly leapt to her shoulder.

Briar gasped at the suddenness of the move, but the creature slid around behind her neck to her other shoulder where it dropped to its belly. Its scales were surprisingly warm against the side of her throat.

"Don't mess my hair," she admonished, "or I'll never hear the end of it."

The creature gave her a whirr of agreement, and she wondered how much it understood. If it had truly been made from a human soul, it might understand her very well. Goosebumps rose on her arms at the notion. To distract herself, she returned to her knees and opened the trunk.

"Let's see what your master has in here," she said to the dragon.

It didn't seem to have a problem with that, so she pushed back the lid.

The trunk did contain clothing—well-made men's apparel from what she could see—but that wasn't all. There were also several books and half a dozen large scrolls of paper. Curious, Briar lifted out the scroll on top and began to unroll it. She soon found herself staring at a mechanical drawing of some sort. The schematic had been drawn by someone who wielded a pen with great skill. There were no marked out lines or retraces. The ink was unsmudged, and each line flowed without waver. The composer had known exactly what he was doing.

Various components and dimensions were labeled in the same elegant hand, but Briar couldn't make sense of most of it. She unrolled the scroll a little more to read the caption. *Life Circuit*. What exactly did that mean?

The little dragon shifted against her neck, perhaps sensing her unease.

Briar's attention dropped back to the drawing. It was a box-like structure, labeled with nothing more sinister than *input* and *output*, and a tangle of lines in the center. The lines were broken up with odd symbols she didn't recognize. A few more moments' study offered no more insight, so she rolled the scroll and reached for another.

She didn't need to read the title of this drawing to understand what it was. The intricately drawn schematic was clearly a railroad locomotive. The title, written in the same elegant hand as the other drawing, declared it The Martel Automatic Locomotive.

"Automatic?" Briar whispered. As in, it did things on its own? Like an automaton?

She studied the schematic closer. Like the other, this drawing was densely labeled with dimensions and terminology she didn't recognize. She saw no mention of anything to do with electric power—as the railroad worker had suggested—but unless it was spelled out, she doubted she would recognize it.

She was about to roll up the scroll when she found something truly disturbing. Near the conductor's compartment was a smallish box labeled *Soul Chamber*.

"My Lord." Briar stared at the schematic. Mr. Martel was a ferromancer.

CHAPTER 3

BRIAR STARED AT THE SCHEMATIC, unable to believe what she held in her hands. If anyone else saw what the railroad's prize engineer was designing—

A loud knock at her door made her jump.

"Bridget?" Andrew's demanding tone carried easily through the door.

Something fell from her shoulder and landed with surprising weight in her lap. She looked down to see the silver lock lying against the fabric of her gown. Andrew had frightened the little dragon back into its other shape.

"Just a moment." She hastily rolled the scroll and returned it to the trunk. Closing the lid, she considered the lock for just a moment before snapping it in place.

She pushed herself to her feet and hurried to the door, pulling it open to reveal Andrew's frowning face.

His green eyes swept over her, but his sour expression didn't change. "Late as always, but at least you no longer look like a man."

Briar crossed her arms. "What's this Molly tells me about your new business venture? You want to build locomotives for the railroad?"

"Yes. It's an amazing opportunity for us."

"Us?" Briar demanded. "The railroad is our competitor."

"No, the railroad is our future. The canals are an antiquated mode of transportation that has served its purpose."

"Antiquated? The canals are what keep your warehouses stocked."

"I'm selling the dock warehouses. And the boat."

Briar stilled. "What?" She must not have heard him right. "You're selling my boat? Your father's boat?"

"I do not make business decisions based on sentiment."

"You can't do this."

"I own the boat; I can. Now come downstairs. I want to introduce you to Mr. Martel." Andrew turned toward the door.

"I don't want to meet him."

Andrew stopped and slowly turned to face her. "Do not test me in this. I am your guardian—"

"I'm an adult."

"And as such," he continued, ignoring her, "it falls to me to provide for your future. I humored your captaining stint because it provided the funds to expand my business. Now that I have the money and the connections, it is time to move into the next phase."

Dread clenched Briar's stomach. "What is the next phase?"

"Expanding the train yards and building a manufacturing plant."

"And how do I factor in?"

"You might be nearly a spinster, but you are not unattractive. A wealthy older man might find you charming, provided you don't speak."

Briar glared at him.

"Or a nice young man who knows no better," Andrew continued. "Come now. If he's returned, I will introduce you to Mr. Martel."

"And which is he, the old man or the young?" Briar asked.

Andrew didn't answer. He left the room, expecting her to follow.

Briar glanced back at the trunk. Did Andrew know his precious Mr. Martel was a ferromancer? Would he even care? As long as Andrew turned a profit, he'd work with a necromancer—if such a talent existed.

"Bridget," Andrew called.

Huffing out a breath—and a few choice words—she started after him. There had to be a way to stop this. He couldn't make her give up her life on the canal. She had grown up on the canal, as had Andrew. But unlike Andrew, she had no desire to become a townie. The canal life was in her blood.

They reached the base of the stairs, and Briar glanced toward the back door, longing to bolt through it. She glimpsed Eli through the window beside the door. He still waited on the back stoop. An idea forming, she called out to Andrew.

"I'll be right there."

Andrew glanced back with a frown, but she hurried on before he spoke.

"I need to send Eli back to the boat. It looks like it'll be a long evening."

Andrew waved permission. "Don't dawdle."

Briar gritted her teeth to hold in her response, and settled for a nod. As soon as Andrew turned down the hall, she hurried to the back door and stepped outside.

"Miss Briar?" Eli's eyes swept over her, widening a little.

"I've been forced to dress as a townie so Andrew can present me to his new business partner."

Eli frowned. "Why?"

"Why do you think? He wants me to find a husband."

Eli's frown deepened. "But he needs you to captain the boat."

"Not after he sells the boat to help finance his new locomotive building business."

"What?"

"You heard me. The business partner he wants to introduce me to? It's none other than Mr. Martel of the new Martel Locomotives."

Eli's bushy brows climbed his forehead.

Briar crossed her arms. "Yeah, the guy who can singlehandedly put the canal industry out of business."

Eli's expression turned considering. "He must be a wealthy man, Miss Briar."

"You're not seriously suggesting that I go along with Andrew's plans."

"Well, no, but—"

"I'm a boatman. I can provide for myself just fine. I don't need a husband."

Eli fell silent.

"And I'm not about to let my cousin destroy my—our way of life."

Eli studied her, a look between concern and amusement warring to be the dominant expression on his face. "You're up to something."

"I learned a little something about Mr. Martel that I suspect my cousin doesn't know."

Eli gave her a questioning look, but didn't speak.

"He spent last night in my room, and his trunk was still there. I went through it."

Amusement was definitely winning on Eli's face.

"I suspect he's a ferromancer."

Eli's jaw dropped open.

"That trunk is currently upstairs and unguarded. With it, we could destroy the railroad's reputation. After what happened in Europe, no one will buy something made by a ferromancer."

"But ferromancers aren't around anymore. They've been gone since I was a kid."

"Apparently one survived."

"I don't want you meeting him, Miss Briar. Them metal mages are said to be cold-blooded killers."

"He's not going to kill me; he wants to work with my family. So while I keep him entertained, you're going to nab his trunk."

"You're going to rob a man who can steal your soul and lock it in iron?"

"Sounds kinda poetic, doesn't it? I'll have to write a song about it when we're done."

"Miss Briar."

"If I turn that trunk over to the newspaper in Columbus, the

Martel Locomotives will be off the market, and we can keep our way of life."

Eli pressed his lips together, clearly seeing the benefit of her plan.

"Now, I need to get back in there before Andrew comes looking for me. You'll take the trunk to the boat?"

"Yes, Captain."

Briar nodded and turned back toward the door.

"Miss Briar?"

She looked over her shoulder.

"Be careful."

"I can take care of myself." She pushed open the back door and stepped into the house. Time to see how she fared against a ferromancer.

BRIAR PICKED AT HER ROASTED duck, trying in vain to come up with some excuse that would allow her to return to the boat to check on Eli. Mr. Martel had not shown for dinner, and she could just imagine the man catching Eli walking through the streets carrying his trunk with the controversial drawing. Beyond that, it had occurred to Briar that she had failed to warn Eli that the lock could transform into a dragon. Boatmen tended to be a superstitious lot, and her crew was no different. Hopefully, Eli would just store the trunk in her cabin for safekeeping.

"Is the duck not to your liking?" Molly whispered, leaning close.

"No, it's fine. I'm not all that hungry." Briar answered in an equally soft tone, aware of her cousin's other guests. She didn't know the three other couples seated around the table, but she was sure they all held positions of importance here in town. Andrew wouldn't have invited them otherwise.

"I feared it had dried out since we waited so long to begin."

Andrew looked up from his plate. "It was rude to begin without our honored guest."

Who was now two hours late. Briar was tempted to add a quip about never being that late herself, but she wasn't in the mood for another fight. Though Andrew probably wouldn't rise to the bait with so many of his wealthy peers present.

The door opened and the housekeeper joined them. "Excuse me, sir, but a message just arrived from Mr. Martel."

Andrew held out his hand, and the housekeeper placed the folded piece of paper on his palm. Bobbing him a curtsey, she hurried from the room.

Molly laid down her silverware with a clatter, her face anxious as she watched Andrew read the letter. He sighed and set it aside.

"What is it, my dear?" Molly asked. "Was I wrong to serve the meal? Is he on his way?" She gripped her hands in her lap.

"No," Andrew's tone was curt. "He won't be joining us this evening. Some business at the train yard has kept him apparently. I assume he took rooms in town." He frowned at the letter. "Whomever he employed to pen this letter should not be allowed to hold a quill."

Briar leaned closer to see the letter and recognized Jimmy's penmanship—or the lack thereof.

She pushed herself to her feet. "I guess I can return to the boat."

Andrew looked up with a frown.

"You don't need me, and I have work to do." She made it through the door and into the hall. Unfortunately, Andrew followed her.

"You don't just get up and leave a dinner party."

"When I'm done eating, I leave the table." She started for the stairs.

"I'm selling the boat, Bridget. You've made your last run."

She turned to face him. "What about the crew?"

"I'm sure they can find another boat to sign on."

"They need to know." She turned away once more.

"I want you here at lunch tomorrow, dressed appropriately."

She gritted her teeth, but managed to remain silent as he returned to the room.

Alone in the hall, and away from her annoying cousin, her worries returned, now with the added concern of why Jimmy was making excuses for Mr. Martel.

Lifting her skirt to her knees, she took the steps two at a time. She ran down the hall to her room and skidded to a stop on the threshold. The trunk was gone.

She snatched up her everyday clothing, and not bothering to change, stuffed it along with her boots into a satchel and ran from the room.

THE MOON WAS HIGH OVERHEAD when Briar arrived at the dock. Lamps had been lit on the deck of her boat, illuminating the transom and the artfully drawn ring of roses encircling *Briar Rose*, the name of the vessel. Most people thought the boat had been named for her, but in truth, her uncle had nicknamed her after the boat. She had loved that. She hated the name Bridget.

The gangplank was down, and she was already aboard before the crew even noticed.

"Cap'n Briar?" Jimmy sprang to his feet, followed an instant later by Zach and Benji.

"What are you doing here, Jimmy?" she asked. Unlike Zach and Benji who lived on the boat during the canal season, Jimmy had a home.

Silence fell over her crew. It suddenly occurred to her that she was still wearing the green gown.

"Cat got your tongue?" she asked, letting her exasperation color her tone.

"Eli called me back," Jimmy spoke up. "He said he came aboard to stow a new trunk for you—then someone tried to nab it."

"Where is Eli?"

"The forward cargo hold—making our guest more comfortable."

"The thief is still here?"

"Aye." Jimmy nodded.

Briar hurried off, following the catwalk down the center of the boat until she reached midship. Once on the other side of the stable, she dropped down into the cargo hold. Without a cargo, the large space was empty. Or it should be. A lantern hung from the catwalk overhead.

"Eli?" For some reason, she kept her voice low—which was silly. This was her boat.

"Captain?" Eli's large form materialized out of the shadows.

"What happened?"

"I got the trunk, like you asked, but no sooner was it stowed than I found this fellow sneaking aboard." He led Briar to where the lantern hung. Opening the shutter, Eli illuminated a man stretched across a couple of hay bales set against the stable wall. A bloody cloth was wrapped around his forehead.

"He's out cold," Eli said.

"Did you hit him?" she asked, a bit alarmed by the blood-covered rag.

"He fought like a mad man. I didn't mean to hit him that hard."

"You're a big guy." Certainly bigger than this fellow, though it was hard to tell in the dim light and with the man lying down.

"It's just a cut," Eli added. "You know how head wounds bleed."

She knew that firsthand. Lifting the lantern from the hook, she moved it closer to the man lying on the hay. "Is this Mr. Martel?"

"He walked onto the boat, demanding we return his property, and you can see how finely he's dressed."

Eli was right. The suit was expensive—and splattered with blood. She moved the lantern up his body, pausing to hold it over his face. His skin was pale, and his forehead bound in that blood-soaked rag, but he didn't appear much older than her twenty-two years.

"I thought he'd be middle-aged, at least," she said.

"This could be his valet."

She unbuttoned his coat and pulled it open to reveal the silk waistcoat. Valets weren't typically dressed this well, but Mr. Martel was most likely a very wealthy man.

A watch chain dangled from the man's pocket. She gingerly pulled it out. The case shone with a soft golden glow, illuminating a curling letter G etched into the surface. She pushed the button, and the cover swung open, the action smooth. The timepiece was clearly well cared for. Inside was a typical watch face, which was disappointing. She expected a ferromancer to have something a little more... elaborate as his personal time-keeping device.

She snapped the watch closed and flipped it over. Another engraving had been worked into the metal, this one more worn. She leaned closer. *Gray, never forget.*

Tipping the watch toward the light, she tried to see if it was signed.

A hand seized her wrist and she gasped, looking down into the slate-blue eyes staring up at her.

She opened her mouth, about to speak, but his eyes rolled back in his head and his hand fell from her wrist.

Feeling guilty that he'd caught her snooping, she tucked the watch back into his pocket.

"Bind him and gag him, should he wake again. Then get to your station. I'm getting underway."

"I thought your cousin was going to sell the boat."

"He can't sell it if it isn't here. And he can't start a locomotive manufacturing business if he has no one to design the things."

"You're going to kidnap Mr. Martel?"

"I wouldn't call it kidnapping."

Eli frowned. "What would you call it?"

"Stopping another megalomaniacal metal mage and preserving our way of life."

Eli frowned at the unconscious man. "He doesn't look old enough to be a meglo-whats-it."

She turned away. "Just do as I ask and get ready to cast off." She left the cargo hold, smiling to herself. It was time to take her destiny into her own hands.

MORNING FOUND THE *BRIAR ROSE* floating along the canal a few miles south of Waverly. A night run wasn't unusual on the canal, but it made things harder. It was more difficult to judge their speed and see obstacles in their path—even with the bow-mounted Bullseye lantern shining on the towpath.

Meeting another boat also presented a challenge. It was hard enough to keep the towlines from tangling in the daylight hours, let alone at night. But the hassle had been worth it. With twenty miles between her and her cousin, he wouldn't be catching up with her anytime soon. He probably wouldn't even notice her absence until she failed to show up for lunch, and even then, he would be more concerned about Mr. Martel's absence.

With the sun well up, and confident that her crew could handle any obstacle now, Briar climbed down the ladder into the cabin she had called home since she was three years old. She crossed the small space in a few strides and ducked into her stateroom—a curtained-off area that held her bunk—to change clothes. The dress was an annoyance on deck, and she was glad to be finished with it. She was half tempted to toss it in the canal, but it would make more sense to sell it. After all, she needed every dime she could get her hands on if she was going to buy the boat.

Leaving her room a few minutes later, she stepped back out into the main cabin and spied Mr. Martel's trunk beneath the table mounted on the wall. Fortunately, it was a small trunk and didn't take up too much room—and there wasn't any room to spare.

Briar was relieved to see the lock still in place. She had been concerned about what the little metal dragon might get into down here. Seeing the lock now, it was hard to believe that it was anything other than what it appeared to be.

She knelt beside the trunk and tentatively touched the lock. The metal surface dimpled at her touch, and she jerked her hand away with a gasp. A swirl of molten silver, and suddenly the little dragon clung to the hasp instead of the lock.

It emitted a happy metal-on-metal scraping noise. The gray-blue eyes blinked up at her, then it leapt across the space that separated them. Like last time, Briar fell on her butt and the little dragon settled on her shoulder.

"I guess I didn't imagine it." Briar reached up to rub a finger beneath the metal chin.

The dragon cooed.

"How are you, Lock?" she asked. "Do you care if I call you that?"

A few clicks and a whirr of hidden gears was the answer. It really did seem to understand her.

Leaving the little dragon on her shoulder, she opened the trunk and pulled out the top scroll, reaffirming that it was real as well. But was it truly ferromancy? She didn't want to take it to the newspaper, create a big stir, then discover that it was a mundane design with some silly labeling. But who could she ask?

She snapped her fingers. "Uncle Liam." Liam Adams wasn't a blood relation, but he and Uncle Charlie had been good friends. She had spent a lot of time with him and his wife when she was a child. They even referred to themselves as her godparents. Liam was well educated and had even lived in Europe as a younger man. Most importantly, he was a talented inventor.

Taking out her pen and paper, she took a seat at her small table and composed a quick letter. Uncle Liam lived in Columbus. If she sent him the plans via the much quicker mail service, he could study them before she arrived.

A knock sounded on the hatch above her. "Cap'n Briar?"

Lock let out a little squeak, then he scampered down the front of her waistcoat to her pocket and slipped inside.

Curious, she reached in the pocket and pulled out the now familiar silver lock. Returning it to her pocket, she climbed the ladder to the upper deck. Eli waited a few feet away.

"What is it?" she asked him.

"Your prisoner is awake."

She frowned, not caring for his choice of words, but she could hardly argue that Mr. Martel was anything else. "Is that a problem?" she asked.

"He's demanding to see you." Eli's thick brows drew together. "And he's really not happy."

CHAPTER 4

BRIAR FOLLOWED ELI ALONG THE catwalk toward midship. The morning air was cool, and since they had just switched mule teams, they were making good time. The bank slipped past at four miles per hour. It helped that they were running light, but she planned to pick up a load. With what she had saved, a few good runs this summer should net her enough to buy the boat from Andrew. After all, he cared only about the money. If she bought the boat and removed the need for him to finance her, she was certain he would be glad to see her go.

The sunlight beat down into the empty cargo hold. Eli had been kind enough to situate their guest beneath the shade of the catwalk, but that would change as the sun moved across the sky.

Briar dropped into the hold and saw that her prisoner was sitting up on his bale of hay. The bloody rag was no longer wrapped around his forehead, exposing a small scabbed-over cut. But a second rag had been cinched around his mouth and his hands bound behind his back.

He watched her approach, his eyes narrowed, but he didn't look so much angry as suspicious.

"Remove his gag," she told Eli.

He stepped forward and did as she asked, tugging the gag from her prisoner's mouth. The younger man worked his jaw a few times, his eyes remaining on her, though he didn't speak.

"I do apologize for the rough treatment," she said to him.

A frown shadowed his eyes, but he remained silent.

"You are Mr. Martel, are you not?"

"Do I look like a railroad engineer?" he demanded, his words accented. Was he British?

"Then who are you? His servant?"

His eyes flickered to Eli before returning to her.

"Eli, would you leave us?"

"Captain, I don't think—"

"He's bound. I'll be fine."

Eli studied her for a moment, then nodded. "I'll be up top." His gaze held their prisoner's as he spoke. The pair stared each other down before Eli turned and entered the bow cabin, which served as the crew's bunkhouse. Using the ladder inside to reach the upper deck, Eli gave them some privacy.

Briar turned back to her prisoner. She could tell by the movement of his shoulders that he was testing his bonds.

"The tying of knots is a skill honed by all boatmen," she told him. "You won't be slipping those."

He rose to his feet. The man was easily half-a-head taller than she was. He hadn't seemed all that big when lying down last night. "You will give me the property you stole." His soft, accented voice was so cold a chill slid down her spine. "And you will allow me to alight from this barge."

"Boat," she corrected. "And no, I will not."

His cold gaze moved over her as if he sized her up—and came away unimpressed. "Solon must be desperate indeed if this is the best thief he could secure."

"Thief?" she demanded.

"I assume Solon agreed to some reimbursement for your trouble. How else would you describe this dark errand you have clearly agreed to do?"

She'd had enough with his cold, condescending tone, and his implication that she took money to commit a crime. This was a valiant effort to save the livelihood of thousands of canal workers like herself.

"If you're not Mr. Martel, then why do you care about what becomes of his property?" Was *he* the thief?

"His interests are my interests."

"You do work for him."

He didn't confirm or deny the accusation.

"Who the hell are you?" she demanded.

He regarded her a moment in silence. "John Grayson. My friends call me Gray."

She remembered the name and monogram inscribed on his watch. Perhaps he was telling the truth. "Well, Mr. Grayson," she emphasized the name, letting him know that he sure as hell wasn't her friend, "I have no clue what you're rattling on about. My intentions are noble. I'm not going to sit by and let the railroad destroy my way of life."

He frowned, but didn't comment.

"I'm sure the public will feel the same when they learn that Martel is a ferromancer."

Mr. Grayson visibly stiffened.

"I see I have your attention."

"What would you know of such things?" His tone remained cold.

"I've seen his plans."

"How would you manage that? The trunk was locked, and I hold the only key."

"You mean this lock?" She pulled the silver lock from her pocket.

"How—" He didn't get to finish his question before the lock transformed into the little automaton. With a squeal of some internal mechanism, it leapt from her hand to his upper arm, scampering upward until it balanced on his shoulder. It moaned, the sound oddly forlorn, then rose up on its rear legs to sniff the wound above Grayson's eyebrow.

Grayson turned his head, muttering something.

The little dragon dropped back to its perch on his shoulder, emitting another soft moan. Then rubbed its nose against the side of his neck.

"I see you are familiar with Mr. Martel's security device."

"I'm the one who procured it, in London."

She eyed him. Was that where he hailed from? "You can buy such things there? Openly?"

"Before the Scourge, yes. Since then, it's not so easy."

She frowned, wondering what he knew of such things. Being near her age, Mr. Grayson couldn't have witnessed the destruction of the ferromancers, even if he did hail from that part of the world.

"So all of it, the Scourge, the ferromancers, it's true?" she asked, marveling that he had traveled so far and had seen so much.

"You're the one who claimed that Mr. Martel is a ferromancer."

"And you're the one with the little metal dragon cooing in recognition on your shoulder."

"Perhaps he is a wonder of mechanical design."

"He's a creature of independent thought and movement. Aren't you, Lock?"

The little dragon cooed.

"You do not name a construct!" Mr. Grayson looked furious.

Briar lifted a brow, pleased by the break in his cool, controlled demeanor. "Why not?"

He opened his mouth, then closed it, seeming at a loss for words. "You just don't."

"Good reason."

"Do not meddle with what you don't understand." He spoke between clenched teeth.

She smiled at his evident agitation. "Come here, Lock." She held out her hand, and the little dragon leapt across the space that separated them. A flap of his wings, and he landed lightly on her palm. Could he really fly?

Briar was tempted to ask, but the muscle ticking in Grayson's jaw made it clear that he wasn't in the mood to entertain questions.

"Captain?" Eli called out.

Lock gave a little squeak and once more scampered down her waistcoat to disappear into her pocket.

"What is it?" Briar answered.

Eli stepped up to the edge of the hold. "We're about to lock through number forty-four. You still want to stop in Waverly?"

"I do. I didn't get to restock in Portsmouth."

"Waverly?" Grayson asked, still frowning.

"Twenty miles north of Portsmouth," she answered.

His dark brows ticked upward, and a speculative look entered his eyes. Was he planning to try an escape?

"Eli, would you be so kind as to secure our passenger? Perhaps out of sight in the bunkhouse?" Briar asked. "Then you'd best get to the tiller."

"Yes, Captain." Eli jumped down to join her, then turned to their *passenger*.

Briar left the hold without looking back.

Leaving Eli on the boat, Briar sent Zach and Benji over to Emmitt's Store for supplies while she and Jimmy visited the mill and the distillery to see if anyone had some cargo that needed to go north. They might as well make the trip a profitable one.

Her inquiries met with success, and she left Jimmy to oversee the loading of the cargo while she walked to the post office to mail her package to Uncle Liam. She didn't miss the irony that the package would travel by rail to reach him.

Finished, she headed back to the boat, cutting behind the train station. A train had arrived recently, and the streets around the station were busy with horses and carriages, picking up or dropping off passengers.

Briar stepped into the street, stopping behind a stationary carriage while she waited for a loaded wagon to pass. She leaned out to see if anything else was coming and glimpsed a pair of men leaving the train station. She pulled back behind the carriage with a gasp. One of the men was Andrew.

Taking a deep breath, she peeked out again. She released the breath when she saw Andrew walking away with the man. Apparently, he hadn't seen her.

Her gaze shifted to the other man, noting his long dark cloak. She stood straighter. Could he be the one she'd seen murder that man in Portsmouth?

"Stop jumping at shadows," she muttered. Half the men in the country probably had a cloak like that. Besides, none of this was her concern. She needed to get back to the dock and get out of here before Andrew realized she'd taken the boat. But what was Andrew doing in Waverly, and who was that man? Could it be Mr. Martel? But what were they doing here and not in Portsmouth?

Briar leaned against the back of the carriage, considering her next move. She couldn't just leave. Not with so many unanswered questions.

Looking out once more, Briar watched Andrew and his companion round the corner at the end of the street. She hesitated, bouncing on the balls of her feet. Unable to deny her curiosity, she hurried after them. It was risky. If Andrew saw her, she'd lose access to her boat, but she had to know what he and Mr. Martel—if that was Mr. Martel—were doing.

She kept her pace to a rapid walk and stopped at the corner. Leaning against the wall, she looked into the next street.

Andrew and his friend had stopped midway down the street beside a hired carriage. They discussed something, but she couldn't hear their words from here. If she could get closer…

She eyed their surroundings, noting a stack of crates near a vegetable stand, and behind that, a narrow alley. If she circled around and came in through the alley, she could hide behind the crates and listen. The distance wasn't too great, so she should be able to eavesdrop without trouble.

Her plan in mind, she hurried back the way she had come, breaking into a jog when she turned down the street that ran parallel to the one where Andrew currently stood. She found the alley she sought, the crates visible at the far end. Rushing forward, she reached her destination without incident.

Fortunately, the vegetable vendor must have stepped away from his stall. She squatted beside the crates, smelling the earthy scent of produce within. If the vendor returned, he would certainly view her with suspicion and demand to know what she was doing.

Briar quieted her breathing and strained her ears in an effort to hear any conversation from the street. She was about to lean out and verify that Andrew was still there when he spoke.

"I had no idea, sir," Andrew said. "It was a business venture, to build locomotives."

"Do not trouble yourself. I believe you," the man answered, his accent much like Grayson's.

"You said you had a counter offer," Andrew continued, the eagerness heavy in his tone. "I came as requested."

"Indeed you did." A soft chuckle followed.

Briar frowned. Was he Martel or not?

"If you would accompany my associate," the accented voice continued, "I will join you shortly to discuss my offer."

"Thank you, Mr. Solon," Andrew answered.

Briar's breath caught. Wasn't that the name of the man Mr. Grayson had accused her of working for? And the bigger question: How did Solon know Andrew?

The sound of a carriage step being lowered carried to her, followed by the squeak of the springs as someone climbed aboard. Andrew? Damn, she had missed the conversation.

She waited, listening for the carriage to pull away.

A scuff of a shoe on pavement was the only warning she got before someone stepped around the crates. Had the produce vendor returned?

She rose to her feet, ready to explain that she was searching for a dropped coin, but took a hasty step back instead. A well-dressed man stood before her, his dark hair just beginning to gray at the temples. But he wasn't a random stranger. She recognized the dark cloak Andrew's companion had been wearing. This was Mr. Solon.

"What have we here?" he asked, his accent confirming who he was. Fortunately, the crates hid her from view of the carriage should Andrew look out.

She looked up into Solon's slate-colored eyes. Something like a smile curled his lips, but the coldness in his eyes gave it a sinister twist. Her ready excuse died before she could utter it.

"You shouldn't have left the safety of the convent," he continued. "And certainly not with a souvenir."

She opened her mouth to demand what the hell he was talking about when he laid a hand over her lower ribcage. For an instant, she thought he was attempting to grope her, then she realized he had placed his hand over her pocket. The pocket where Lock was hidden.

"Do you mind?" She reached out and gripped his wrist. Cool metal met her fingers and she glanced down, expecting that he wore some kind of bracelet. He didn't. His wrist and most of his hand were covered in, or maybe made of metal. The same shiny silver metal that made up Lock.

She jerked her hand from his cool wrist. Oh dear God, a ferromancer.

"I know this soul," he whispered. His cold eyes narrowed. "You cannot have him, witch." He took a step closer.

"If you mean this poppet in my pocket, I stole it fair and square. Get one of your own, metal ass." She stepped toward him and brought her knee up. Hard.

For a split second, she feared his man parts might be made of metal, as well, but he doubled over with a grunt an instant later. His bizarre metal hand left her ribs for his crotch.

Briar didn't stick around for the obligatory cursing that was sure to follow. She turned and ran.

The business district was in full swing this morning. She darted through the busy streets, forcing herself to take the most congested and roundabout path back to the docks. If the ferromancer gave chase, she hoped to lose him in the crowd.

A few glances over her shoulder revealed that no pursuit had come. At least, not one she could see. Could he track her in some other way? Lock? She'd have to ask Mr. Grayson. He seemed to know a few things about ferromancers. But if he knew, would he tell?

When she felt certain she hadn't been followed, she slowed to a fast walk and hurried to the docks. No need to have folks talking about the crazed canal boat captain sprinting to her boat and setting off. That would certainly make her easier to follow.

Arriving at the boat, she jogged up the gangplank and hopped on board. She found her crew securing the cargo in the aft hold.

"Prepare to cast off," she told them between deep breaths.

"Captain?" Eli turned to face her. "What's wrong?"

She didn't want to alarm them. "My cousin is in town."

"Looking for you?"

"I don't think so." She wiped her damp brow. "But should he pass the docks, I don't want him to see the boat."

"We'll hitch the team," Benji said, hurrying from the hold with Zach on his heels.

"Is our passenger still comfortable?" she asked Eli.

"Last I checked." A frown wrinkled his brow. He no doubt realized that there was more to this.

She gave him a small shake of the head to deter any questions. Jimmy would freak out if he even suspected there was a ferromancer around.

"If you would be so kind as to see us underway, I'll go speak with him."

"What is your business with him, Captain?" Jimmy asked. "He works for the railroad, right?"

"I'm trying to puzzle that out." She gave him what she hoped was a confident smile. "Get us underway, Jimmy, so my cousin doesn't stop me from solving this mystery."

Jimmy grinned. "Aye, Captain." He turned and hurried from the hold.

Eli still watched her with suspicion. "What are you up to, Miss Briar?"

"I'm just trying to make it so we can buy this boat. Nothing more. Get the boys moving?"

Eli didn't look convinced, but he gave her a nod and moved off to do as she asked.

Glancing toward shore, but seeing neither Andrew nor the ferromancer, Briar made her way to the bunkhouse in the bow of the boat.

Mr. Grayson looked up when she stepped into the narrow confines of the cabin, a frown shadowing his eyes and the cold stare once more in place.

"I just met your friend," she told him, her breath still coming a little quickly.

Grayson frowned.

"Mr. Solon," she clarified.

Grayson came to his feet, his brows lifting. He tried to step away from the trunk he'd been seated on, but Eli had tied a rope around his bound hands and secured it to the support post.

"You failed to mention that he was a ferromancer," she said.

Grayson demanded something, but she couldn't make it out around the gag.

"Sit," she said.

He glared at her.

"Sit and I'll remove the gag."

He huffed—or tried to through the gag—and dropped back to his seat on the trunk.

She stepped forward and tugged the cloth from his mouth, allowing it to drop around his neck.

"You're certain it was Solon?" he demanded.

"He was addressed by name. And… he has a metal hand."

Grayson sighed, his shoulders dropping. "Damn," he muttered.

"He knew I had Lock with me."

"Do *not* call constructs by name, and why are you walking around with it?"

"I forgot he was in my pocket."

Grayson leaned back and muttered something to the ceiling. It wasn't English.

"What language was that?"

"Latin."

"Do you know a few phrases or do you actually speak it?"

"That's hardly pertinent. What did you say to Solon? Did you tell him I was here?"

"No. I kneed him in the nuts and ran."

Grayson stared at her. "You what?"

"In case you were wondering if ferromancers have iron balls, question answered. They don't."

Grayson blinked, then tipped back his head and laughed. Up to this point, he had been so remote and cold that his mirth threw her. Of course, judging by his clothing and speech, he probably wasn't used to such coarseness—especially from a woman.

Her cheeks heated. "Since you work for one, I thought you might want to know."

"You still insist that Martel is a ferromancer?"

"My instincts say yes, but I've sent the plans to a friend—"

"You mailed the plans?" His tone was somewhere between outrage and disbelief.

46

"Yes. My friend is knowledgeable and can help me make the determination."

"He's an expert in ferromancy?" The sarcasm was heavy in Grayson's voice.

"He lived in Europe, but his expertise is in the area of mechanical design."

Grayson leaned back against the support post.

Briar eyed him. "Are you worried?"

"That this friend of yours will reveal Martel to be a ferromancer, no, I'm not worried." A small smile played at the corner of Grayson's mouth.

It was Briar's turn to frown. Did he think so little of Liam's knowledge, or was Martel really not a ferromancer? Had she kidnapped a man and stolen a famous engineer's plans for no reason? Or was Grayson lying?

"Solon said he recognized Lock's soul," she said.

Grayson's confident expression vanished, and he once more watched her with suspicion.

"So, it's true? Automatons really are made from stolen souls?" She pulled Lock from her pocket. He seemed to know when they were alone, and instantly transformed into the little dragon.

Grayson didn't answer.

"He's so beautiful," she whispered, rubbing Lock beneath his chin, getting a purr from him. "How did Solon recognize his soul?"

"Its soul," Grayson corrected her choice of pronoun.

"Do you not know or are you just refusing to tell me?" She studied the silent man. A new idea occurred. "Did you take Lock from Solon? Is that what you meant when you said you procured him in London?" After all, Solon shared Grayson's accent.

Silence met her question.

The boat lurched into motion, and she absently spread her feet to keep her balance.

"We're leaving?" Grayson asked.

"Yes. I made the unpleasant discovery that your friend is meeting with my cousin."

"He's not my friend, and who the hell is your cousin?"

"Andrew Rose."

Grayson's brows lifted. "You're Bridget Rose?"

"My friends call me Briar."

"Charming, Miss Rose. What do your enemies call you? A thorn in their side?"

"Ha ha. How do you know my name?" Then she remembered. "Oh, right. Andrew had some big plan to marry me off to your Mr. Martel."

"Was that his plan?"

"Yes."

"Something tells me you weren't as thrilled with the idea."

"That Andrew intended to sell my boat, build locomotives for the enemy, and give me to some ferromancer? I was delighted."

"So, you stole his boat, pilfered those locomotive plans, and kidnapped me? Seems it would be simpler to just knee Andrew in the nuts."

"It has proven to be less than effective," she answered, ignoring the heat in her cheeks. Why did it make her feel so coarse and common to discuss such things with him? It never bothered her with the crew. She rubbed Lock beneath his chin to hide her discomfort and got another coo from him.

"I wouldn't think Mr. Martel would be any more thrilled with the idea," she said.

Grayson sighed. "It might be a bit late for that since you've already captured a bit of his soul."

CHAPTER 5

B RIAR LOOKED UP FROM TICKLING Lock's chin. "What? Are you saying Lock is…"

"I told you not to name it."

"You might have told me why!" She stared at the little dragon in horror. Lock blinked, delicate silver eyelids descending over those gem-like eyes. He sprang up to her shoulder and with a coo that sounded too much like a question, rubbed his cheek against her throat.

"What does this mean? What do I do?" she demanded.

Grayson looked amused at her discomfort.

"Is that who Solon recognized?" she continued. "What's the connection? And why is my cousin involved with both of them?"

Grayson's frown returned. "That I don't know."

"Captain?" Jimmy called down from the hatch above them.

Lock scampered down her chest and vanished into her pocket.

"What is it?" she called.

Jimmy opened the hatch in the roof above them. "We have a problem."

Her heart surged. "Andrew saw us?"

"No. At least, I don't think so. It's the rudder."

A thump sounded, and Briar stumbled to the side as the boat hit something.

"What the hell?" Briar demanded.

"We docked beside Darby last night," Jimmy said.

"Shit." Briar headed for the ladder.

"I can fix it," Grayson called after her.

Briar hesitated. "You don't even know what's wrong."

"I can fix it." He held her gaze.

Jimmy snorted. "He just wants you to untie him."

"A boat floundering at the dock would have to draw attention," Grayson said. "I don't know about you, but I'd like to avoid attention."

In other words, he didn't want Solon finding him. Not that she blamed him. God, had Solon really stolen a part of Mr. Martel's soul and locked it in a little metal dragon?

Without commenting, Briar left the cabin and hurried along the catwalk to join Eli on the tiller deck. The boat was currently butted against the dock a short distance from where they had begun. They weren't noticeably floundering in the middle of the canal—as Grayson feared—but they weren't underway, either. And with the canal visible from the busy streets to either side, Andrew could catch sight of them if he were to come this way.

"Eli?"

In answer, he lifted up on the tiller, and the handle rose up from its setting. It wasn't supposed to do that.

"How did that happen?" she asked.

"I thought it felt a little soft ever since we left home, but I hoped it just needed tightening. When we bumped that sand bar coming out of lock forty-four, I heard a pop, but since we docked immediately, I didn't notice a problem."

"You think Darby did this?"

"Aside from brushing that sandbar, we haven't hit anything."

She ran a hand over her braided hair, glancing toward shore. "Can we rig something just to get us out of town?"

"It's below the water line. We'll need to dry dock and have it repaired."

She knew that, but had hoped Eli might have a little canal

magic up his sleeve. Speaking of magic... She glanced back toward the cargo hold.

"Mr. Grayson claims he can fix it."

Eli's eyes narrowed. "The ferromancer's servant?"

"Maybe he learned a few tricks."

"He's tied up in the bunkhouse. How does he even know what's broken?"

"I already pointed that out." She eyed a hired coach moving along the street. Fortunately, it turned off before reaching them. "I'm going to let him try."

"Miss Briar—"

"We can't just sit here in plain view."

Eli rubbed a hand over his face, but he had no argument for that. He followed her back to the bunkhouse.

"The tiller no longer controls the rudder," she said the moment she stepped into the cabin. "We'll have to dry dock and have it repaired."

Grayson nodded as if he understood just what she meant. "I can fix it."

"You're very confident."

"Yes."

She turned to Eli and gave him a nod. He didn't look happy about it, but he walked over to untie Grayson's bonds. Once free, Grayson rose to his feet, rubbing his wrists.

"Don't get any ideas," Eli told him, his voice low.

Briar wasn't certain if Eli was just being overprotective or if something had transpired between the two of them when Eli first took him captive. Whatever it was, Eli definitely disliked the guy.

"You have me at a disadvantage, friend," Grayson answered.

"You're not my friend."

Briar rolled her eyes. "If you two are done posturing, there's a rudder to be fixed and a cousin to elude."

"Yes, Captain," Eli grumbled.

"Where's the trunk you stole?" Grayson asked her, ignoring the rest of it.

Briar eyed him. Was that why he'd volunteered? He wanted to learn the location of his employer's trunk?

Grayson sighed at her hesitation. "There's a tool kit in the bottom."

"How would you know that?"

"I packed the trunk."

"You really are Mr. Martel's valet?"

"Do you want me to fix the rudder or not?"

"Eli, please show Mr. Grayson to the tiller deck." She wanted to add that he was free to toss him in the canal if he gave Eli any trouble. But Eli would probably take her up on it. The rudder wouldn't be fixed and they'd have the added attention from onlookers while Mr. Grayson was fished out of the canal. She doubted if a dandy like him could swim.

Gritting her teeth against the annoyance of this whole situation, she marched off to her own cabin to retrieve the tools her *passenger* had requested.

Aware that he had been the one to pack the trunk, Briar sifted through the contents, noting how neatly everything had been arranged. Mr. Grayson would do well on a canal boat where every inch of space was a commodity to be used in the most economical way. Had he grown up in a similar environment?

When she returned to the tiller deck, she found only Eli in attendance.

"Where's—" She didn't get to finish as Mr. Grayson appeared— on the other side of the rail. He'd been hanging off the back of the boat.

He hoisted himself over the rail to stand before her. "Ah, good. You found it." He nodded at the bag she carried.

He'd doffed his coat and rolled up his shirtsleeves, but he still looked out of place in the silk waistcoat and well-tailored trousers. His gold watch chain winked in the sunlight.

"It's not as bad as I feared." He accepted the bag from her.

"You can fix it?" She found that hard to believe.

"With a forge and some quality steel, absolutely. With what I have here, I can get us to that forge." He opened the bag and began to sift through the contents with a lot of clinking of metal against metal.

"Bullshit," Eli grumbled.

"Would you like to make a wager?" Grayson asked, not looking up from his bag.

"Enough," Briar cut in. She was going to quickly lose patience if these two had to work together for long.

Grayson pulled out a clamp along with some nuts and bolts. The silver metal wasn't as glossy as Lock's scales, but it had a similar sheen.

"That doesn't look like iron," she said.

"It's an alloy. It's stronger and more versatile." He handed her a wrench. "Hand that down to me when I'm ready?"

She accepted the wrench with a frown. "What's an alloy?"

Grayson sat on the rail and took a moment to toe off his boots and socks. "Commonly, it's a combination of two or more metallic elements. Steel, brass, and bronze are examples." He rolled up his pant legs and swung one leg over the rail.

"And what's that?" She nodded at the clamp he picked up.

He flashed her a grin, then dropped over the end of the boat. "*The Briar Rose?*" His voice carried back to her.

She stepped up to the rail to watch him climb down the back of the boat. "Yes."

"You named your boat after yourself?"

"No. I'm named after the boat."

He gave her a considering look she couldn't interpret before turning back to his task.

She swung one leg over the rail and watched him work. He really did seem to know what he was doing. It was no time before he was asking—no commanding Eli to test the tiller and for her to hand him the wrench.

Looping her knee over the rail, she leaned out to eye the repairs. The shiny metal seemed oddly out of place and made her aware that the boat could use a fresh coat of paint when they docked this winter. Would the boat be hers by then? Would she be able to afford to have it painted?

Grayson climbed back up and took a seat across from her. Without comment, he handed her the wrench.

She lifted a brow.

"I figured you wouldn't want me to carry around a potential weapon."

"Do you often use a wrench as a weapon?"

"Not often." He was studying her again, his expression impossible to read.

"And what—"

Grayson abruptly twisted around to glance over his shoulder.

She lifted her head to follow his gaze when he sprang at her, pulling her from the rail to drop them both to the deck.

Briar grunted as she landed face down against the worn boards, Grayson's arm around her shoulders holding her down. Like her, he was on his stomach. It had happened so fast that her heart just now began to pound.

"What the hell?" Eli demanded.

"Look," Grayson whispered, pointing between the posts supporting the rail that surrounded the tiller deck.

Briar looked where he pointed and the breath caught in her throat. Along the street, not a dozen yards from her boat, a hired coach had stopped. As she watched, Solon stepped out.

"Miss Briar?" Eli was reaching for her. "Did he—"

"Eli, get us out of here. Quickly." She didn't know why she whispered. Certainly Solon couldn't hear them.

Eli glanced back toward the street.

"That's the man Andrew was meeting," Briar said. "Move, Eli."

He stepped away from the rail and, taking the newly repaired tiller in hand, shouted out to Benji to get the team moving.

Briar cringed at Eli's shout, then reminded herself that it was no different from any other boat moving along the canal.

She peered out between the posts. Andrew wasn't in sight, though he could be in the carriage.

Solon wasn't looking directly at them. He kept turning his head as if searching for something.

"He can't… sense Lock from there, can he?" she whispered to Grayson.

"No." Grayson never took his eyes off the man.

"Then what caught his attention?" she demanded. "Or do ferromancers routinely stop in the middle of the street to stare around?"

The corner of Grayson's mouth curled upward, hinting at amusement, though he didn't take his eyes from the bank—or answer her question.

With a lurch, the boat started forward. Benji's shouts of encouragement to the team echoed back across the water.

"Hope this rudder holds," Eli said.

"Insulting," Grayson muttered.

"You can take your arm from around the captain," Eli added.

Briar's attention had been so focused on Solon that she hadn't noticed that Grayson still held her against the tiller deck.

"Eli's right," she said when Grayson didn't immediately move.

"My apologies. Captain." Grayson still looked amused, though he did take his arm from her shoulders.

"Why do I feel like everything you say with that snooty accent is a joke at my expense?" she demanded.

"You kidnapped me. You've given me no cause to address you with anything except derision, snooty accent notwithstanding."

"If you would take the tiller, Captain," Eli spoke up, "I can tie the dog in the bunkhouse once more."

"I fixed your ship." The coldness was back in Grayson's tone.

"Boat," she corrected. "Because it benefited you."

"And you."

She started to get up, but he placed a hand on her shoulder. "A few minutes more. That red hair is distinctive. It might catch his attention."

Solon was still looking around, though to her relief, he seemed most interested in the street around him.

"Can't this heap of waterlogged timber go any faster?" Grayson demanded.

They were already up to speed. "Four miles an hour is as fast as any *boat* is allowed to go," she said.

"Tell me you're kidding."

"Any faster, and the wake would erode the bank."

Grayson just stared at her, clearly appalled.

"What's going on, Captain?" Eli asked.

"See that man standing beside the hired coach?" she asked. When Eli agreed, she continued. "He's a ferromancer. The real thing. He even has a hand made out of metal."

Eli paled. "And he's meeting with Andrew?"

"Yes, I don't know why. It gets worse."

"How can this get worse?"

"I kneed him."

"You do have a gift for trouble," Eli muttered before turning his attention to the streets around them. "Stay down, Captain. We'll be out of the city shortly."

"I just don't understand what got his attention," she said to herself as she watched Solon.

Abruptly, the ferromancer turned and climbed back into his carriage. A pause, and it rolled off, back into the small tangle of streets around the canal.

Briar released a breath and was surprised to hear Grayson do the same. Carefully, she climbed to her feet and he rose beside her.

"Captain? You want to take the tiller?" Eli asked.

Wordlessly, Grayson offered his wrists.

Briar frowned, feeling guilty about holding a man against his will. But if she could prove that the railroad was using ferromancer technology to further its empire, she had to do it. Even if Mr. Martel proved to not be a ferromancer, Solon certainly was. And with her cousin's clandestine meeting with him, there had to be a connection.

She took the tiller and glanced back at the town they were leaving. She didn't watch Eli lead Grayson away.

BRIAR PROPPED HER ELBOWS ON the table and rested her chin on her hand. The lantern swayed with the gentle rocking of the boat, casting its light across the ledger she was supposed to be updating. They had tied up for the night, not wanting to chance a sandbar or submerged log in the darkness. Eli feared the rudder repair wouldn't survive a collision. They would reach Chillicothe by morning and have it repaired properly.

With a sigh, Briar leaned back in her seat. "What do you think, Lock?"

The little dragon looked up from where he sat on one corner of the table, his gem-like eyes seeming to question her.

"I feel bad about tying him up, but what am I to do?"

Lock hopped across the ledger, then climbed her arm to reach her shoulder. With a soulful moan, he rubbed his cheek against hers.

She smiled at the gesture of comfort, then rubbed him beneath his chin. "Mr. Martel must be a gentle soul if you're part of him."

Lock cooed.

"Of course, that also means Grayson lied. He didn't buy you in London. Perhaps he stole you from Solon there?"

Lock just rubbed her cheek with his.

"What a shame you can't talk. I would love to know more— about both men." She remembered the beauty of the locomotive she'd seen in Portsmouth. Mr. Martel was an artist. What a shame he was a ferromancer.

She got to her feet and after pausing to rub out the stiffness in her lower back, she closed the ledger and returned it to the shelf above the table.

Changing into her nightgown, she extinguished the lantern and climbed into her bunk.

Lock crawled up the blanket and curled up on her pillow. She fell asleep stroking his glossy scales.

BRIAR WOKE AT DAWN—WHICH WAS later than her customary time to rise—not feeling very well rested. Her sleep had been fitful and she had woken often. Each time she did, Lock would snuggle closer, ultimately making a bed in her hair. How his fine claws and intricate scales and joints didn't become entangled in it, she had no idea.

Leaving her cabin, she headed for the bow to rouse the crew—if they weren't already up. Crossing the catwalk, she glanced down into the cargo hold. Last night, Eli had returned Mr. Grayson to the bales of hay where he'd been originally tied, but at the moment, they were empty.

She hurried toward the front of the boat, noticing for the first time the absence of her crew. Though with the night run the night before last, they had likely been as exhausted as she was.

Reaching the bunkhouse in the bow, she rapped on the hatch. Had Mr. Grayson escaped while the crew slept?

When no one answered her summons, she began to fear something more sinister. Had Grayson escaped and killed the crew? Why hadn't he come for the trunk—or her?

In the quiet, she heard the low rumble of male voices. She backtracked to the stable at midship. Dropping to the lower level, she stepped up to the door and found Zach and Benji inside, tending the mules.

"Hey, boys," she greeted them. "Where's the rest of the crew—and our guest?"

Zach elbowed his brother. Unable to speak, Zach had to rely on Benji for communication—which made it hard since fifteen-year-old Benji tended to turn bright red and go mute around her as well.

"They took the prisoner into the woods," Benji answered.

"Why?"

"I, um, think they went looking for an outhouse, Captain." Benji's cheeks turned pink.

"Oh." She hadn't stopped to consider that. "I guess our passenger amenities leave something to be desired."

Zach nodded, a faint frown on his features, giving Briar the distinct impression that he wasn't pleased with the way she had handled this.

She sighed. He was right.

"In the absence of Jimmy, I guess I'd better go start breakfast."

Zach gave her an alarmed look.

"I know. But I didn't get a chance to advertise for a new cook." Mrs. Jenkins, the elderly woman who had been cooking for Briar and her crew since before her uncle passed away, had decided to retire and move in with her daughter in Millport. They'd had a rough time since then.

By the time Jimmy returned, she had burned the bacon, and her attempt at eggs had yielded a runny goo dotted with bits of shells.

The crew ate in polite silence, but Briar knew they were as disgusted as she was.

"We'll dock in Chillicothe to fix the rudder," she said as Jimmy gathered the dirty dishes, most with food still on them. "Let's ask around and see if we can't find a cook."

"Aye, Captain," Jimmy said, taking her plate last. She'd left just as much food as the others. "We'll—" He didn't get to finish his statement as a thump followed by the sound of breaking dishes came from below decks.

"Damnation!" Grayson's angry shout carried to them.

Eli immediately came to his feet.

Briar stepped into his path. "I'll take care of this."

"Captain," Eli began.

"I think you've tormented the poor man enough."

Eli frowned. "He's a dangerous man, Captain."

She studied him. "Is there more to this? You seem to have taken a particular dislike to him. He's just an engineer's valet."

Eli crossed his large arms. "He doesn't fight like a valet."

Briar lifted a brow. "I assume you refer to your initial confrontation? He may not be a valet at all. He might be a bodyguard." He was very protective of his employer's belongings, though she wasn't so certain that bodyguards packed trunks.

She moved past Eli, but his large hand came to rest on her shoulder.

"I wish you would listen to me," he said softly.

"Why start now?" She gave him a smile to let him know she was teasing. "I'll be fine. He's not going to molest me on my own boat."

Eli sighed and took his hand from her shoulder. "Call if you need assistance."

"Ever the big brother." She smiled and shook her head, then left him standing there. Much like Andrew, Eli hadn't yet noticed that she had grown up.

BRIAR FOUND MR. GRAYSON ON his feet, pacing at the end of the rope that secured his hands and bound him to the side of the cargo hold. At least, Eli had bound his hands in front of him today.

The remains of his breakfast plate were on the other side of the cargo hold, a trail of runny eggs and charred bacon marking its flight across the hold.

She bent to retrieve the pieces of broken plate, and when she straightened, Grayson had stopped his pacing to glare at her.

"Have you come to torment your caged beast?" he demanded.

"You are acting like one."

"I have done you no ill. As a matter of fact, I helped you. Yet you treat me like an animal. No, I've seen your mules. You treat me worse than an animal."

She sighed. "Look, I know the conditions aren't the best—"

"I'm sleeping on a bale of hay. I've worn the same clothes for two days, and I can't take a piss unless someone holds my—" He stopped, seeming to remember who he was speaking to.

There was some truth to what he said, and she certainly wasn't proud of how things had transpired. "I'm really only interested in those plans." She studied him. "I don't have to take you, but if I release you, you'll run back to your master and—"

"No man is my master." He regarded her with those cold eyes as if debating whether to do her some harm. With that look in his eye, she wondered if Eli might be right about him.

"We'll be docking in Chillicothe. I aim to get the rudder repaired, so it could be a lengthy stop." She studied him. "I could have the boys take you into town."

"And what? Pummel me in a back alley so they don't get blood on your precious boat."

"Take you to the Valley House Hotel. They have hot baths— and a laundry service. My treat."

His eyes narrowed. "What's the catch?"

"No catch." She let her anger out a notch. "I never wanted any of this, but I'm not going to stand by and let some damn ferromancer and the railroad he works for destroy my way of life. If you have ever fought for something that was important to you, then you might understand. And if you're just an innocent caught in the middle of this, then I'm truly sorry, but I've never backed down from a fight, and I'm not going to start now."

He didn't respond, but he looked a little less angry.

"As for the breakfast," she continued, "my cook retired last week, and I've yet to hire on a new one. Your breakfast was no different from what the rest of us ate—or tried to."

"There's no one on this boat who can fry an egg?"

"Sadly, no."

"That is sad."

"And I suppose you could?" she demanded.

"Unless you prefer your egg poached, perhaps with a hollandaise sauce?"

She had no idea what he was talking about, but wasn't about to admit it. She arched a brow instead.

"I'd be happy to demonstrate." He held out his bound hands.

She sighed. "I can't release you."

He dropped his hands. "I won't leave without the construct."

She placed a hand over the pocket where Lock hid. "You mean this piece of Mr. Martel? Why are you so set on protecting him?"

"Why are you so set on destroying him?"

"I've given you my reason, but I've yet to hear yours. Why would you serve a man who can lock your soul in iron?"

"You know nothing about any of this."

"Then educate me."

He pressed his lips together, studying her. For a moment, she thought he might speak, but his shoulders dropped a moment later and he remained silent.

"That's what I thought." She turned away. "I'll send someone down for you when we arrive," she said over her shoulder.

He didn't respond.

She left him standing there and went to get the crew moving. The sooner this errand was finished, the sooner she could get back to her life.

CHAPTER 6

CHILLICOTHE WAS LARGER, AND MUCH busier than Waverly had been. It also supported a more varied market and offered more services, especially to the canal industry. Fortunately, the parts for the rudder were readily available, and there wasn't much of a wait for the repair. Aside from the expense, it would be a relatively painless process.

She had expected Grayson to take her up on her offer immediately, but he stayed around to watch the rudder repairs. She wondered at that until he stepped forward to collect the metal pieces he'd used for the temporary fix. Were they valuable? Or would he get in trouble if Mr. Martel found something missing?

Once the small pieces were tucked in his pocket, he was happy to depart with Zach and Benji for his promised bath.

"Are you certain about this?" Eli frowned after Grayson.

"He's my problem," she snapped, tired of the constant nagging. "Stay with the boat. I'm going to find us some cargo—and maybe a cook."

"Miss Briar," Eli tried to stop her.

"Let it be." She didn't give him a chance to respond before walking off.

THE STOP PROVED TO BE a profitable one when Jimmy was able to secure a load of bricks and some lumber for the trip north.

They would no longer be running light, but the time frame for the delivery was reasonable and Briar expected no problems.

By mid-afternoon, the boat repairs were finished and they were able to begin loading the cargo. With both holds filled with lumber and brick, Briar realized she'd have to find a new place for Mr. Grayson. The crew's cabin only held four bunks, and those were occupied. The stables were out, and Briar hoped the cook's bunk in her cabin would soon be occupied. It looked like Mr. Grayson would have to make do with the deck, which should suit him fine. The crew often slept on the deck on warm summer nights—provided it didn't rain.

Briar glanced up at the blue sky overhead. It certainly didn't promise rain anytime soon.

A jingle of tack made her glance over, and she was surprised to see Benji leading one of the mules ashore.

"Did Mr. Grayson finally finish his bath?" she asked him. "That took long enough."

"I believe he was waiting for his clothes to be laundered."

She grunted. "Is Zach still with him?"

"Yes, waiting at his door."

She sighed. "I guess I need to go get his dandy butt moving." They were ready to shove off. "Go ahead and hitch up the team. We'll head out as soon as I return."

"Yes, Captain."

She left him to field any questions the crew might have as to her whereabouts, and went to round up her squeaky clean passenger.

The baths were located at the back of the Valley House Hotel. Briar had visited more than once when docked for the night and not in the mood to haul her own hot water.

She found the attendant folding a stack of freshly laundered towels. "Bath, ma'am?"

"No. I've come to collect a crewman. The name's Grayson."

"The handsome gentleman in the fine clothes?" The attendant's eyebrows lifted. "He didn't look like a boatman."

He certainly dressed like a gentleman, but she wasn't so sure about the rest of it. "He's more passenger than crewman. Which room?"

"Room two." The girl handed her a stack of towels. "He'll be wanting these."

Briar started to point out that she wasn't here to bring him a towel, but figured it was easier than sending the attendant in a dozen times to get him moving.

Tucking the towels under her arm, she thanked the girl and went in search of room two. She found it at the end of the hall, but to her surprise, Zach wasn't waiting outside the door.

A bit of unease tightened her stomach as she remembered Eli's warnings. If Grayson had taken advantage of Zach...

She knocked on the door.

"Yes, come in." Grayson called out, his accent making it clear she had the right room.

She opened the door and stepped inside. The small room was steamy and uncomfortably warm, the stone floor slick with moisture. A curtained partition blocked half the small room from view, including the large brass tub she knew rested on the other side.

The door closed behind her with a soft click.

"Did you get more hot water, Zach?" Grayson called out before she could speak.

Briar gripped the towels she held, her anger flaring. How dare he use kind, gentle Zach as his servant. Zach was his guard.

She stepped around the curtain and found that Mr. Grayson was indeed still in the tub. Submerged to the chest, his bare arms rested on the sides of the tub, while his head lay on a folded towel, his eyes closed.

"Zach is not your manservant," she told him.

Grayson sat up with a gasp, moving so quickly he sloshed a

little water over the sides of the tub. "Dear God, woman. Do you always walk in on a gentleman's bath?"

"A gentleman?" She smiled, amused by his reaction. Her amusement faded as her eyes were drawn to the livid scar down the center of his chest, made visible now that he was no longer reclining. "Jesus," she whispered. "What happened to you?"

"Do you mind?" He pressed a hand to his chest as if ashamed. "You are determined to leave me no shred of dignity."

"Dignity? I came here to tell you that you need to cut the primping short. We're ready to leave."

"Time to tie me to the wall once more? Is that what you're saying?"

"No. The cargo holds are full. I'll have to tie you to the deck." She refused to let him rattle her. "So get moving. I want to cast off."

"Then I won't keep you." Without warning, he shoved himself to his feet.

Heat washed over her face, and she knew her cheeks were scarlet.

The scar on his chest ran nearly the length of his sternum, stopping just above the well-defined muscles of his stomach. She didn't see any other scars.

"Are you going to hand me a towel?" he asked.

She jerked her eyes back to his face.

One corner of his mouth curled upward. "Well?"

She dropped the towels on the floor and turned to go. She'd taken one step when Zach stepped around the curtain, a steaming bucket in one hand.

"We're leaving in five minutes," she said, then hurried past him. She escaped into the hall and pulled the door closed behind her.

The bath attendant stepped from the next room, carrying a basket of towels. "He about done in there?"

"Almost."

The girl nodded, then headed back toward the front of the building.

66

Briar hesitated, not wanting to share the hall and be forced to hold a conversation.

"I know," Grayson's voice carried through the door. "I shouldn't have done that, but she just barges in here and starts asking about my scars. That's private, you know?"

Zach didn't answer of course, but Briar had no doubt that he understood Grayson's view. Zach's neck and from what she heard, a good deal of his torso bore scars from his attempt to rescue his parents and siblings from their burning boat almost five years ago. Benji had been the only one he had saved.

"You can punch me, if you like," Grayson continued. "I deserve it."

Briar tensed, but no sound of flesh hitting flesh reached her.

She hurried away from the door, shamed by what she had done. It was another example of her bad behavior toward Mr. Grayson. If he proved to just be a servant of Mr. Martel, she was going to feel terrible.

In her mind's eye, she could see his scar again. She flashed back to that murder she'd witnessed in Portsmouth. The villain had cut open the victim. What if that glint of something metallic had been a ferromancer device, pulled from the victim's body? Did they implant such devices in their slaves?

Horrified by the prospect, Briar stopped just outside the hotel, trying to collect herself. She remembered the way Solon had stopped in the street. Something had clearly drawn his attention. Grayson had claimed it wasn't Lock. What if it had been Grayson himself? Had Solon... felt some ferromantic device implanted in Grayson? Something implanted by Mr. Martel?

If Grayson had fallen prey to such a heinous act, no wonder he was ashamed of that scar. It was glaring evidence of the fact that he had been violated. His comment on her leaving him no dignity suddenly made sense.

Unable to face him—or her crew—at this moment, she stepped

away from the hotel and followed the busy sidewalk into the next street, away from the docks.

She rubbed her hand over her waistcoat pocket where Lock rested. The little dragon had crawled inside on his own after she dressed this morning. If Martel was vile enough to implant some device in Grayson against his will, how could he create something as sweet as Lock from his own soul?

She turned down the next street, noting the people around her going about their business, oblivious to her turmoil. She wished she could be one of them again and continue in blissful ignorance of these foreign metal mages.

"You can't change the past," she muttered. Ignoring the problem would not make it go away. What she needed was knowledge, but her only source was Grayson. She certainly wasn't going to ask him.

Briar turned down another street letting her feet carry her where they would while her mind tried to sort out the problem. She wasn't the kind to sit back and wait for a solution. She preferred to address her problems with decisive action. But she had no idea what action to take.

She came to a stop outside a watchmaker's shop, her eyes drawn to the half-dozen pocket watches on display in the window. Such intricate works of mechanical marvel were nothing compared to what rested in her pocket.

"Now why would you circle the city only to end up here?" a male voice asked from behind her.

Briar turned, not so certain she was the one addressed, and discovered a man standing close by. She didn't know him, but his long dark cloak was decidedly out of place on this warm summer afternoon.

"Were you speaking to me?" she asked.

He reached up and she tried to take a step back, but came up against the display window she had been perusing.

He didn't seize her. Instead, he pulled her thick braid over her

Ferromancer

shoulder. "Red hair, dressed like a man, and—" He placed a hand over the pocket that contained Lock.

Briar gasped. Was he another ferromancer?

She turned to run, but he caught her arm and in the next instant, jerked her off her feet. A blur of movement, and suddenly, they stood in the alley beside the shop.

"Wh—" She didn't get to finish the question as he covered her mouth with his hand.

"Mr. Solon sent me to fetch you," he explained.

She stared at him. He worked for Solon? And the next, more terrifying question: why were they following her?

"He speculated that you had taken the train out of Waverly, but that was too obvious. Martel is a sly one. He hired a carriage, didn't he?"

He thought she was with Martel? Because of Lock?

As if answering her question, his opposite hand slid down to her waistcoat pocket and slipped inside.

"With this, he'll come to us," he said.

She couldn't let him take Lock. She gripped his wrist and tried to pull his hand away, but she couldn't budge him. The willowy man was fiendishly strong. Seeing no alternative, she bit him.

An odd metallic taste filled her mouth. Not blood exactly, but it could be. She pulled back in surprise at the same moment he pulled his hand from her mouth.

He seized her shirt collar before she could step back and, twisting it in one hand, lifted her until her face was on level with his.

At five-six, Briar wasn't a big woman, but she wasn't small enough for him to handle this way.

"Stupid ferra witch. Did you think that would work on the soulless?"

She didn't follow any of the references, but she wanted to point out that it had worked. He had taken his hand from her mouth. She opened her mouth to tell him so, but he twisted her collar tighter, blocking her ability to breathe.

Before the lack of air sent her into a full-blown panic, he slung her aside. The alley wall met her with surprising speed, and the side of her head hit before she could even get her hands up.

She landed in a heap, her ears ringing and a new metallic taste in her mouth. Her own blood.

Her attacker squatted beside her and, seizing the front of her shirt, pulled her into a seated position. He leaned in, his pupils contracting as he focused on her. This close, she could see that his steel-gray irises were made of fine, overlapping layers of what appeared to be metal, sliding smoothly over each other.

"If Solon didn't want your heart, I would take it," he whispered, then laid a hand over her heart. His fingers dug into her flesh even through her shirt and waistcoat.

She took a breath to scream, but he released her before the sound emerged. With the release of the pressure, her scream became a grunt of relief. She didn't get to revel in it as he pulled Lock from her pocket and rose to his feet.

"Lock," she whispered.

The silver lock transformed into the little metal dragon, but the man's fist closed around him before he could spring away.

"How cute." The man laughed—an odd joyless sound.

Lock screeched as the man's fist closed.

"No," Briar sobbed, trying to get to her feet. The world refused to stay still, and she only made it to her hands and knees.

Lock screeched again, but it wasn't a cry of pain. He sounded pissed. He twisted in the fist that held him and, much as she had earlier, bit him.

The man didn't release him. "Damn vermin."

"Indeed," a familiar, accented voice said from behind him. "Alleys tend to be full of them."

The man spun away from her, clearing her line of sight to where Grayson stood a few feet away. His eyes narrowed. "Now it gets interesting."

CHAPTER 7

"Grayson," Briar called, trying to focus through the dizziness. "I don't think he's human."

Her attacker spared her a glance. "I must have thumped her harder than I realized."

"She isn't what you think," Grayson said.

Before she could puzzle out what he'd meant, Lock shimmered into a new shape. She couldn't make out exactly what it was, but she glimpsed a serrated edge. The man shouted and dropped him. Lock changed shape before he hit the ground and with a flap of his wings, landed lightly on the packed dirt of the alley.

"Cute trick," the man said to Grayson, showing no evidence of pain or any reaction to the blood dripping from the damage Lock had done to him.

"Protect her," Grayson said to Lock, then stepped to the side. He stomped one foot, catching a discarded metal rod Briar hadn't noticed by one end and flipping it in the air. He caught it with casual ease, holding the rusty piece of metal ready at his side.

Her assailant barked another joyless laugh. "He said you weren't—"

Grayson attacked.

Briar pulled in a breath, shocked by his speed. His opponent, for as fast as he was before, couldn't get out of the way in time. Grayson caught him with a glancing blow in one hip, but it hit hard enough that she heard a crunch.

The man took a limping step to the side, but made no effort to flee. He cocked his head as he studied Grayson. Without warning, he sprang.

Briar gasped at the suddenness of it. She wanted to shout a warning, but the fellow was already upon Grayson, except, at the last moment, Grayson simply sidestepped him.

His attacker went stumbling past and Grayson spun, the metal rod lashing out so quickly that it was hard to follow. The blow hit the man in the head with a sickening crunch. He stumbled to the side and smacked the wall much as she had earlier. But unlike her, the collision didn't take him down.

Shoving himself off the wall, the fellow sprang at Grayson once more. This time, Grayson didn't try to avoid him. He stepped forward to meet him, shoving the rod ahead of him. The rod slid into the man's stomach. Grayson continued forward, one hand still on the rod while the other caught the man by the throat.

The man threw back his head as if to scream, but no sound emerged. An instant later, it looked like a lightning storm had erupted in his mouth. Silver light sprang forth, first from his open mouth, then his eyes.

Eerily silent, he collapsed, his head thumping off the ground. His face was toward her, and she could still see the silver light faintly glowing in the depths of his eyes.

Grayson dropped to a knee beside him and pushed him over onto his back. He shoved the rod, still buried in the man's stomach, upward. A series of brittle snaps echoed in the deserted alley. It took Briar a moment to realize they were ribs.

Using the hole he'd made, Grayson ripped open the man's shirt exposing his pale chest and stomach—and the livid scars covering both. It appeared the man had been cut open many times. But this time, Grayson was performing the surgery.

She watched in horror as Grayson used one hand and the rod to pry open the man's chest. In a terrifying recreation of what she had witnessed in Portsmouth, Grayson reached in and pulled out a blood-smeared silver object attached to a multitude of thin wires. This close, Briar was able to see that it was a heart.

Dear God, had she been right? Did ferromancers really implant metal objects in their slaves? Objects that looked like organs?

Grayson closed his fist, but unlike the man's attempt to crush Lock, Grayson had no trouble crushing the silver heart. It began to collapse beneath his fingers, emitting a flare of golden light as if Grayson held a tiny sun.

Suddenly, Grayson gasped and glanced back over his shoulder. Footsteps approached from the street accompanied by a low, tuneless whistle.

Briar tried to turn her head to look, but the world swung around her. Before she could right her vision, hands gripped her shoulders. She gasped, attempting to pull away.

"Easy, it's me," Grayson said. He didn't give her a chance to answer before pulling her to her feet.

Darkness haloed her vision until she seemed to be viewing the world through a tiny pinhole.

Grayson lifted her from her feet, shushing her feeble protest. "Solon is coming," he muttered against her ear.

She could smell her assailant's blood on him. She wanted to pull away, but didn't have the strength. Grayson carried her out the far end of the alley, his pace rapid. She didn't see where he went next because she was soon forced to close her eyes in an attempt to combat the dizziness.

His pace finally slowed, and he set her down, her back against the wall of a building. Another alley? Lock cooed from her shoulder, his tone reassuring.

"Miss Rose?" Grayson touched her cheek, and once more, she caught another whiff of her assailant's blood.

"It was you," she whispered to Grayson.

"Shh. Just sit still." He lifted a hand to the throbbing place above her temple.

She groaned as his touch awakened the pain, but she had to know. "You killed that... man near the train yard, in Portsmouth."

Grayson sighed. "You have a very bad habit of sticking your nose where it doesn't belong."

"Tell me the truth," she whispered.

"It wasn't a man. Not anymore."

"Like the guy here?"

"Yes." His tone sounded resigned.

"Did someone try to do that to you? Make you a... thing?"

"In ferromancer parlance, they are known as the soulless." He leaned closer, carefully parting her hair to check her head wound.

"You still have a soul?" she asked.

"Yes, Miss Rose, I do. And I do wish you would be a little more careful with it."

"I'm sorry." She wasn't exactly sure what she was apologizing for. Perhaps for her ill treatment of him.

"Me, too," he muttered. "Now sit still. This might sting a bit."

She was about to ask what he was doing when a prickling sensation took the place of his probing fingers. Then pain hit. She hoped she didn't scream before she blacked out.

"CAPTAIN?" ELI'S CONCERNED FACE SWAM into focus.

"Eli?" Briar's voice was rough, and she wondered at that—and why she was lying on the deck.

"How are you feeling?"

"Like I've been run over by a large carriage with a team of eight." She sat up, biting back a groan. Her aching head protested the movement.

Eli gripped her elbow, but released her when it seemed she wouldn't fall over.

She sat on a makeshift pallet of blankets not far from the tiller deck.

"Do you remember what happened?" Eli asked.

She frowned at that, trying to recall. The boat was in motion, and she could see Benji and the team on the towpath ahead of them. By the look of the sun, it was early evening, but she had no clue how she'd gotten here. She remembered an alley, a man with inhuman strength, and Grayson.

She took a breath to answer and smelled something delicious. She recognized their surroundings as a stretch of canal several miles north of Chillicothe. This was a seventeen-mile level between locks, but they hadn't reached the village of Yellowbud yet.

"What's that smell?" she asked.

Eli scowled. "Mr. Grayson demanded he be allowed to make dinner. He said you'd been injured and would need the meal. He's below deck now, cooking."

"In my cabin?" Yes, it was where anyone who performed the task cooked, but it was also where she kept his trunk. She laid a hand over her pocket and pulled in a breath. Lock wasn't there.

"He's down there with Jimmy," Eli answered. "We don't leave him unguarded."

"I can't believe you're letting him cook."

"He said he could have just left you and escaped, but he brought you back—at no small risk to himself." Eli sighed. "The boys seemed to think that proved him trustworthy." Eli's expression made it clear that he didn't think so. "What happened in Chillicothe, Miss Briar?"

Glancing around, and finding themselves alone, she leaned closer. "I was set upon by a ferromancer's henchman. The same ferromancer I encountered in Waverly."

Eli's eyes widened. "He's following you?"

"So it would seem."

"Dear God."

She started to tell him about the metal heart and Grayson's actions—both in Chillicothe and in Portsmouth—but she hesitated. Eli hadn't met the... soulless. He would probably call Grayson a murderer.

"I know you're just trying to save our way of life on the canals," Eli continued. "But I think it's time we cut our losses. Burn those plans and get rid of the ferromancer's servant. He's nothing but trouble."

"He saved my life, Eli." She wanted to go on, to tell him about Grayson's scar and her suspicions about his true relationship with his boss, but she didn't think Grayson would appreciate her divulging so much. He had told her that he wasn't soulless, but something had clearly been done to him.

She didn't want to argue about Grayson's actions, past or present, with Eli—or herself. Fortunately, the hatch opened and Jimmy climbed out. Once he reached the deck, he turned back and accepted a covered Dutch oven. He turned away from the hatch and saw her.

"Captain!" Jimmy gave her a wide grin. "You're up." He set down the oven and turned back for a cloth-covered basket. Meals were a bit inconvenient when the cargo holds were full, but the money they made was dependent on how much they could haul. All available space went to cargo, and the crew made do.

"Have I got a surprise for you." Jimmy carried the cloth-covered basket over to her.

"I have a suspicion of what it might be." She lifted the cloth and glanced inside. "Biscuits?" She couldn't believe it.

"Well, he likes to call them scones." Jimmy waved a hand at the hatch as Grayson climbed out, carrying a larger basket laden with the dishes and flatware.

Grayson had doffed his coat and rolled up his shirtsleeves. His dark hair was damp around his face, and his cheeks a little flushed from working over the hot stove.

She got to her feet and walked over to greet him. "Do I have you to thank for all this?"

"You were injured. You need to eat." He spoke the words without inflection. "No one else was capable of preparing an edible meal." She puzzled at the coolness of his tone. Was he annoyed that he'd had to do it? "It appears you outdid yourself."

He didn't answer. Instead, he reached a hand toward her face, and she instinctively stilled. Carefully, he brushed the sore spot on the side of her head. "The swelling seems to have gone down."

His gaze dropped to hers with that pronouncement. The sunlight off the canal caught in his eyes, making them almost glow. She looked more closely, afraid to see those intricate plates she had seen in the eyes of the soulless man, but Grayson's irises were the typical human ones, the light making them more blue than gray this evening.

He lifted his brows, and she realized she had been staring into his eyes a little too long.

She stepped back. "Now that you boys are out of my space, I'll clean up for dinner."

"Don't take too long, Captain," Jimmy said. He and Eli were already setting up the folding table. "This will go fast."

"Tie up and call Benji in," she said. "He should get some, too."

"Yes, Captain," Jimmy agreed.

Eli took a more decisive action and moved to the rail to shout at Benji.

She left them to bring in the boat and climbed down into her cabin. The room was very warm, even with the open windows, but it smelled wonderful.

Crossing the room in a couple of quick strides, she squatted beside the table and found the trunk tucked underneath where she'd left it. She started to lift the lid, then noticed the silver lock hanging from the hasp.

"Lock?"

A swirl of metal, and the little dragon now hung from the trunk. With a squeal, he leapt to her shoulder.

"It's good to see you, too." She rubbed him beneath his

chin, then turned back to the trunk. Lifting the lid, she saw that everything was still in place. Why had Grayson relocked his master's trunk? Was there something in here of value? She had seen nothing.

"I don't understand that man."

Lock purred and rubbed his nose against her cheek. He rose up on his rear legs and sniffed her hair where the injury was, then offered a sympathetic moan.

"I'll be fine," she reassured him. "Now, I'd best get ready for dinner."

Lock chattered in agreement, then leapt down to the table. Leaving him there, she hurried to her partitioned part of the cabin. Her appetite was returning with a vengeance, and she didn't want her crew to scarf down everything before she got there.

GRAYSON HAD MADE PLENTY, SO going hungry wasn't a concern—overeating was. He had made something like pot roast, though he called it by some French name. Whatever it was, she had three helpings, but the meal seemed to be just what she needed.

By the time the dishes were washed and put away, she was feeling like her old self. Even the headache had faded.

"Are we to continue on, Captain?" Eli asked. It was twilight, the western horizon a brilliant red and gold while the first stars were just visible in the east.

"No," Briar answered. "Let's bring in the team and tie up for the night. It's been a crazy couple of days, and I don't know about you, but I could do with a night off."

"We're not that far from Yellowbud," Jimmy pointed out. The canal town of Yellowbud boasted several taverns.

"I know," she answered. "But you'll all be unfit tomorrow, and I want to make it at least as far as Circleville."

"We'll drink in moderation," Jimmy promised.

"Since when?" she glanced at Eli and he chuckled. Jimmy never seemed to keep that promise. "Let's just have a quiet night here on the boat," she offered.

"Will you play for us?" Jimmy asked.

Briar smiled. "I could probably be persuaded."

Jimmy grinned. "We've still got that bottle of bourbon. Maybe we'll play some cards, after."

"Fine," she relented. "Let's tie up for the night, then I'll go get my fiddle."

"You play violin?" Grayson asked. He had been quiet throughout the meal and cleanup. Though he had surprised her with his willingness to work.

"Yes." She frowned. "That seems to surprise you."

"It does."

She wasn't certain what to make of that. "Do you play, sir?"

"No. I don't seem to have an aptitude for music."

"And here I was beginning to think there wasn't anything you couldn't do."

"There are a few things." His cool tone was matter of fact. She had expected a smile. Was he angry with her?

"No one can play like the captain," Jimmy spoke up.

"Jimmy," she complained, embarrassed by the praise. "I'm sure someone as worldly as Mr. Grayson has heard better."

Grayson seemed to consider this, then turned to Jimmy. "What task would you have me do?"

"We need to bring the mules in. Give me a hand with the bridge plank," Jimmy said, then led him across the catwalk toward the stable.

"Looks like he's charmed Jimmy," Eli said.

"Would you give it a rest?" she demanded.

Eli held her gaze, then turned and walked away.

Briar watched him go. Maybe they should push straight through to Columbus and be done with this miserable task.

"I really thought bringing down the railroad would be more enjoyable," she muttered.

CHAPTER 8

YING OFF FOR THE NIGHT went quickly as they all performed their work with the expediency born of repetition. Like her, every crew member had grown up on the canal. The surprising aspect was how well Grayson performed. Perhaps he'd had a similar upbringing. She wondered what kind of life he'd led to give him such a varied skill set. At their first meeting, she had thought him a pampered dandy with his fine clothes and disdain for her way of life. Perhaps that was just the appearance he gave. Maybe now that he was out from under his master's thumb, she was seeing the real man.

Night was fully upon them when they returned to the deck over the rear cabin. Eli retrieved the cards while Jimmy got the bourbon. The cards were for later, but the bourbon was poured before she finished tuning her fiddle.

It had been a while since they had gathered like this. Usually, it was at the end of a profitable run, or in celebration of a birthday or some other event. Tonight, there was no reason. Well, maybe she was celebrating the fact that she had lived through her first encounter with the soulless.

She glanced at Mr. Grayson who sat apart from the others. Zach had given him a glass of bourbon, but he wasn't drinking it down like the others. Perhaps it wasn't to his liking.

His eyes met hers, and she realized that once again, she had been studying him for too long, trying to puzzle the man out.

Feeling awkward, she drew her bow across the strings, letting the familiar motion pull her away from the moment. The fingers of her left hand worked their way along the fingerboard. An eerie little tune sang out from beneath the bow.

The crew fell silent, and she stopped.

"What song was that?" Jimmy asked.

"It wasn't one," she answered. "Just a warm up." She did that sometimes. It seemed the emotions she was feeling—like her uncertainty about Grayson—came through in an original tune.

"What do you want to hear?" she asked, trying to get back to the familiar and out of this odd funk.

"Cluck Old Hen," Jimmy suggested.

She nodded, then bent over her fiddle. The upbeat ditty burst from the strings, and the boys were tapping their feet and singing along in no time.

The evening continued in that manner as the bourbon flowed and Briar lost herself to the music. She asked for fewer requests and played the tunes that spoke to her. Though the festive atmosphere had cheered her and the songs remained upbeat and lively.

Sweat wet her brow by the time she finished the last refrain of Blackberry Blossom.

The boys clapped and whooped, bringing a blush to her cheeks. Hopefully, they'd just think it from the warm temperature and exertion. Captains didn't blush at every little compliment.

"That's it for me," she told them, trying for a stern tone. "We've got to get back to work tomorrow. Can't be staying up all night."

"Aye, Captain," Jimmy agreed. "A quick game of cards it is."

She bit her lip to keep from smiling. After she'd agreed to the game, she knew nothing would deter him from it.

As the crew sat down to their game, she glanced over to see what Mr. Grayson made of all this. The barrel he'd been sitting on was empty.

Heart rate surging, she looked around. She was just about to point out his absence when she spied him sitting on the rail at the bow. Had he gone to the other end of the boat for some quiet?

Taking a moment to pack away her fiddle, she picked up her glass—now only half full—and went to see what he was up to.

Following the catwalk, she crossed to the roof of the bow cabin, but Grayson didn't look up. He straddled the rail, his attention on the canal and the dark banks to either side. The moon wasn't full and left a lot in shadow.

"Are you standing guard?" she asked.

He didn't startle at the sound of her voice, so he must have heard her approach. "I don't believe Solon knows where we are."

"We?" She threw a leg over the rail and sat down across from him.

Grayson's eyes met hers. "Yes."

The directness of his answer caused goosebumps to pebble her arms—even in the balmy air.

"Why is he interested in me?" She hoped her tone didn't reveal her unease.

"You assaulted his person."

Even with Grayson's phrasing, her cheeks heated—which was annoying. Why did she keep blushing tonight?

"But the true reason is the construct," Grayson added in the same matter-of-fact tone.

She laid a hand over her pocket. "Lock?"

He held her gaze.

"You still refuse to call him by name," she said, annoyed by the fact. "He answers to it, you know."

"I know."

There was movement within her pocket, and an instant later, Lock climbed out. A little whirr of what she took to be happiness, and he scampered across the few feet of rail that separated her from Grayson, and sprang up onto his shoulder.

"He recognized the sound of your voice," she concluded. "Or does he speak English?"

"He neither speaks nor understands any language. He reacts to the whispers of your soul."

"What? How is that even possible?"

"I don't know how you made the initial connection, but you went on to name him and care for him. There is great power in both."

She watched Lock rub his cheek against Grayson's. "There's a connection between the two of you as well."

"Yes." Grayson seemed indifferent to Lock's attention. Actually, he seemed indifferent to this whole conversation. It reminded her of what he was like the first night on her boat. Well, maybe not that cold.

"How do you know so much about all of this?"

"I've had an extensive education in many things. It is my adaptability that has kept me alive."

She frowned. Was that what he was doing? Adapting? At times, he seemed so friendly, but now he was distant.

"You look as if you don't believe me," he said.

"Oh no, I believe you. I'm just wondering who the real Mr. Grayson is. You had seemed to be warming to us, but tonight, you are so distant."

"Stopping the soulless is…" he hesitated, as if he searched for a way to describe it. "Unpleasant."

"Yes, it was. You pulled a metal heart from his chest."

Grayson didn't comment.

"I saw other scars on him, and his eyes… they weren't human."

"No, he had lost his humanity."

"Is that what ferromancers do? Replace a man's organs with metal ones? Is that how they make the soulless?"

"Yes." Grayson's matter-of-fact tone gave her chills. He seemed so different.

"What's wrong with you?"

"I told you. Stopping the soulless is not pleasant."

Lock cooed and pressed closer to him, trying to comfort him—or warm him. It suddenly occurred to her that Grayson had dispatched that soulless man in Portsmouth just before he was taken onto her boat.

"It's an affliction," she concluded. "A side effect."

"I guess that's a way to look at it."

"How can I help you?"

His brows lifted. "You would help me?"

She scooted closer. "You saved me tonight—at no small risk to yourself. Should I not return the favor?"

His forehead furrowed.

"Am I to take your silence to mean there's nothing to be done? Or are you not sure how to respond to someone offering to help you?"

His gaze once again locked with hers, and she had a strong suspicion it was the second answer.

"Last time," she continued when he didn't answer, "you seemed to cheer up after I told you about kneeing Solon. I would be happy to do it again, but if he doesn't know where we are, that seems a bit foolish."

The faintest of smiles touched his lips before fading.

"Come on, give me something. There must be—"

"Play for me." His request was not what she expected.

"The fiddle? I don't mind, but I just spent most of the last hour playing."

"Not the folk songs you played earlier. I want to listen to your soul."

"My—"

"Like your warm-up piece."

"Oh." In other words, something she made up. Something from the heart.

She glanced back at the crew. They were laughing, intent on their game, though Eli frowned in her direction from time to time.

"You don't want to?" Grayson asked. There was no animosity in his tone, just resignation, as if he accepted that he would have to ride out this malady.

"I've never played like that for anyone," she admitted, and damn if her cheeks didn't heat once more. Hopefully, the low light hid it.

"Sharing something created from the soul is a terrifying experience," Grayson agreed. "But when the labors of your soul are appreciated, that brings the purest of joys."

"Spoken like a true artist." She smiled. "What is your talent?"

"You've seen it."

She waited, but he added nothing else. "You get very cryptic when you're like this. If I want a straight answer, I guess I'll have to play for you."

"So it would seem."

Shaking her head, she pulled her leg back across the rail and rose to her feet. Was she really going to do this? Maybe she could play some obscure ballad for him. After all, he wasn't from this country, so he was unlikely to recognize every song.

Feeling a bit better about the idea, she returned to the stern to fetch her fiddle.

"Captain?" Eli called to her when she started for the bow. "What are you doing?"

"Mr. Grayson killed a man in my defense today. It's left him feeling a little out of sorts. I'm going to try to cheer him." She gestured with her fiddle.

Eli didn't look happy, but he didn't immediately reply.

"That's good of you, Captain," Jimmy said. "I know he's supposed to be our prisoner, but we're all human, after all."

Not all, she wanted to say. Instead, she gave Jimmy a smile. "You're right."

Patting Eli's thick shoulder, she left them to their game and returned to the bow of the boat.

Grayson had returned to studying the dark banks of the canal and didn't glance over when she returned. A small lump just inside his open shirt collar and a glimpse of a silver tail marked Lock's presence.

She smiled at the little dragon's antics to warm him. Setting her case atop the rail, she took a moment to rosin the bow, then pulled out her fiddle. She brought the instrument to her chin and drew the bow across the strings. Yes, still in tune.

Now what? She had come this far with the conviction that she could play him some obscure tune and he'd be none the wiser, but that felt wrong. He had given of himself today. Could she not do the same?

Closing her eyes, she drew the bow across the strings once more. The fingers of her left hand moved across the fingerboard, the progression of notes becoming a melody. She imagined the hopeful tune a balm to Grayson's battered soul. A sharing of gratitude on her part.

She released the music trapped within the strings—or more accurately, within herself. Expressing as she could never express in words, the terror she had felt before Grayson's arrival in that alley in Chillicothe, and her relief once he joined her. But she couldn't quite set aside the confusion and, if she was honest, unease he stirred in her. Who was he?

The last note rang out, echoing over the still waters of the canal. Briar lowered the bow and released a breath.

"Perhaps, one day, I will tell you," Grayson whispered.

She opened her eyes to find him standing before her, though strangely, his closeness didn't make her jump. It was as if she'd been aware of him all along.

"What will you tell me?" she asked, her voice just as soft.

"Who I am."

Her heart sped up with her realization that he had truly heard her through her music.

One corner of his mouth curled at her reaction. "And I'm glad I was close enough to lend you aid," he added, growing more serious. "I do not want to think about Solon getting his hands on you."

She clutched the fiddle to her chest, so stunned that she didn't know what to say.

Grayson's brow wrinkled, perhaps noting her distress.

"Captain?" Eli was crossing the catwalk toward them.

She gave herself a mental shake and stepped away from Grayson.

"I appreciate the song, Captain," Grayson said, his tone cheerful. "I've never heard such fine playing, neither in London nor Paris."

"You exaggerate," she whispered.

"I do not." He turned to Eli who had stopped beside them. "Any bourbon left?"

"Not for you." Eli glared at him.

Grayson raised his hands in a gesture of surrender. "Then I'll be grateful for what I got." He started to turn away, then stopped. "Here." He reached beneath his shirt collar and lifted out a heavy silver chain that held a medallion. Light caught on the surface, and she saw the depiction of a dragon. "I believe this belongs to you."

When she just stood there, Grayson dropped the chain over her head. The medallion slipped beneath her open shirt collar, the metal oddly warm as it settled against her breastbone. Lock.

She looked up, meeting Grayson's eyes.

"Keep it close to your heart." A wink, and he turned and walked away.

"What the hell was that all about?" Eli demanded.

She wanted to say she had no idea, but that wouldn't sit well with him. "It's a defense," she said, feeling inspired. "Against ferromancers."

"Why would he have something like that?" Eli frowned after him. "He works for one."

"I'm beginning to wonder about that," she admitted. She lowered her voice and continued, "I think he might hunt them."

Eli's thick brows lifted. "You think he might be part of the Scourge?"

"It's possible." What if he hadn't been working for Martel? What if he was hunting him? But how had he known the contents of Martel's trunk? Ugh. Just when she thought she'd figured him out, another complication arose.

Eli's frown shifted to the back of the boat where Grayson was joining the others at the card table. "If that were the case, I would think killing a man wouldn't bother him a bit. The Scourge was supposed to be a ruthless organization. Some say they were as bad as the monsters they hunted."

"You're determined to dislike him." She walked to her case to put away her fiddle.

"And you seem determined to praise him. If I didn't know better, I would think you liked him."

She snapped her case shut and turned to face him. "You over step yourself, Mr. Waller."

"Miss Briar."

"This conversation is over." She didn't give him a chance to respond before returning to the back of the boat. "The rest of you finish up and get to your bunks. I want to make good time tomorrow."

A hail of *Aye, Captains* answered her pronouncement, except Grayson, of course. He'd taken a seat on one of the barrels surrounding the table, his expression far too amused for her taste.

She turned away and hurried down the hatch to her cabin.

The hatch thumped closed behind her and she released a breath. She set her fiddle case on the table, noting the way her hands shook. What had just happened?

She took a seat on the edge of the spare bunk, trying to sort out the events of the last ten minutes. She had played an original song for Grayson—something she had never done—and he had understood every note. The connection she'd felt with him afterward had been so... intimate. Too intimate. And the way he'd slipped the medallion around her neck—

"Oh." She lifted the heavy silver chain over her head, pulling the medallion out to gaze at it in the better light of the lantern. The dragon etched on the silver surface was an exact depiction of Lock. She lay the necklace beside her on the bed. "Lock?"

The chain appeared to retract into the medallion, then morphed into the familiar metal dragon she knew so well.

"Oh wow. You really do have other forms." She hadn't imaged what she saw in that alley.

He gave her a little whirr of agreement, then sprang up to her shoulder. With something like a purr, he rubbed his cheek against hers.

She reached up to brush a finger beneath his chin. "I just don't know what to make of you. Or him."

Lock purred, then hopped down onto the bed. With a flap of his silver wings, he leapt across the short distance separating them from the table.

Finding no answers, Briar got to her feet and walked to the curtained nook that held her bunk. There was nothing to do but follow her own instructions and get to bed. She shrugged off her waistcoat and the shirt followed. She hesitated before pulling on her nightgown, noting with unease the bruises the soulless had left on her when he clutched her heart. What would have happened if Grayson hadn't found her? Had he once suffered a similar experience?

Her mind flashed back to the scar she'd seen on his chest— before he'd climbed from the bathtub as bare as the day he was born.

Her cheeks heated again with the memory.

"Dear God," she complained, pulling on the nightgown. What

was with all the blushing? It wasn't like he was the first naked man she'd ever seen. He was just the first one she didn't mind looking at.

She groaned and dropped onto her bunk. "It's the bourbon," she told herself, though she had only one glass. "And the stress." It had been a very stressful day—well, couple of days.

With a click of tiny claws, Lock slipped beneath the curtain and hopped up on the bed with her. Scampering across the sheets, he climbed onto her pillow and gazed up at her.

"Yes, you're right," she told him. "I just need some sleep."

She lay down, and Lock crawled over to curl against her shoulder. Did an automaton need to sleep? She'd have to ask Grayson—if he would tell her.

"So many unanswered questions," she muttered, letting sleep overtake her.

SHE WAS BUTTONING HER WAISTCOAT when a knock on the hatch door drew her out of her room.

"Captain?"

She instantly recognized Grayson's voice. "What is it?" she called out, unease tightening her stomach. Did he have some indication that Solon had found them?

"The crew has informed me that I am now cook—until one can be hired. The equipment I need to do my job is in your chambers."

She climbed up the ladder and pushed open the hatch. "Cabin," she corrected, climbing out.

He held the hatch for her, smiling at the correction.

"Well, go ahead." She waved a hand at the open hatch.

"You would allow me to visit your… cabin? Alone?"

"Yes. This is a canal boat. Any semblance of private space is merely a courtesy from your fellow boatmen, not an actual physical space. Besides," she lowered her voice as she continued, "you are already aware of the one thing I consider private. He's curled up on my pillow."

Grayson's smile grew. "He sleeps with you?"

"Don't be perverse, sir." She hesitated. "Unless there's a reason he shouldn't."

"No, and I wasn't being perverse. Merely surprised."

She lifted a brow, but he didn't comment further.

"Well, go on," she said. "I assume you know where everything is." After all, he had cooked dinner yesterday.

"Yes, ma'am."

"Then get to it, and I'll get this boat underway."

A final grin, and Grayson disappeared down the ladder.

She turned away, smiling to herself, and discovered Eli at the tiller deck, frowning at her.

"What?" she demanded. "He's making breakfast."

Eli wordlessly turned back to the rope he was coiling. She hated being at odds with him, but she had to trust her instincts. And her instincts kept telling her that Grayson wasn't the bad guy.

CHAPTER 9

"CAPTAIN?" ELI CALLED TO HER from the tiller deck. Briar looked up from her mopping. "What is it?"

"We're coming up on lock thirty-four."

She dropped her mop in the bucket and turned. He was right. The land flattened out considerably once north of Chillicothe, and she could easily see the lock in the distance.

"Looks like we won't be doubling up," Eli added.

Shielding her eyes against the bright morning sun, Briar squinted. Eli was right. The miter gates were closed on their side, indicating that the water within the lock would need to be lowered to their level.

"Looks like we'll need to fit the lock." She remembered how Uncle Charlie used to complain about that, but he remembered the days when the Ohio & Erie used to employ lock tenders. There were still men who held the title, but their job was to maintain the upkeep of the locks, waste ways, and sluices. They didn't open and close the locks for the passing boats.

"Where's Jimmy?" she asked.

"Below deck, with Mr. Grayson. Apparently, he offered to fix Jimmy's watch." Eli frowned. "I hope he doesn't break it beyond repair. That watch belonged to Jimmy's father."

"Mr. Grayson can fix watches?"

"So he claims."

This she had to see. Walking to the hatch, she called down to Jimmy. "We're about to lock through."

"Coming, Captain," Jimmy's voice echoed up from below. A moment later, he climbed through the hatch.

"How are the repairs going?" she asked.

"He just took it all apart." Jimmy's brow wrinkled in concern.

"I'll go check on his progress if you don't mind taking care of things up here?"

"Thank you, Captain." Jimmy looked relieved already. "I never expected that old watch to ever work again, but I'd like to keep it in one piece, all the same."

Not sure how Jimmy expected her to remedy the situation, Briar shook her head. Being captain wasn't just about navigating the boat or keeping the books. Sometimes, she was just expected to make things right—even if she was the youngest person on this boat, save Benji. Still amused, she climbed down the ladder into her cabin.

Mr. Grayson sat at the table hunched over a towel that held an assortment of tiny gears and other pieces.

He glanced up, then turned back to what he was doing. "Turn the sausages for me?" He paused long enough to gesture at the stove, but kept his focus on the watch.

All right, not everyone aboard her boat saw her as captain.

"At least you phrased it as a question." She walked to the stove, inhaling the wonderful scent of freshly cooked sausage.

"I didn't figure you wanted me to burn your breakfast," Grayson answered.

She picked up a fork and carefully turned each sausage in the heavy cast iron pan. Finished, she walked over to the table to see what he was doing. It appeared that he was reassembling all the tiny pieces and was perhaps, nearing completion of the task. She must have misunderstood when Jimmy said he'd *just* disassembled the watch.

"I hope you know what you're doing." She stared at all those parts crammed in such a tiny space. How had he remembered what went where? "That watch is important to Jimmy."

"It didn't work and hasn't for some time." He picked up a gear with a small set of tweezers. The black tool bag he'd used to repair the rudder was open on the table beside him.

"It belonged to his father," she explained. "He drowned when Jimmy was seventeen."

"The watch was submerged?"

"I… guess."

"There was some corrosion," Grayson continued, seeming untroubled by the morbidity of his conclusion. "The inner workings were cheaply made. Fortunately, I had some replacement parts."

Now that he'd drawn her attention to it, she noticed that the watch's inner workings were bright and shiny, unlike the dull metal of the case. "You mean, Mr. Martel had some spares."

"Yes." He picked up one of the gears and carefully aligned it with the one he had just mounted. "It'll run forever when I'm done, submerged or not."

She lifted a brow, though he didn't look up to see it.

He picked up a tiny screwdriver and leaned closer.

She watched him work for a few minutes. "That's amazing."

"Thank you."

A laugh escaped her. "Not you. I meant that all those intricate little parts can fit together and keep time."

He glanced up then back down once more. "Though complicated, it's a simple mechanical principle."

"Show me?"

"If you like, but pull the sausages out of the pan for me?"

"Oh." She had forgotten all about them. She hurried back to the pan and was relieved that none had burned. Transferring them to a plate, she set it on the back of the stove to stay warm before returning to the table.

"Here, look at this." Grayson absently scooted over, making room for her on the bench.

She sat down, not so certain she cared for this closeness. She considered moving to the seat across from him when he leaned over to show her what he was doing. She realized she wouldn't be able to see the tiny mechanism from over there.

"The basic principle is the storage of power in a wound spring, the mainspring"—he tapped a circular housing with his tweezers—"and releasing that power in a controlled way." He launched into a surprisingly technical explanation about the movement of the balance wheel and the alignment of a host of gears and pinions that transferred the stored power in the spring to the calibrated movement of the hands.

Briar soon forgot about his closeness, leaning in to better see and asking questions. She'd always been interested in the inner workings of mechanical things. Uncle Charlie had taken her to task more than once when she'd disassembled something just to see how it worked. But she'd never had the nerve to tear into a timepiece.

Grayson, on the other hand, had clearly done this before. His movements as he worked were confident and precise, and his knowledge of the topic made it obvious that he had some training, or at least, a lot of experience.

He tightened the final screw and set aside his screwdriver.

"And that's it?" she asked.

"Yes. It will keep perfect time now." He pulled his own watch from his pocket and passed it to her. "Allow me to reattach the hands, then you can compare them."

She pressed the button to open the cover and display the watch face. "So you're going to validate your claim with your own pocket watch?"

"That watch was a gift, crafted by a master watchmaker. You'll find none finer."

She studied the smooth motion of the second hand. "Are you telling me it's ferromancer made?"

He lifted his gaze from Jimmy's watch. "It's those sorts of comments that have cost many a talented craftsman his life." A muscle ticked in his jaw with his restrained anger.

His anger surprised her. "I'm sorry. You work for one, and I encountered another's minion yesterday. I have ferromancy on my mind."

He released a breath. "You're right. I apologize for the outburst." He returned to his work.

"I'd hardly call it an outburst." She watched him for a moment. "So, who was he?"

"Who was who?"

"This watchmaker who died. The one who gave you this watch."

Grayson glanced up. "I never told you that."

"I put two and two together." She held his gaze. "Will you tell me? Is he the one who taught you how to fix watches?"

Grayson sighed. "His name was Fabrice Martel—no relation, before you ask."

She smiled at that.

"He had immigrated from Paris and ran a little shop on the outskirts of London. He took me in as an apprentice when I was eight."

She lifted a brow. "That sounds young."

"I had—have an aptitude for mechanical things."

"I'm beginning to see that."

"No ferromancy involved," he hurried to add.

She smiled. "I wasn't going to ask. I might be hard-headed, but I'm not stupid."

"I'm beginning to see that," he threw her words back at her, a glint of humor in his gaze.

She resisted the urge to roll her eyes. "How long did you work for this man?"

96

"Three years. Aside from the convent, it's the longest I've lived anywhere."

"You're an orphan?"

"More or less."

She frowned, not sure what to make of his answer. Perhaps he still had parents, but they had given him up for some reason. She wasn't going to ask for details, but his answers only created more questions.

"I'm surprised that a pocket watch still impresses you after being around ferromancers and creations like Lock," she said.

"Fabrice couldn't mold the gears with his mind or feel the imperfections in a hairspring, yet he produced watch after watch of meticulous perfection." Grayson spoke the words with passion and a clear admiration for the man and his talent. "You met the soulless. That's what ferromancers create."

"Not all."

Grayson glanced over, a frown now on his face.

She reached up and pulled off the necklace. "Whatever your relation and feelings toward him, you must admit that Mr. Martel is different." She laid the medallion on the table. "Lock?"

Like the night before, the chain retracted into the medallion and an instant later, Lock sat in the center of the table, blinking at them with his gem-like eyes.

She held out her hand. and with a whirr of what might be happiness, he rubbed his cheek against her finger.

"I find pocket watches—or any mechanical design—fascinating," she admitted. "But I don't see how you can compare that to this."

"You're enamored with the construct because it can move on its own."

She ignored his blatant effort to avoid using a male pronoun. "That aspect is incredible, but if I understand you right, his animation has nothing to do with his design." She brushed a finger along Lock's neck beside the raised scales that ran down his spine and along his back. "Look at this intricacy. Each individual scale is a work of art. There's the life-like motion of his limbs and the design of his joints. Then there are the wings…"

Lock spread one wing as she ran a finger over the upper edge.

"Add to that the fact that he can morph into other shapes." She looked up and found Grayson watching her, not Lock. "Can other ferromancers do this?"

"All have the ability to create constructs."

"Of this beauty?"

A slight smile curled his lips at her word choice. "Yours is unique among constructs."

"I knew it." She trailed a finger along Lock's tail. "This is probably incredibly stupid, but I want to meet your Mr. Martel. I've studied his plans, and though I can't make sense of them, it's clear the man is an artist."

"An artist?"

"Yes. I snuck into the shed that housed his locomotive in Portsmouth. I had intended to vandalize it, but it was so beautiful, I couldn't bring myself to do it." She laughed at herself. "I might have a crush on your boss—vile ferromancer and all."

When Grayson didn't reply, she looked up. He still watched her, but she couldn't read his expression. There was a hint of amusement, but also, something more.

"What?" she asked, suddenly self-conscious about all she had shared. "I'm kidding. You know that, right?"

"Of course." He returned his attention to Jimmy's watch, replacing the face.

A knock sounded on the hatch, and Briar sprang to her feet.

Lock let out a soft cry and dropped to the table, morphing in mid fall, but he didn't become the lock or the necklace. A beautiful silver pocket watch now lay beside Jimmy's.

"Captain?" Jimmy opened the hatch. "We've locked through. How's breakfast coming?"

She was stunned that she'd been down here so long—and that she'd forgotten breakfast.

"Breakfast is ready," she answered. "Tell the crew?"

"Yes, Captain." Jimmy didn't immediately close the hatch. Instead, he descended the ladder, stopping a little over halfway down. His gaze shifted to Grayson. "I was wondering how you made out with my old watch."

"Quite well," Grayson answered. He picked up Jimmy's watch, the steel watch chain dangling from his fingers, and carried it over to him.

Jimmy left the ladder to accept the timepiece. "It works?" Jimmy eyed the exterior of his watch, no doubt wondering if any pieces were missing.

"See for yourself." Grayson caught her eye, a slight smile on his mouth.

Jimmy opened the cover and stared at the watch face. He took so long in responding that Briar moved to his side to verify that the watch hands were still moving.

"It really works," Jimmy whispered.

"You'll find it keeps perfect time," Grayson answered.

Jimmy stared at the watch for a complete revolution of the second hand. "I never thought..." He cleared his throat. "My granddad bought this watch with the money he made digging the canal. He always credited it with helping him land my grandma— her seeing that he was a man of means and all with his fancy watch." Jimmy chuckled.

"It's a fine piece," Grayson said. "It just needed a good cleaning and a little adjustment."

Briar looked up, but Grayson kept his attention on Jimmy. From what he'd told her, it sounded like he'd had to replace a lot of the cheaply made components.

Jimmy snapped the watch closed and offered Grayson a hand. "Thank you, sir. What do I owe you for your trouble?"

"It was no trouble." Grayson shook his hand. "I enjoy fixing things."

"So we've seen." Jimmy chuckled. He returned the watch to his waistcoat pocket and carefully reattached the chain. Briar didn't realize how incomplete Jimmy had looked without that familiar chain dangling from his pocket.

Jimmy kept his head down, seeming to have some trouble getting the chain situated as he wanted.

"Mr. Grayson and I will bring up breakfast," she said to fill the awkward silence. "Will you set up the table and call in Zach?"

"Aye, Captain." Jimmy looked up. He blinked several times, but he was smiling. He thanked Grayson again, then hurried up the ladder.

"I told you that watch meant a lot to him," she whispered to Grayson.

"You did."

She returned to the table and picked up the silver pocket watch. An image of a dragon was carved into the cover. Like the image on the medallion, it was a perfect representation of Lock. Opening the cover, she exposed the silver face and moving hands. "He actually keeps time?"

"Yes." Grayson stopped beside her. "This will probably become its favored form since you expressed an admiration for the object. Who knew it was such a flirt?"

"You insist that he is a thing, not to be named or assigned a gender, yet you attribute him with such a human expression."

"Are you calling me a hypocrite, Miss Rose?"

"Yes, I am." She slipped the silver watch into her pocket.

Grayson followed the motion, his expression more amused than offended.

"Help me carry up breakfast," she said, trying to put some distance between them again. "Otherwise, the crew might mutiny."

"Aye, Captain." Grayson still grinned.

CHAPTER 10

FTER BREAKFAST, THEY LOCKED THROUGH number thirty-three without a problem, then traveled the two miles between it and lock thirty-two, also known as Aqueduct Lock, so named because it would lift them the nine and a half feet to the Circleville Aqueduct to passed over the Scioto River.

"Wow." Grayson stopped beside her, eyeing the approaching lock and the covered aqueduct beyond it.

Briar glanced over. "Are you impressed or poking fun?"

"I was admiring the engineering that went into designing this," Grayson said. "Granted, by today's standards, it's a bit antiquated, but I recognize quality work when I see it."

She glanced over, ready to protest his *antiquated* comment, but he wasn't smirking at her as she expected. Instead, he was studying the structure they approached.

"At over four hundred feet long, it's said to be longest aqueduct on the Ohio & Erie." They had crossed other aqueducts on this trip, but this was by far the most impressive.

"Though I must admit," Grayson continued, "I find it amusing that a bridge has been built to transport one waterway over another."

"How else would we cross it?" she demanded. "Rivers have currents, and they rise and fall with the floods and droughts. Plus we need a towpath to—"

"Mr. Grayson?" Jimmy called from the bow, interrupting their argument. "Would you give me a hand on the balance beams?" Jimmy waved a hand toward the long wooden beams that projected from the top of the lock's miter gates. One person on either side had to push their gate open using the beam. It seemed Jimmy had selected Mr. Grayson to be his helper.

"Certainly," Grayson called, his tone cheerful and almost eager. He turned back to her. "Perhaps we can continue our conversation after we've…"—he consider his word choice—"locked through?"

"If you like." She tried to hide her amusement. He might consider their system antiquated, but he was still eager to learn all he could.

She joined Eli on the tiller deck where they waited for the lock to lift them to the level of the aqueduct.

"I don't like being at odds with you, Miss Briar," Eli spoke up.

She sighed. "Nor I you."

"I just don't trust that Mr. Grayson," he insisted.

"Why is that, Eli?"

He didn't immediately answer, frowning at where Grayson and Jimmy were now manning the balance beams.

"Is it because he works for the railroad, or a ferromancer?"

"I should think either reason would do."

"You don't think we should judge the man on his own merit?" she asked.

"We don't know what the merit is. He doesn't show us his true self."

She frowned, debating on how much to tell. "Dealing with that ferromancer's minion in Chillicothe affected him. It made him… cold. I learned that he'd had a similar encounter shortly before he came aboard our boat."

"A similar encounter? In Portsmouth?"

"Yes, so if your trouble with him stems from his varying personality, that's why."

Eli didn't answer, once again turning his attention to Grayson, who was now pushing the gate open.

"Eli?"

"I don't like that these ferromancers have come to our country, our hometown."

"I'm not too happy about that, either, but that doesn't make Mr. Grayson a bad person. He might not work for that ferromancer willingly."

"And if he does?"

She didn't have an answer for that.

Benji had reattached the towline to the mule team, and Grayson and Jimmy were returning to the boat. It was time to get underway.

"We can continue this discussion later," she told Eli. "Prepare the rudder." When locking through, the rudder was pulled closer to the boat to allow it to fit better in the lock.

"Aye, Captain."

She left him to it and crossed the catwalk to the bow of the boat where Jimmy and Grayson were coiling the bow lines that had held the boat stationary while in the lock. She waved to Benji, signaling him to get the team moving.

Grayson straightened from coiling the rope, then looked up at the roof over their heads. "I assume the roof was built to protect the structure from the decaying effects of the weather?"

She had never stopped to wonder why the aqueduct had a roof. "That sounds like a reasonable assumption."

Jimmy glanced up at the roof. His considering expression suggested that he'd never thought about it, either.

"Iron trusses would remove the need for a roof," Grayson continued, "but I guess timber was more plentiful when this was built."

"The area was little more than a wilderness when it was built."

He grunted, and she guessed the concept was foreign to him. She doubted there were any uncharted wildernesses where he came from.

"The more I think on it," he said after a moment, "the more impressed I become. To construct such a structure, in the wilderness, with little more than shovels…" He stopped to shake his head. "It's truly an engineering marvel."

She had the distinct impression this was high praise coming from him. "We'll make you a boatman yet."

"I'm beginning to understand the appeal," he answered.

Jimmy laughed and clapped Grayson on the shoulder. "Who needs the soot-belching railroad?" Still chuckling, he turned and walked off.

"But what if the train doesn't belch soot?" Grayson asked her.

"I suppose that would be an improvement, but no train will ever surpass this." She lifted her arms to encompass her boat and the canal they floated on.

"I do admire your passion." He held her gaze for a moment, then turned and followed Jimmy.

She watched him go. Perhaps he wasn't as enamored with the canal as he appeared to be.

THEY DOCKED IN CIRCLEVILLE, AND after Briar located the owner of the appropriate warehouse, they began the slow process of unloading the bricks they'd picked up in Chillicothe.

Briar leaned against the rail, watching the workers transfer the brick to the waiting wagons. Nothing seemed amiss, but after her last two excursions, she couldn't help but wonder if Solon would show up here, too.

Grayson stopped at the rail beside her. "Would I have time to visit the market?"

"The market?"

"I was going through our stores and planning the next meal. I could use some shallots and perhaps some tarragon."

"Tara what?"

"It's an herb."

"This is a canal boat, Mr. Grayson. You need to keep it simple. How are you with beans?"

"I'll need some salt-pork."

She straightened. "That should be easy to find. There are several pork-packing houses in town."

"How about some leeks?"

She started for the gangplank. "Not on my boat."

"I meant the vegetable."

"Good luck finding that." She led him down the gangplank, but stopped at the bottom. "Do you think Solon followed us here?"

"I can't say, but you should really consider leaving the construct on the boat. The water and the complete lack of technology will insulate it."

She laid a hand over her pocket and looked up.

"That wasn't a criticism on the canal," he hurried to add, "just a statement of fact."

"I know. I was curious about your *insulating* comment. How does that work?"

"I believe we've escaped Solon's notice because he wouldn't expect us to travel by canal boat. He'll be looking for a carriage or searching the train stations. He'll be drawn to metal and more modern surroundings."

"Why's that?"

"It's a ferromancer's nature." Grayson shrugged. "He'd be uncomfortable on your boat."

She smiled, liking the sound of that. "Good to know."

BRIAR WALKED BESIDE GRAYSON AS they left the docks to walk up Canal Street. A heavily loaded wagon was blocking the road, backing up traffic. It had lost one of its rear wheels and wouldn't be going anywhere soon. A group of men was busy unloading the wagon in an effort to lighten it enough to jack it up and replace the wheel.

Grayson stopped a moment, watching them.

"We'll never get your herbs standing here," she reminded him.

"Why aren't they using an iron hub?" He waved a hand at the wagon. "They're far superior to wood."

"I'm sure they have a good reason." She caught his sleeve and pulled him away from the wagon. "You're easily distracted."

"It's frustrating to watch people struggle to accomplish something when there are better ways to complete the task."

"Like the railroad?" she asked.

"I will refrain from comment since I do not wish to be tied to the deck once more."

"That's a cowardly attitude. After your recent escapades, I assumed you more courageous than that."

"Against the soulless, certainly. Against a red-haired canal boat captain named for a thorn bush... Well, I'm not *that* courageous."

"What does the red hair have to do with anything?"

"You fit the stereotype, my lady. If I touted the railroad's advantages, I'm sure I would end up with a knee in a place where I would prefer not to have a knee."

"I'm not that unstable."

Grayson lifted a brow.

"And I wasn't named after a thorn bush. I was named after a boat."

"Another reason to avoid a debate on the pros and cons of one transportation method over another."

"You really are an exceedingly annoying fellow," she told him. "Maybe you should have been named for a thorn bush."

"Hm. Perhaps." He tapped his chin. "How about Hawthorn? It has a roguish air, don't you think? Except, I believe it is technically a tree rather than a bush."

She shook her head, unable to hide a smile. "You are in good spirits today, Mr. Grayson."

"It's Hawthorn, remember? I will need a cane and a top hat to wear at a jaunty angle."

She laughed. "That doesn't sound very roguish."

"A top hat is to be worn vertically upon the top of the head and a cane is an affectation for someone my age."

She glanced over. Was he just making this up on the fly or was he really quoting some upper-class etiquette she knew nothing about?

"Ah, I assume this is our destination?" He nodded at the building before them. General Store had been painted in large block letters across the front of the building beneath the second-story windows.

"It is," she answered.

"A bit more expansive than I expected." He pushed open the front door and held it for her. "Perhaps I can find some tarragon after all."

Briar rolled her eyes.

GRAYSON WAS A THOROUGH SHOPPER, browsing through the various foodstuffs and spices with a critical eye. She finally had to tell him to make his selections so they could get back to the boat before too much of the day was wasted.

"You'll thank me when you taste dinner." He laid his selections on the counter, but the shopkeeper didn't pick up a pen and paper to calculate what was owed him. Instead, he began depressing a series of buttons on a large metal box.

"Might I inquire as to what you're doing?" Grayson asked.

The shopkeeper glanced up with a smile. "I'm totaling the sale." He pulled a lever, and with the ding of an unseen bell, a drawer at the base of the machine slid open.

"It's a cash register," the shopkeeper continued. "A friend of mine in Dayton designs them."

"A cash register?" Grayson laid a hand atop the contraption.

"It totals the sale, stores the money, and alerts the shop owner when a clerk is completing a transaction."

"Ingenious," Grayson said. "Would you allow me to take a closer look?"

"Of course." The shopkeeper stepped aside, inviting Grayson to join him behind the counter.

Briar watched the exchange with amusement. Grayson was like a kid with a new toy, and the shopkeeper, the proud papa showing off his mechanical wonder. Though with a few presses and a closer examination of the gadget, Grayson was soon asking questions the shopkeeper couldn't answer. After watching Grayson repair Jimmy's watch, Briar wasn't surprised.

"Allow me to give you my friend's card," the shopkeeper said when Grayson mentioned that he wished for a screwdriver to take a closer look.

"Perhaps you're interested in purchasing one yourself to take back to England? My friend would love to introduce his invention to a foreign market."

"To England?" a woman inquired, setting a bottle of scented water on the counter. She gave Grayson an inquiring look. "Might you be a countryman, sir?" Her accent sounded much like Grayson's, and she was certainly dressed as well as he was.

"I might be," Grayson answered with an easy smile. He stepped back around the counter to face her. Briar thought he would offer to shake hands, but he gave her an elegant bow instead. "Jonathan Grayson, at your service."

"A pleasure." She held out her hand, and he took it. "Miranda Kendrick."

"Of the London Kendricks?" Grayson asked, still holding her hand.

"My late husband's family. I hail from Oxfordshire."

"Lovely countryside."

"You've been there?" She looked delighted. "My father is a professor at Oxford." She continued on, naming people and places completely foreign to Briar, though Grayson seemed to have no trouble following her.

Briar had always considered herself worldly. Growing up on the canal, she had always been on the move and frequently exposed to new people. She'd been educated on the boat by her uncle and could read, write, and perform arithmetic as well as anyone, but she was feeling decidedly out of her element when Grayson and his new acquaintance discussed the wider world.

Briar stepped past them to settle her bill with the shopkeeper. Grayson was still deep in conversation when she finished.

"The boat will be leaving shortly, Mr. Grayson," she cut in.

"Indulge me a moment, Captain?" he asked. "It's been a while since I've heard word of home."

The woman's gaze fell on her, and her delicate brows rose. "You're a woman." She stared at Briar in open astonishment.

"What gave it away?" Briar demanded.

The woman didn't answer, perhaps taken aback by Briar's sharp tone.

"I've booked passage on her boat," Grayson spoke up.

"One of those canal boats?" The woman looked appalled.

"I wished to see the countryside at a more leisurely pace. I assume you are traveling by rail?"

"Of course. It's a bit more rustic than I anticipated, but nothing like you must be enduring."

Briar opened her mouth, but Grayson stepped in front of her.

"Are you staying at a local hotel?" he asked the woman. "Perhaps you would allow me to walk you to it?"

"I would like to continue our conversation," she agreed.

"Mr. Grayson—" Briar didn't get to finish as he abruptly faced her.

"Might I have a word, while Mrs. Kendrick settles her bill?" He gripped her elbow and not giving her a chance to respond, turned her toward the door.

"We don't have time for you to chat up some English tart," Briar told him as he walked her to the door.

"She came by train," he said, keeping his words soft. "Perhaps the same train our friend was on. She would certainly notice another Englishman and would know if and where he disembarked."

"Solon," Briar concluded, feeling a bit foolish. That was what Grayson was doing? She glanced back at the counter where Mrs. Kendrick was paying for her scented water.

"Yes," Grayson answered, following her gaze. "Not that I'm opposed to chatting with a pretty woman."

"She's at least ten years your senior." Though it wasn't all that obvious with that dark hair and alabaster skin. No freckles marred the bridge of her nose—unlike Briar's.

"That just makes her more interesting, but all that is a moot point since you are so anxious to leave. I will constrain my conversation to talk of her travel companions."

Briar wanted to point out that she hadn't agreed to this scheme, but the woman in question had paid for her purchase and walked over to them.

"Mr. Grayson?" She stopped beside him. "Do you have leave to escort me?"

"Captain?" Grayson gave Briar an inquiring look.

"You have a quarter of an hour, then we depart—with or without you."

"I will be aboard," Grayson promised. He turned to his companion, and offering her his arm, led her from the store.

Briar frowned after them a moment, then stepped outside. Grayson and his new friend had already rounded the corner, but the woman's accented voice carried back to her.

"...rustic charm, but it leaves me longing for an educated conversation."

"Yes," Grayson agreed.

"Yet you chose to travel in such a barbaric way, with a woman who dresses like a man."

A carriage rattled past, and Briar missed the next snippet of conversation, though Grayson's laugh carried back to her.

She was half tempted to go confront the pair of them and even took a step in that direction before she made herself stop. It was pointless to confront the over-dressed twit. It was unlikely the haughty woman would even punch her back. Hell, Briar would probably lay her out with one blow.

Grumbling to herself, Briar pulled out her new silver pocket watch and, noting the time, headed for her boat.

CHAPTER 11

GRAYSON ARRIVED WITH EXACTLY ONE minute to spare. The mules were hitched, and Zach awaited her signal to head out. Watching Mr. Grayson stroll coolly along the docks toward their vessel tempted Briar to give the command, but when Zach lifted a hand to wave at Grayson, she knew he would hesitate to start the team, thinking she hadn't seen their passenger. Perhaps she should have assigned Eli to be driver. He certainly wouldn't care if they left Grayson behind.

"Good of you to join us," Briar said as Grayson jumped from the dock to the boat. They had already pulled in the gangplank.

"Heard you were chatting with some Englishwoman," Jimmy said as Grayson stopped beside him. "Any success?"

"A gentleman doesn't kiss and tell," Grayson answered.

"How does that pertain to you?" Briar asked.

Grayson just smiled, appearing in too good a mood to be bothered by the barb.

"Did you learn anything of importance?" she asked him.

"I did."

Briar lifted her brows. "Go on," she demanded when he didn't continue.

"The man in question was on her train, but disembarked in Chillicothe."

"We already knew that."

"Yes, but what we didn't know was that he traveled with two companions."

"He has two soulless?" They had only encountered the one in Chillicothe.

"The second man was a well-dressed red-headed gentleman."

Briar stared at him. "Andrew? He was in Chillicothe?" With Solon?

"Your cousin was in Chillicothe?" Jimmy asked. "Does he know you've taken the boat?"

"I'm sure he does by now," she answered before turning back to Grayson. "Were you able to learn why Andrew was there?"

"That, I have no way of knowing," Grayson answered. "My new friend had only a passing word with them before they departed her train."

"I'm glad that your conversation with her wasn't a waste of time."

"Certainly not a waste of time," Grayson agreed. "She also gave me the address of her friend's residence where she'll be staying in Columbus. She invited me to call when in town."

Jimmy chuckled. "I figured he knew his way around the ladies."

Briar caught the wink Grayson gave him. "I believe we have a boat to get underway," she reminded them, then turned to Grayson. "Can the crew expect dinner, or has your romantic interlude left you out of sorts?"

"I'll manage, Captain. Do I have your leave to begin? I shall need the afternoon if the cassoulet I'm planning is to be done in time."

"You have my leave."

Grayson nodded and headed for the hatch.

"What's a castle-whatever?" Jimmy asked, walking beside him.

"Cassoulet. It's a dish made from beans, and sausage, named for the vessel in which it is cooked. I'll have to settle for a Dutch oven, but I'm sure I can make it work."

The two men parted ways at the hatch, and Jimmy moved off to see about his duties.

Briar glanced over at Eli who stood a few feet away. "The sooner this errand is finished, the better."

"I couldn't agree more, Miss Briar."

She nodded. "Then man the tiller and we'll get the boat underway."

"Aye, Captain." With a grin, Eli walked off to do as she commanded.

"I bet that overeducated tart couldn't command a canal boat," Briar muttered, walking off to do just that.

THEY DOCKED THAT NIGHT AT Lockbourne, planning to make the twelve-mile trip up the Columbus Feeder Canal the next morning. The docks were always busy in Ohio's capital, and it would be easier to navigate in the light of day. Besides, Lockbourne was home to one of the nicest taverns along the canal. Her crew would be disappointed if they passed it by during prime operating hours.

Guard Lock Tavern was a favorite among boatmen and a great place to catch up with friends along the canal, should they be docked at the same time.

Briar took her fiddle ashore with her, knowing she would just be returning to fetch it if not. Old Clem, the tavern's proprietor always asked her to play when she stopped in.

"Good thing we got your fiddle," Jimmy said as they followed the road from the docks. "Clem's gonna be disappointed in our lack of appetite this evening."

Grayson's cassoulet had been well received at dinner this evening. Even Eli had offered a begrudging compliment when Grayson served him a fourth helping. Briar would never have guessed her crew would be so open to the different dishes that Grayson prepared, but he was a good enough cook that he could get away with it. What a shame she couldn't find someone like him to hire permanently.

Jimmy proved to be right. Old Clem didn't put up too much protest when they turned down a meal. Briar wasn't so certain it was her fiddle, or Eli ordering a bottle of Clem's finest. Though Clem had stroked his beard and given Grayson a speculative look. If most of his patrons hadn't been in the whiskey already, she figured Grayson's appearance in his fine clothes would have warranted a moment of silence.

With Jimmy's hand on his shoulder, Grayson was soon part of one of several card games going on near the back of the room.

"Who's the dandy?" Clem asked her.

"Just a passenger we picked up." Briar laid her fiddle case on the bar and took out the instrument, preparing to play.

"I thought you ran a freighter." Clem set a glass of whiskey beside her fiddle case.

"I do, but we were running light."

"And he clearly has the ability to pay."

"Yep." She took a deep drink from her glass, relishing the burn.

"Hope he throws some of that money around here."

She offered an indulgent smile and pulled her bow across the strings. She had yet to see any money from Mr. Grayson, but then, perhaps his abrupt departure from Portsmouth had prevented him from bringing any along. Not that it mattered now that he was working for his keep. His new lady friend probably wouldn't find him nearly so attractive if she knew he was cook for a bunch of barbaric boatmen.

Briar launched into "Turkey in the Straw," and the tavern patrons were soon clapping and stomping their feet. Some who'd had a little longer with their whiskey got up and danced.

The evening wore on, the whiskey flowed, and Briar lost herself to the merry tunes that told the story of this life she loved. This was her family, her high society, and she chided herself for letting another make her feel it was less.

She threw back another glass of Clem's belly-warming payment for the entertainment, and allowing the captain of the *Red Bird* to hand her up onto a nearby table, she began a boot stomping rendition of "Cripple Creek," accompanied by boisterous shouts and some off-tune singing.

Her own crew was scattered around the room, enjoying the camaraderie of old friends and no doubt swapping tales of the goings on along the canal.

Grayson still played cards and by his changing companions, she suspected he must have been doing well. Though that didn't surprise her. He seemed to do everything well.

The tavern door opened, and Briar looked up to see who entered. Her bow screeched to a halt as Darby and his crew stopped just inside the crowded room.

The harsh sound of her last note and the sudden absence of the music brought a hush to the room.

"I see you're dancin' the tables again Briar Rose," Darby said, intentionally dropping the *Captain*.

"You back to vandalize my boat a second time, Dale Darby? Were you *that* ashamed that my crew tossed yours into the canal?"

Darby's face turned red. "You ain't got no call for them accusations."

"I'd call you out right now except you won't fight me."

"But I will," a female voice said from behind him.

Briar smiled when Hester Darby stepped past her willowy father. She topped her father by several inches and outweighed him by an even greater margin.

She gave Briar a gap-toothed grin. Darby must have stopped by the house to pick her up just for this encounter. How thoughtful.

Briar stepped down off the table, almost missing the chain she'd tried to use as a step. Fortunately, a hand caught her elbow before she ended up on the floor.

"Are you certain this is wise?" an accented voice asked.

To Briar's annoyance, Grayson held her elbow. When he'd left his card game, she hadn't seen.

She jerked her elbow from his grip, stumbling a little before she could turn and shove her fiddle and bow into his hands.

"Put that away for me," she told him.

"You've had quite a lot to drink," he whispered. "I don't think you realize she's twice your size."

"And slow as a pregnant cow," she shot back. "I whipped her last time we fought."

A hint of amusement curled his lips. "Were you this inebriated?"

She pushed past him. "Outside," she told Hester. "I won't have you busting up Clem's furniture when your fat ass smashes into it."

Like her father, Hester's face instantly turned red. Briar thought she'd charge her right there, but she allowed her father to herd her outside.

Briar followed, along with every person in the tavern. Nothing more exciting than a good fistfight—especially between two women.

The sun hadn't yet set, but it had clouded up considerably. The gusting wind promised a coming storm.

"I'm gonna pound you to dust," Hester told her. Though her father had sneered at Briar's attire, Hester had adopted the same style of dress in her trousers and waistcoat, though Briar fancied she could make three sets for herself from the fabric involved.

"That's what you said last time," Briar reminded her.

They stopped in the dirt yard before the tavern. The crowd gathered on the front porch and the yard, forming a rough circle around them.

"Take 'er down, Captain Rose!" a man shouted from the crowd. It wasn't one of her crew.

"You spread your legs for him, too?" Hester sneered. "Everyone says that's how you got to be captain."

"I inherited my boat," Briar said through clenched teeth.

"Heard your cousin owns the boat. I also heard he's real pissed that you took it."

Briar stepped closer. "Where'd you hear that?"

"He came to the docks in Portsmouth looking for you Monday afternoon. Heard he's offered a reward for news of your whereabouts."

So Andrew had gone back to Portsmouth after he met Solon in Waverly? Had Solon gone with him? Maybe Andrew had agreed to take him to Martel. Apparently, they hadn't found him if the pair was later seen in Chillicothe.

"Also heard about your fancy man," Hester continued. "He paying to ride your boat, or something else?"

Briar slammed her fist into the woman's big mouth.

The blow caused her to stumble back a step, and a cheer rose around them.

Hester turned her head and spit the blood from her mouth. "Forgot how strong you were, bitch."

She charged toward Briar, a meaty fist pulled back for a punch that never connected. Briar ducked the blow.

Briar spun to face her, stumbling a little. Grayson might have a point about the inebriation, but Briar figured she'd have to be unconscious before Hester could get the better of her. After facing the soulless, Briar found the current contest like fighting in slow motion.

Her mind took her back to that fight, and she remembered how well Grayson had handled himself. She never had asked him about where he learned to—

Hester closed with her more quickly than she expected, and Briar wasn't able to move fast enough, taking a glancing blow across the cheek. Damn, she hit hard.

"Pay attention," Briar muttered to herself. She regained her balance, but the blow to the head must have knocked loose her brain that was already floating in whiskey fumes.

Her vision doubled, and for just a second, there were two

Hesters coming at her. The two images merged into one just in time for Briar to avoid Hester's next punch.

Briar stumbled back, shaking her head in an attempt to clear it. She had to end this soon.

On Hester's next swing, Briar didn't spring back. She simply leaned to the side, narrowly avoiding the blow. She came back with a punch of her own that the larger woman couldn't avoid—or was too slow to avoid.

Briar caught her with a solid blow to the chin, the punch so hard it stung her hand.

Hester's head snapped back and her body followed, though she managed to keep her feet under her as she staggered backward.

Ignoring the whoops and shouts from the crowd, Briar followed the stumbling woman and landed a second blow to one pockmarked cheek.

This time, Hester dropped to a knee.

"Had enough?" Briar asked.

Hester came off the ground with a roar like an angry bull—or maybe an enraged cow.

Briar saw it coming, but she was standing too close, and her impaired reaction time didn't allow her to move quickly enough.

This time, Briar took the blow on the chin. The power of the punch knocked her off her feet and she landed on her back hard enough to knock the air from her lungs.

"Had enough?" Hester asked, standing over her.

Briar rolled onto her hands and knees and, shaking her head, shoved herself to her feet.

She had heard the expression *seeing stars*, but this was the first time she had experienced it.

She tried to blink away the sparkling lights, just catching a glimpse of Hester closing with her. She turned her head, but didn't avoid the blow. Her balance still wasn't what it should have been, and she staggered several steps to the side before she regained her equilibrium.

"This ain't a fair fight," Eli's voice rose above the rowdy crowd. "Call off your cow, Darby. I'll fight the best you got."

"Sounds like your big man's worried about you," Hester said. "I bet I can guess how you keep him so loyal."

Briar charged her, a small voice telling her it was stupid, but she couldn't seem to help herself. She caught Hester with solid jab to the stomach, but there was just too much padding for it to prove effective. All she got was a grunt from Hester and then the bigger woman was on her.

A blow to her own stomach doubled Briar over, then the woman grabbed a fistful of her shirt and jerked her close.

"I'm sick and tired of you showing up my Da," Hester said in a low voice. "It'll be different if you can't use that pretty face to get your way." Hester lifted her arm, and Briar caught a glint of metal in her fist.

"She's got a knife!" someone shouted.

The world seemed to slow as Hester's arm descended, the knife aimed for Briar's face.

CHAPTER 12

BRIAR TRIED TO PULL BACK out of the way, but her body wouldn't respond.

Lock stirred in her pocket. If the little dragon emerged...

Suddenly, Grayson was beside her. He caught Hester's wrist at the last moment, but only managed to knock the downward plunge of the blade off course. Instead of slicing into Briar's cheek, the knife bit just below her collarbone then sliced across the front of her shoulder.

Hester released Briar's shirt, allowing her to fall on her butt. Though instead of reaching for the wound, Briar pressed her hand over her pocket, fearful that Lock would reveal himself.

Grayson's back was to her as he still held Hester's wrist, the blood slicked knife in her hand. She cried out as Grayson must have squeezed, and the knife fell in the dirt at his feet.

With something close to a roar, Eli shoved Grayson aside and took Hester by the collar.

"Eli," Briar called to him, but didn't get to finish as he slung her across the ring of onlookers. She collided with her father's thin frame, and they both ended up on the ground.

"Take your trash and get out of my sight," Eli told Darby, his voice rough and dangerous.

Darby's crew hurried over to help him and his oversized daughter to their feet. Darby's face was red and Briar thought he might speak, but one look at Eli, and he seemed to have second thoughts.

Grumbling to themselves, captain and crew began to turn away.

"Darby, is it?" Grayson's voice wasn't loud, but something in his tone brought a hush over the crowd. Even Briar felt an instinctive need to remain as small and quiet as possible.

Darby slowly turned to face Grayson. "Yeah?" his voice was soft and quivered on the single word.

"Don't forget this." A flick of the wrist, and Grayson sent Hester's knife whirling end over end toward the wide-eyed man.

The knife thunked into the tree behind him, having missed Darby's cheek by a hair's breadth.

"I missed on purpose," Grayson said, his tone as cold and devoid of human warmth as the soulless man's laugh.

Chill bumps rose on Briar's arms, and she suspected she wasn't the only one. No one moved or spoke.

Grayson turned his back on the old man and walked over to her. "Are you all right?" The coldness was gone almost as if it had never been there. He offered her a hand.

"Yes." She reached up, but Eli shouldered Grayson aside and took her hand instead. He pulled her to her feet, the movement making her wounded shoulder and throbbing head pound in unison. Unable to find her equilibrium, she stumbled forward, and Eli caught her against him.

"Are you sure about that?" Grayson asked her, a smile in his voice.

Beyond them, she saw Darby turn and eye the knife. She feared he might pull it out and hurl it back at Grayson, but he walked past it, hurrying toward the canal bank.

"You're bleeding, Miss Briar," Eli said.

"The knife nicked my shoulder."

"Nicks don't bleed that much. We need to get you to the boat." Without warning, he picked her up and her head spun with the sudden movement.

"Eli, I can walk."

"I wouldn't take that bet," Grayson said, his tone too cheerful.

"Eli, please," she whispered.

He swung her to her feet, and this time, the world flipped upside down.

Hands caught her before she hit the ground, and once again, she was lifted off her feet. The dizziness hit so hard, she feared she might be sick. Squeezing her eyes closed, she prayed she wouldn't vomit in front of the entire inn.

"I commend your respect for her wishes," Grayson said, his voice too close, "but sometimes, you have to do what is best for her, my friend."

With horror, Briar realized that Grayson held her.

"You're not my friend," Eli growled.

"You can put me down, Mr. Grayson," she tried to cut in.

"Sorry, Captain." He turned and started walking. "I'm not yet yours to command."

She puzzled over the *yet*. Was he thinking of joining her crew? They would certainly welcome his cooking talents, but she couldn't imagine a man like him serving as cook on a canal boat.

She started to ask him about it, but he was setting her down. Good. She didn't want to be carried away from the tavern like some delicate flower. She walked away from her fights.

"Easy." Grayson gripped her uninjured shoulder. "Can you sit up or should I lay you down?"

"I'm fine," she ground out, annoyed with his over protectiveness. "I'm not some damsel in distress that needs rescuing."

"We all need to be rescued at some point, Miss Rose. If one of your crew were injured and you were able, would you not carry him to safety?"

"Yes, but I'm fine. I can walk to the boat."

"You're on the boat." He was definitely smiling.

She blinked, trying to force her eyes and mind to work together. A hazy image of the deck of her boat swam into focus, the crew gathered around where she sat on a barrel.

"Mr. Grayson is right," Jimmy spoke up. "There's no shame in letting your friends help you. Goodness knows, Eli has slung me over his shoulder more than once and hauled me home from a tussle."

She groaned and bowed her head, giving up on the argument. They didn't understand.

A tug on the shoulder of her waistcoat almost upset her uncertain balance—and reawakened the pain.

"Sorry," Grayson muttered.

"What are you doing?" Eli demanded.

Grayson leaned in to examine the wound. "This is going to need stitches."

"You ain't doing it," Eli said.

Grayson sighed. "Is there anyone else onboard with the necessary training?"

"I'm sure there's a woman on one of the boats who—" Eli began.

"Like bloody hell," Grayson cut him off. "I'm not going to stand by while some woman and her dirty needles tests her sewing skills on Miss Rose."

"You ain't doing it," Eli repeated.

"Are you suggesting that I plan to take advantage of an injured woman?" The coldness was back in Grayson's voice. "I'd call you out right now, friend, but I happen to consider her welfare more important."

"Would you two quit?" she complained. "If it needs stitches, I'll do it myself."

"It's your right shoulder. You're right-handed," Grayson pointed out. "Don't—"

A loud crack of thunder cut off what else he might say. A large raindrop hit her cheek and another splashed against her forehead.

"Someone help me get her down to her cabin and out of this rain," Grayson said.

"And that's really not appropriate," Eli said.

"Then join me," Grayson growled the words. "You can punch me if my stitching seems inappropriate."

"I'll do it," Jimmy spoke up. "You'd take up too much room, big guy." He thumped Eli's shoulder.

Briar knew what Jimmy was doing and gratitude warmed her heart. Eli didn't do well around blood. Even a minor injury would turn him green. Eli claimed he'd always been that way, and they had just accepted that aspect of his personality. Everyone had a weakness. Blood was Eli's.

"Come along, Captain." Grayson started to pull her good arm across his shoulders.

"I can walk." She pushed him away, then slid to her feet. She had to grip the barrel to stay on her feet.

"Take my arm, Captain?" Grayson offered his arm. "Your big man is going to pummel me if any harm befalls you. I assume that includes taking a tumble down the hatch."

"Ha ha." She tried to make fun of it, but gripped his arm as he asked her to. She was still so light headed, but didn't know if it was from the whiskey or the punch in the face. Probably both.

"You want to climb down first in case she misses a step?" Grayson asked Jimmy.

"You're all a bunch of overprotective ninnies," she told them.

"What exactly is a ninnie?" Grayson asked.

"A type of goat?" Jimmy offered.

"I think that's a nanny," Grayson said. "But perhaps it's a dialect thing."

"How long have you lived in this country?" Jimmy asked as the pair helped her down the ladder.

"About three years, but I spent most of that time on the east coast."

Briar managed not to fall down the ladder and let them guide her to the cook's bunk. It was roomier than the narrow space that served as her room. Besides, she preferred to keep her space private.

Becca Andre

"Are you still with me?" Grayson asked, squatting beside the bunk.

Had he asked something and she hadn't replied? "Yes."

"I'm going to need you to remove the waistcoat and pull your shirt off your shoulder."

She didn't know how to respond to that.

"Or you could go put on that green gown you were wearing when we first met. As I recall, it left your shoulders bare."

"I'd rather not," she said.

"I'll turn my back, Captain," Jimmy said, doing just that.

"As will I." Grayson held her gaze for one long moment, then rose to his feet and gave her his back. "But if you fall over, please try not to hit your head on the wall."

"I'm not going to fall over," she complained. She started undoing the buttons on her waistcoat, suddenly self-conscious—which was silly. As Grayson had pointed out, she had worn dresses that were more revealing. Except she wore a corset under her dresses. In her boatman's attire, the fitted waistcoat served that purpose.

Gritting her teeth, she managed to work the waistcoat off her shoulders and down her arms. The right shoulder of the garment was bloodstained and split where the knife had penetrated the fabric. She'd have to wash and mend it later.

Undoing the top three buttons of her shirt, she was able to slip it off her shoulder, revealing the oozing wound just below her collarbone.

"I'm ready," she said.

Grayson turned to face her, and after the briefest of glances, moved the pillow to the opposite end of the bed and encouraged her to lie down. "With the injury closer to me, you'll get prettier stitches," he said.

"I was so concerned." She didn't bother to hide the sarcasm.

"I wouldn't want to deter you from wearing another off-the-shoulder gown."

"Mr. Grayson?" Jimmy cut in, a hint of a reprimand in his tone.

"Just a little harmless banter to put her at ease," Grayson answered. He picked up the folded blanket from the foot of the bed and pulled it over her.

She lifted a brow. "Do you fear I'll take a chill?" The rain hadn't been that soaking.

"It's not for you." He gave her a wink.

Her cheeks heated, but he got to his feet before she was required to comment. Walking over to Jimmy, he began to discuss what he needed to play doctor.

She pulled the blanket a little higher. Oddly, the comment warmed her rather than pissed her off. The blow to the head must have messed her up more than she realized.

Grayson returned a few minutes later, carrying a bowl of water and a wet cloth. He sat down on the side of the bed and began dabbing the wound.

She gritted her teeth until he stopped. "How bad is it?"

"It's not as deep as I feared, but stitching it will help it heal cleaner."

She grunted, not looking forward to that.

"This man Darby. He's the one who damaged your boat?"

"Yes. We've never gotten along, but when he flat refused to yield the right of way on our arrival in Portsmouth, it came to blows."

"Ah." He rinsed the rag, then began wiping away the blood around the wound—which wasn't as painful. "Is that when you first fought his daughter?"

"No, that was years ago. She thought I was trying to court some man she wanted."

A smile curled Grayson's lips, though he didn't look up from what he was doing. "Were you?"

"No." Briar frowned. "I have no patience for that foolishness."

"Fighting over a man or just courting in general?"

"I already have my cousin trying to rule my life. I don't need another man helping him."

Grayson looked up. "Do you mean to say that you've never been courted?"

"Men have tried. I don't entertain them."

"Many a man has tried," Jimmy joined the conversation, carrying over a pair of towels. "But no man can tame our Briar Rose." He gave her a smile.

"Maybe I don't want to be tamed, Jimmy O'Shea."

"It's not so bad."

She rolled her eyes. "Ignore him," she told Grayson. "He's newly married."

"Congratulations," Grayson told him. "Your wife doesn't travel with you?"

"We set up housekeeping in Portsmouth, and since we only run the Scioto River Valley—the stretch from Columbus to Portsmouth," he added for Grayson's benefit, "I usually get in every week, and most of the winter."

"What an interesting life all of you lead," Grayson said.

"None better," Briar agreed.

The teapot whistled and Jimmy returned to the stove.

"You seem to move around a lot," she said to Grayson.

"Not by choice." He picked up his bowl and rag. "You have the right of it, Miss Rose. Don't let any man—or woman—take away your freedom. It's a precious thing."

"You sound like you envy us."

"I do."

"You envy this barbaric means of travel where you can't expect an educated conversation?"

He smiled and she had no doubt that he realized that she'd overheard his conversation with the Englishwoman. "This mode of travel has grown on me, and I happen to enjoy our conversations."

She frowned.

"I was playing a role," he said.

"You seemed pleased when you told Jimmy you got her address."

He lifted his brows.

"Another role to play," she concluded.

He dipped his chin. "I told you: it's my ability to adapt that's kept me alive."

"Then how do I know you're not playing a role now?"

"You don't." He gave her a smile that was almost sad. "There are only two other people in this world who know more about me than you do."

"I know nothing about you."

"So I've led you to believe." He gave her a wink, then walked over to join Jimmy at the stove.

Briar frowned at his back, not sure what to make of that conversation. He was a man who envied her freedom, yet moved around the world at will. And if she was one of the few who really knew him—well, that was just sad.

THE STITCHING PROCESS WAS A miserable, grueling procedure that left her jaws aching from clenching her teeth. Grayson had been as gentle as he could, but no degree of gentleness could alleviate the pain of having a needle poked through torn flesh.

Once he finished, her relief was so great that she instantly fell into a dreamless slumber.

Unfortunately, she didn't wake feeling all that rested. Her head thumped with a morning-after headache. It didn't help that her shoulder and chin were sore from her fight with Hester Darby.

Briar blinked her eyes, staring up at the unfamiliar ceiling until she remembered that she'd fallen asleep in the cook's bunk.

Speaking of sleeping... loud snores echoed through the cabin. She hadn't heard such noise since she shared the cabin with her uncle and cousin.

"No, you can't move like that," Grayson's accented voice was soft, but the answering whirr of gears wasn't.

Briar turned her head and saw Grayson sitting at her table. Before him was her uncle's chess set.

"Knight takes bishop," Grayson said.

Another indignant metallic squawk drew her attention to Lock, who to her amazement, sat on the table across the board from Grayson.

"It does too move like that. Pay attention. The knight moves two spaces forward, then one to the right or left. The bishop moves diagonally."

An angry whirr came from the little dragon, his tail whipping in agitation.

"You knock the pieces off the board again, and I'm making you into a fruit press."

Lock snapped his jaws.

"Try me."

"Are you teaching him to play chess?" Briar asked.

Grayson spun to face her, the motion so fast that she knew he hadn't known she was awake.

Abruptly, he smiled. "You have already corrupted it, so I thought I could put it to good use. I was wrong."

Lock snapped his jaws again.

Briar smiled at the little dragon's spunk, then sat up. She couldn't quite subvert the groan.

"How are you?" he asked.

She rubbed her temple. "I'm swearing off alcohol."

He chuckled and got to his feet. Stepping over where Jimmy still snored on a blanket on the floor, he walked to the stove and poured a cup of steaming liquid from the teapot. She didn't smell coffee.

"What's that?" she asked when he brought her the cup. She held it to her nose and inhaled the pungent scent.

"Willow bark tea," Grayson answered.

She brought the cup to her lips and took a tentative sip.

"I added some honey and—"

"Ugh." She pulled the cup from her mouth. "Does the nasty taste scare away the headache?"

"Drink it down. Don't be such a baby."

She made a face at him, but did as he instructed, holding her breath to avoid the taste. It still lingered when she finished, and she coughed.

"Disgusting," she breathed.

"A necessary evil." He took the cup back and set it on the table.

Lock moved closer to poke at it just as Jimmy rolled over, releasing another loud snore. Lock morphed into the pocket watch.

"I see why Jimmy's wife doesn't join him on the boat," Grayson said. "It's her only chance to get a good night's sleep."

"Is that what kept you awake?"

"No." He didn't elaborate, sitting down on the side of her bunk. "May I see?"

She glanced down and realized that her shirt was no longer off her shoulder, but the top buttons were still undone to the center of her breastbone. Fortunately, it hadn't gapped open too much.

"All right." She tried to ignore the heat in her cheeks. She was curious about the injury herself. She hadn't gotten a chance to examine it after he finished.

Working the shirt back off her shoulder, she glanced down at the neatly stitched wound. It was close to four inches long, starting just beneath her collarbone and stretching across the front of her shoulder.

"Not bad," he said. "I prepared a poultice. Let me warm it." He returned to the stove, stepping over Jimmy's sleeping form again.

The tea warmed her belly, and she swore her aches and pains had lessened. She leaned back against the pillow and closed her eyes, listening to the oddly soothing sounds of Grayson working at the stove.

Her bunk shifted, and she realized he had sat back down beside her.

"That was quick," she said, noting how the words were slightly slurred.

"I think you dozed off."

She blinked her eyes to look up at him, but he was studying the wound. "What else was in that tea?"

"Honey and rum."

"Great. Rum knocks me on my ass."

He smiled, but didn't look up from what he was doing.

She pulled in a breath as he smeared a warm dollop of his poultice on her wound.

"Sorry," he muttered.

"S'all right."

Another smile curled his lips, drawing her eyes to his mouth. He had a nice mouth—which was an odd thing to notice. She didn't recall ever noticing such a thing on a man.

"I think I'm drunk," she told him. "So much for swearing off alcohol."

"Sorry about that, too." He kept his eyes on his work, his long dark lashes brushing his cheeks when he looked down.

"You'll thank me in the morning," he said.

She realized that she believed him. "Why do I trust you?"

He looked up, his slate-blue eyes more gray than blue in the low light.

"I don't know you," she insisted. "And you don't know me, yet you've put yourself in harm's way twice to save me—or at least, my physical form." She wasn't so certain that her life had actually been in danger.

He offered another smile with those very nice lips. "Maybe I like your physical form."

From any other man, she would have taken insult, yet when he said it, it warmed her more than the tea.

"I should slap you," she told him, striving for some semblance of normalcy.

"You should," he agreed. His expression turned serious, yet the new look upon his features did not detract from them. How strange that she'd never noticed what a handsome man he was.

"You should command me to go," he whispered.

"I should." But she didn't. A part of her mind insisted that she was no longer thinking straight, but she ignored it. Pushing all logic aside, she leaned up and brushed his lips with hers.

For the briefest moment, he hesitated, then his mouth was moving against hers.

It seemed he must have breathed life into her because her body came alive in a way she had never felt before. Then he opened his mouth and trailed his tongue along her lower lip in a shocking, yet deeply intimate gesture.

"Open for me," he said against her lips. "Let me in."

He licked her lower lip once more, and she opened her mouth. His tongue slipped inside, but it wasn't as disgusting as she would have expected. After a brief moment to overcome the strangeness of the situation, she copied him. She liked the way he tasted—which was really bizarre.

He groaned, the sound sending another wave of heat through her body. She didn't protest when he pushed her back against the pillow, his mouth still deeply engaged with hers. This time, she groaned.

"Briar," he breathed her name against her lips. "We must stop." His words didn't match his actions as he continued to kiss her.

"Why?" the question was muffled against his mouth.

"You don't know what you're doing."

"You could teach me."

"I was referring to the fact that you're drunk." He lifted his head, but he remained braced on his hands above her, his eyes shadowed, but his wonderful mouth damp and flushed.

She didn't want him to stop. Reaching up, she attempted to wrap her arms around his neck, but the pain in her right shoulder made her stop.

He pulled back. "Don't. You already have too much power over me."

She frowned, not understanding what he meant by that.

"Tomorrow, we will arrive in Columbus where you will learn that those plans contain no ferromancy. You will return them and the construct, and we will go our separate ways."

Her addled mind tried to make sense of what he was saying. "You're leaving."

"Yes," he spoke the word firmly as if convincing himself more than her.

"This is just another role to play," she said.

He neither agreed nor disagreed. Getting to his feet, he gave her his back. "Construct," he said to Lock. "Watch over her."

Without another word, Grayson climbed the ladder and disappeared through the hatch.

Lock sprang from the table to the bed and crawled up the blanket until he reached her pillow. He rubbed his cheek with hers, his soft coo questioning.

"I don't know," she answered. "Maybe I'll wake up and this will all have been a dream." Whether it would turn out to be a good dream or bad, she wasn't certain.

CHAPTER 13

BRIAR WOKE TO THE SMELL of bacon and the awareness that the boat was moving.

She sat up, clutching the blanket to her chest. It was full daylight beyond the cabin windows, and through a gap in the curtains, she could see the banks slipping past at the usual speed.

"Good morning, Captain." Jimmy sat at her table, a mug in hand.

"We're moving," she said.

"Aye. We knew you wanted to make Columbus this afternoon, but we didn't want to disturb your healing slumber. Are you feeling better?"

"Yes, I think so."

Jimmy smiled and got to his feet. "Good, but if you're head's a thumping, Mr. Grayson makes an amazing tea that will take care of that." He gestured with his mug.

"Careful with that. He gave me some last night, and it knocked me out."

"Really?" He looked into his mug. "This is my second cup."

"There's rum in it," she explained.

"Yeah, but just a little." He looked up. "Maybe he made yours stronger since you were injured and all. I bet it would have been hard to sleep."

She frowned, wondering if that had been Grayson's motive.

"Are you upset that we're underway without your command?" Jimmy asked, misinterpreting her frown. "It was my idea."

"No, Jimmy. Thank you for getting us moving. I really made a mess of things yesterday."

"Nah. You did great. It wasn't your fault that Darby cow had a knife."

She sighed. That wasn't exactly the event she was referring to, but she couldn't go into that with him.

"Would you give me some privacy so I can freshen up?"

"Sure." He got to his feet. "We saved you some breakfast. It's in the covered pan on the back of the stove. Mr. Grayson made something he called om-mu-lets. You need to hire him."

"I'm afraid he has other plans."

"A shame. That man would make someone a good wife." Chuckling at his own joke, he left the cabin.

A questioning coo broke the silence, and she noticed movement beneath her pillow.

"Yes, you can come out now, Lock."

The little dragon crawled from beneath her pillow. He gave himself a shake, his silver scales shimmering in a glittering wave over his body as the sunlight caught on the shiny metal.

"Goodness, you're beautiful." She held out a hand, and he hopped into her palm. "I'm going to miss you when Mr. Grayson takes you away."

Lock moaned, his silver wings drooping.

"But maybe I can arrange a way to meet you again." Once the boat was hers, perhaps she could write Molly and get Mr. Martel's address. But first, she needed to know if he was a ferromancer.

She set Lock down on the table and headed for her room to change. Today, she would go see Uncle Liam and determine once and for all if Grayson was telling her the truth.

BRIAR TOOK HER TIME GETTING ready. She even sat down to eat breakfast. Jimmy had been right about the egg concoction Mr. Grayson had prepared. It was wonderful.

When there were no more excuses for her to remain in her cabin, she went topside.

Jimmy was mopping the crew's bunkhouse, while Benji cleaned the stables. She found Eli at the tiller, but before she could ask him where Mr. Grayson had gone, she saw him out on the towpath, walking with Zach and the mules.

"Morning, Miss Briar," Eli greeted her. "Jimmy said you were much improved."

"I am." She took a seat on the rail beside him.

"You seem a bit out of sorts, though."

She glanced over, and he lifted his bushy brows in question. In the past, she could always share her troubles with Eli and he could help her work through them. But she knew he'd be furious if she admitted that she'd kissed Mr. Grayson. It was times like these that she wished she had a woman to talk to.

"I'm still a little groggy from yesterday's beating." That did stick in her craw as well. It just wasn't as vexing as this issue with Grayson.

"It happens, Miss Briar. You'll whip her next time."

Briar smiled at his optimism. "I guess I better get to work, especially after lying around all morning."

"Don't over do it. That wound needs a good day or two to get the healing well started. Me and the boys will do the big stuff."

She sighed and, well aware that he wouldn't relent, went off to find some little things to do.

SHE WAS OILING A MULE harness when they reached Four Mile Lock on the Columbus Feeder Canal. The lock was so named because it was only four miles from Columbus. They should be there in a little over an hour.

After helping Zach and Benji swap out the team, Grayson came aboard.

"Shall I lay out a midday meal?" he asked her. "I had planned a simple repast since we'll be docking this afternoon."

He didn't seem to have any trouble speaking to her. Maybe the whole exchange hadn't left him uncomfortable. She, on the other hand, grew annoyed with the way her gaze kept dropping to his mouth when he spoke. She needed to have this out.

"I'll help you," she said, then continued before he could refuse. "The crew has assigned me light duty until this scratch is healed."

He smiled at that. "Very well." He walked to the hatch, then held it open for her. She climbed down and he followed, the hatch thumping closed behind him.

"You're getting the plans back today?" he asked before she could speak. He stepped past her and walked to the stove.

"Yes. My friend, Mr. Liam Adams lives in Columbus."

"Ah." He pulled out the cutting board and unwrapped the ham.

She frowned at his back a moment.

"How's the shoulder?" he asked.

"Fine." She took a breath. "About last night—"

"My wits abandoned me. I apologize."

She spread her hands, though he didn't see the gesture. "This is awkward as hell," she complained.

"You've never kissed a man before, have you?"

"What does that have to do with—"

"You would know that the easiest solution to avoid the awkwardness is to pretend nothing happened."

She guessed that was what he'd been doing. "You are the one with the experience." She stepped up beside him. "How can I help?"

"Slice the bread?"

"What bread?"

"Oh." He took down a basket and unwrapped a crusty loaf.

"Where did that come from?"

"I made it this morning."

"Damn, that tea of yours must have knocked me out cold."

He didn't comment, probably because that tea had led her to kiss him. Pretending it didn't happen. Right.

She carried the loaf back to the table and began to slice it. Lock crawled out of her pocket and hopped down onto the table to inspect what she was doing.

"What about Lock?" she asked. "Will I ever see him again?"

The little dragon sprang up onto her shoulder and huddled against her neck.

"Probably not. The railroad is expanding westward. That's most likely where I'll go."

"Those are Mr. Martel's plans?"

"Yes."

She glanced over, but he still had his back to her. She considered asking more, but returned to her task. The silence stretched, becoming uncomfortable. Finally, she couldn't stand it any longer.

"What does Mr. Martel have on you?" she asked. "Is he the one keeping you from your freedom?" She remembered well his envy of her life, even though a lot of other details were hazy.

"It's no concern of yours." He carried over the baskets, one already filled with sliced ham and a round of cheese. He began to gather up the bread she'd sliced. "Do you want to get the plates?"

She huffed, but did as he asked.

Looping the baskets over his arm, he started to climb the ladder, but she caught his sleeve.

"My freedom wasn't just given to me," she said. "I had to fight for it."

"And I admire that in you."

"Then let me help you."

"You can." His gaze held hers. "By letting me and your Lock go." He climbed the ladder and left her standing there.

She noted that it was the closest he'd ever come to calling Lock by name. But it seemed a hollow victory.

She left Eli and Jimmy to oversee the unloading of the lumber, and walked with Zach to the Columbus canal office. Her silent companion glanced around as they walked, and she wondered if he was taking his bodyguard duties a little too seriously. Ever since the assault in Chillicothe, the crew had been insistent that she venture nowhere alone.

"I saw Mr. Grayson on the towpath with you this morning," she said as they walked. "You seem to have befriended him."

Zach nodded.

"That's nice." She wished Zach could tell her what Mr. Grayson spoke of—if anything. Most people fell silent when they spent any time around Zach.

"I'll certainly miss his cooking when he goes."

Zach glanced over. A considering look, then he nodded and faced forward once more. He went back to scanning their surroundings, and she glimpsed the scars that ran down the right side of his neck and disappeared beneath his shirt.

She sometimes wondered what he'd been like before the accident. Did the silence bother him? She always made a point to speak to him and not to imitate his silence, but it was hard to hold a conversation when she was the only one talking.

"Ah, here we are," she said as they reached the canal office. "I'll pay our tolls. Hopefully, the boat will be unloaded when we return."

Zach nodded then took a seat on the bench beside the front door. She left him there and walked inside.

"Captain Rose." Mr. Baker gave her a wide smile from his place behind the counter. "This dreary old room just got a whole lot brighter."

She forced a smile and walked over to greet him. It seemed people either sneered at her captaincy, or used it as an opportunity to flirt with her. There wasn't a whole lot of in-between.

"Good to see you, as well, Mr. Baker." She handed over her manifest, then waited while he took his sweet time tallying up the toll she owed. Before he was even halfway finished, she wanted to jerk the pencil and paper out of his hand and tally the numbers herself. As Uncle Charlie had told her frequently, patience was not one of her virtues.

Mr. Baker finally gave her a total, dropping a not too subtle hint that dinner with him might lower her fee. She managed to politely decline instead of punching him.

"Oh, and before you go, I have a letter for you." Mr. Baker pulled out a small beige envelope.

She recognized the stationery and the curly monogram on the back. An *A* for Adams.

Her heart beating faster, she accepted the letter. "Thank you, Mr. Baker."

If he had more platitudes, she didn't catch them. She was already out the door.

Zach started to get up when she stepped outside, but resumed his seat when she dropped onto the bench.

"Adams left me a letter," she explained, already ripping open the envelope. A single sheet of matching stationery had been folded once and tucked inside.

My Dear Briar:

I will be departing Columbus on the sixteenth. I promised to take Agatha to see her sister, and I dare not disappoint her. If you should arrive after the sixteenth, I must ask you to visit me in Millersport. I will have your schematics with me.

I hope I have not inconvenienced you.

Your Friend,
Adams.

Briar turned to Zach. "Today is the fifteenth, right?"
He nodded, and she released a breath.

"Good. That will save me some trouble."

He gave her a questioning look.

"Oh. Sorry." She would have passed the letter to him, but he wouldn't be able to read it. "My friend will be leaving the city for Millersport tomorrow. Unless I wish to visit him there, I must go see him now."

Zach rose to his feet, then gestured for her to lead the way.

"You don't need to escort me. They live only a few blocks from here."

He shook his head, refusing to abandon his guard duty.

Briar sighed and got to her feet. "Since when did my crew become a bunch of over protective ninnies?"

Zach simply held her gaze, his jaw set in determination.

"Fine," she muttered. "You can play bodyguard a little longer. But unless I get attacked by an overzealous pigeon looking for a few bread crumbs, you're going to have a dull time of it."

Zach just shrugged.

CHAPTER 14

THEY REACHED MR. ADAMS'S MODEST townhouse a short time later. Zach refused to accompany her inside, so Briar left him sitting on the curb and climbed the steps to Adams's front door. Agatha must have been watching because the door opened the moment Briar stepped up on the front stoop.

"Briar Rose! I had hoped you would arrive today." The elderly woman pulled her through the door and into a tight hug. Briar returned the gesture as the door swung shut behind her.

"I've missed you," Briar admitted.

"And I, you." Agatha kissed her cheek, then released her. "Look at you. More beautiful every time I see you."

"You say that every time you see me," Briar answered.

"Well, it's true." The older woman winked. "Have you found a husband yet?"

Briar gave her a loving, but exasperated head shake. "Aunt Agatha, please." Briar hoped her blush wasn't too noticeable.

Agatha was watching her, then without comment, reached up and touched the silver necklace around her throat. "What's this? A gift?"

"No, it's…" Briar stopped, not sure how to answer that. She couldn't tell Agatha the truth, but she couldn't lie to the woman who was the closest thing she had to a mother. Grayson's words from this morning came back to her. If he had his way, she would be parted from Lock very soon.

Agatha took her hand, quickly picking up on her uncertainty. "Come talk to me." She tugged Briar toward the parlor.

"That isn't necessary." Briar pulled her to a stop.

"Nonsense. I saw that look in your eyes."

"What look?"

"Uncertainty, hurt, frustration. What's his name?"

Briar sighed. "Really, it's not—"

"Come now." Agatha gave her hand a squeeze. "You know you can tell me anything."

"Yes." Briar fumbled for some excuse. "It's complicated."

"Of course it is, dear. These things are always complicated." She patted Briar's hand. "I won't pry, but I'm here if you need me."

Briar gave her another hug, wishing she could tell her about this mess she had created, but she couldn't quite bring herself to admit that she'd kidnapped a man.

"Is Mr. Adams in?" Briar asked, trying to change the topic.

"He's in his workshop, of course." Agatha's tone was resigned. She knew she couldn't get Briar to talk if she didn't want to.

"I'll go see him. He has something that belongs to me."

"Yes, those plans." Agatha's smile was bemused. "He hasn't stopped talking about them since they arrived."

"What did he say about them?" Would he have said anything to Agatha if they were ferromantic?

"He rattled on with a lot of technical jargon I didn't follow," Agatha answered, "but he's clearly enjoyed them. You know what the man's like when he finds some new mechanical wonder to study."

Briar smiled. She could easily imagine that. She suddenly regretted not bringing Grayson. He and Adams would certainly get along.

SHE FOUND MR. ADAMS WHERE she expected: hunched over his workbench. An assortment of gadgets and half-assembled contraptions covered every surface. Bookshelves lined with well-used tomes and rolled sheets of drafting paper competed for space in the cramped, but oddly comfortable room. Next to her boat, this was Briar's favorite place to be. She had spent many a happy hour tinkering with Uncle Liam in this workshop.

Stopping on the threshold, she tapped on the open door.

"Dinner already?" Liam asked, his words colored by the Scottish brogue that still clung to him, even after decades in this country.

"Not just yet," Briar answered.

Liam looked up, a wide grin on his ruddy cheeks. Judging by the color on his face and his disheveled salt and pepper hair, he'd been working for some time.

"My Briar Rose." He pushed himself off his stool and hurried over to her. "I didn't realize you had arrived."

"Only just now." She exchanged a quick hug with him.

"Hm. Well, I guess you are here to divest me of my newest treasures." Liam released her and stepped back.

She smiled at his word choice, remembering Agatha's comment on Liam's obsession with them. "Yes, I'm here for the locomotive plans," she answered, turning serious. "What did you think of them?"

"They're extraordinary. I've barely been able to sleep because of my desire to exam them in minute detail."

"And?" Briar bit her lip, waiting for Liam's answer. Had all this been worth it? Could she defame the railroad and save the canal?

Liam's gray eyes met hers. "I think I know why you acquired them, but I fear I must disappoint you. The man who designed them is a mechanical genius, not a ferromancer. Though I would wager that he has studied their technology."

Disappointment snatched away her excitement. "You're certain?"

"Yes, my dear." He studied her. "How did you acquire them?"

"My cousin has decided to go into the business of building locomotives. I took those from his business partner."

"In hope of proving that he was using ferromancy."

She sighed. "Yes. I had hoped to ruin the railroad's reputation and save the canal."

Liam pressed his lips together, his expression amused, yet sad. "Briar."

"I had to try."

"I understand."

She smiled. "I knew you would." Liam was the kind of man who took action against a wrong, even when that action wasn't completely on the up and up. He'd never given her any details, but he had once admitted that he'd had to do some wrong to see good prevail.

He turned away and lifted the leather tube she'd used to send him the plans. "What are you going to do now?"

"Return the plans," she answered. "If what you say is true, these plans are the product of hard work and creative genius. Even if the designer sells them to the railroad, I can't take them from him."

Liam gave her a soft smile. "That's my lass. Take the high road."

"I'm trying."

He nodded and offered her the tube. "Then I won't impede you."

She accepted the plans and slipped the strap over her shoulder. "Thank you." She stepped forward to give him another hug. "I'm so glad I came to you before turning these over to the newspaper."

Liam chuckled. "Yes. They would have believed as you do."

She stepped back and looked up at him. "They would have gone after the railroad."

Liam sobered. "The railroad would have tried to save face, most likely by having the plans' engineer hanged."

Briar stared up at him, remembering well Grayson's tale of the watchmaker. Had she almost doomed another brilliant mind with accusations of magic?

"I see you understand," Liam said. "You have the heart of a witch hunter, but I would never wish that life on you."

Briar wasn't sure what to make of that statement. Perhaps Liam was trying to be enigmatic. "You're right. I don't think I could live with myself if I caused the death of an innocent." She slipped a thumb beneath the strap over her shoulder. "I'll return these plans and be through with it." Even if she did have to listen to Grayson say *I told you so*.

"That's my girl." He patted her shoulder.

"Briar?" Agatha called from the doorway. "Will you be staying for dinner?"

Briar turned to face her, ready to explain that she needed to get back to the boat, but the leather tube clipped a ruler on the edge of Liam's workbench and knocked it to the floor.

"I'm afraid I can't stay," Briar said, leaning around the side of the bench to retrieve the ruler. The heavy medallion slipped from beneath her shirt and bumped against her chin. "I need to visit Bennett's Mill to see if I can secure some cargo for the return trip."

"But you've only just arrived. I had hoped we could visit," Agatha said. "You get to Columbus so infrequently."

Briar straightened and returned the ruler to the workbench. "I know. Maybe I can spend some time with you this winter." After the boat was hers.

"Oh, we would love that," Agatha said. "Right, dear?" she directed the last at Liam.

"Absolutely," Liam answered. "It has been too long since you've stayed with us. I've missed your help with my inventions."

Briar turned to face him, smiling at his enthusiasm. She longed to tell them about Andrew's plan to sell the boat, but she knew they'd insist on helping her. She also knew they couldn't afford to offer that kind of help.

Liam's smile faded, and for a moment, Briar feared he already knew about her plight. Then she realized that he was studying her throat.

"Where did you get this?" He reached out and touched the silver chain, lifting it until he could hold the medallion in his hand.

Briar felt a faint buzz of static around her neck. Fearing Lock was about to change forms, she pulled the medallion from Liam's hand and took a hasty step back.

"Briar?" Liam looked concerned.

"Don't trouble her about that," Agatha quickly came to her defense. "I think our Briar might have an admirer." She gave Briar a knowing grin.

"Aunt Agatha," Briar complained. She tucked the medallion beneath her shirt, hoping that Lock would feel more secure now that he was out of sight.

"Is this true?" Liam demanded. His stern tone surprised Briar.

"It's nothing. Really." Briar struggled for some explanation. "He's just a friend."

"Friends don't give ladies such expensive pieces of jewelry," Agatha said, her blue eyes twinkling with restrained happiness. Agatha was ever on a husband hunt for her.

"I want to meet this man," Liam said, his tone still demanding and perhaps a bit angry.

"Calm down, dear." Agatha moved to his side and laid a hand on his arm. She glanced up at Liam, looking as puzzled by this outburst as Briar felt. "I'm sure our Briar will introduce him to us when she's ready."

"Truly, it's nothing," Briar said, then continued when Agatha grinned. "But if it were, I would most certainly introduce him to you both."

"You see," Agatha said to Liam. "You needn't worry."

"She's alone in the world," Liam insisted.

Briar laughed. "No I'm not. I have my crew."

Liam frowned, not looking all that convinced.

"And speaking of my crew," Briar added, hoping to move the

conversation away from her fictitious suitor, "I need to get back to the boat."

"Of course." Agatha agreed. Still gripping Liam's arm, she pulled him with her as they started for the door. Agatha kept up a front of small talk as they made their way to the foyer at the front of the house, asking about Briar's trip and whether the recent storms had been a problem.

Briar answered her questions, grateful to talk about something so mundane. Perhaps Grayson's departure wouldn't be a bad thing. She would be relieved to be finished with this business. Her life could finally get back to normal.

Reaching the front door, Briar exchanged another hug with Agatha, and promised again to spend the winter with them. After all, she would need somewhere to stay. As soon as she bought the boat, she was finished with Andrew.

Liam still looked unhappy, but he exchanged a hug with her.

To Briar's surprise, she felt Lock stir again, and pulled away quickly. "I'll be in touch," she promised, and with what she hoped was a reassuring smile, she beat a hasty retreat out the front door.

"Don't do that, Lock," she whispered as she descended the stairs. "I would have had a devil of a time trying to explain you to them."

A buzz of static around her neck made it clear that he had heard.

Smiling, she reached up and ran her fingers along the chain. She was going to miss him so much when Grayson left. But she would return the plans. As she'd told Liam, it was the right thing to do.

ZACH REJOINED HER AS SHE reached the street, and they headed back toward the docks. Lost in her contemplation of recent events, Briar was surprised when Zach touched her arm. When she looked up, he nodded at the leather tube slung over her shoulder.

Becca Andre

"Sorry. I guess you're wondering what I learned." She sighed before continuing. "The schematics contain no magic. So much for my plan to defame the railroad."

He patted her forearm.

"Guess I'd better go tell the crew—and let Mr. Grayson say, *I told you so.*"

Zach walked beside her, unable to offer any sympathy for her plight.

She thought back over Liam's words. A mechanical genius. Of course, Mr. Martel would be one. He had created Lock. Had he drawn these plans so that others could build the locomotives?

"Or had them drawn for him." She stumbled to a stop.

Zach touched her shoulder.

"What if Mr. Grayson is the engineer and Mr. Martel is just the front man? Liam said the schematics weren't magical, but that the guy designing them was a genius. Mr. Grayson is certainly good at fixing most anything."

Zach nodded.

"The question is: does Mr. Grayson work for him willingly or not?"

Zach gave her shoulder a squeeze and released it.

She didn't know how to interpret that, but she knew where to go for answers. The schematics might not contain ferromancy, but it wasn't her only evidence that Martel was a ferromancer. She still had Lock. But was she willing to expose him to the world?

Laying a hand over the medallion beneath her shirt, she hurried back toward her boat.

The docks were a busy area with multiple boats being loaded and unloaded. She and Zach were forced to wind their way through the commotion.

Briar caught a glimpse of the *Briar Rose* through the wagons and dockworkers, noting the absence of the timber in the cargo hold.

"Looks like we're unloaded," she told Zach, leading him around

150

the back of a paneled wagon to reach the gangplank. She glanced up at the side of the wagon and blinked in surprise at the large block letters that spelled out Police.

Fearing the worst, Briar took the leather tube from her shoulder and shoved it into Zach's hands before she ran across the gangplank, but didn't need to cross it to have her fears confirmed. Two blue-coated policemen had Jimmy, Eli, and Benji corralled against the side of the stable where she'd once tied Grayson. But her eyes were drawn to the red-haired man in the fine suit.

"Let them go, Andrew." She crossed the gangplank and hopped down into the hold, aware of Zach following her.

Andrew turned to face her. "And here's the thief now."

"Let them go," she repeated. "This was all my idea. I didn't tell them I didn't have your leave to take the boat."

"You *stole* it."

"I borrowed it—to raise the money to buy it from you."

"So you intend to use the profits made from my own boat to purchase it?" An ugly smile creased his face. "That's still theft—of both my property and my profits."

She closed the distance between them. "This boat is as much mine as it is yours."

"Father left it to me. You've seen the title."

She fisted her hands, longing to punch him. "Uncle Charlie wanted the boat to remain in the family and in operation. I honored his wishes."

"The boat is still mine," Andrew said.

Briar was aware of the policeman stepping up behind her. "You're going to have me thrown in jail?" she asked Andrew.

"That's where thieves go, Bridget."

She was stunned. She'd known Andrew would be pissed, but she would never have imagined he'd go to such extremes. Wouldn't the imprisonment of a close relation shame him?

She started to ask when the man behind her gripped her shoulder.

"I see you still have it," an accented voice said at the same moment he began to lift the necklace over her head.

Briar gasped and grabbed his wrist. A metal wrist. "Solon."

"Behave," he told her, his opposite hand clamping down on her shoulder. His fingers dug into her injury, and she grunted in pain.

Solon lifted the necklace over her head and gripped it in his fist.

"Let her go!" Eli shouted, shoving aside the policeman that tried to stand in his way.

"Mr. Owens," Solon called out. "Please lend me your assistance."

Thumps came from the gangplank, and Briar turned her head to look. Her mouth dropped open as she watched the newcomer jump onto her boat. It was the soulless man Grayson had faced in Chillicothe.

He caught her look and flashed her a grin.

"If you would be so kind as to subdue the large fellow," Solon said.

"Certainly, Mr. Solon."

"Eli, don't—" She didn't get to finish the command before Eli charged the considerably smaller Mr. Owens.

The space between them vanished rapidly. Mr. Owens made no effort to move out of the way. Eli reached him, but just before his hands could close on him, the smaller man threw a punch. The move so fast that Briar barely followed it.

The blow took Eli in the chin and snapped his head back. His feet shot out from under him, and he landed on his back with a hollow boom that shook the whole boat.

"Jesus," the policeman who had tried to seize Eli said. Perhaps he had considered stepping in, but changed his mind.

A pause, and Eli rolled onto his side, then pushed himself up on his hands and knees. He shook his head as if trying to clear it.

"You may take them away," Andrew said to the policeman. "The silent one, too." He gestured at Zach who'd stopped a few feet away.

152

"Please go quietly, Eli," she said. "Don't make this worse than it is."

"On your feet, sir," the policeman said, though he didn't come much closer.

Eli shoved himself to his feet. His eyes met hers and she gave him a nod. Certainly, she could get Andrew to let them go.

"Move along there," the policeman repeated.

Eli's gaze moved to Solon's hand on her shoulder. He took a step toward them, but when Mr. Owens stepped into his path, he stopped.

"Eli—" Briar didn't get to finish as Eli threw a punch.

Mr. Owens leaned to the side, narrowly avoiding the blow. His hand shot out, and before Eli could pull back his own arm, Owens had seized his wrist.

Eli blinked in surprise, but didn't get a chance to react before Owens slung him aside. Eli hit the stable wall hard enough to bust a couple of boards before he crumpled to the deck.

Mr. Owens tugged his waistcoat straight and started toward him.

"Don't hurt him anymore," Briar pleaded.

Suddenly, Grayson dropped down from the catwalk above them, landing lightly on his feet between Eli and Mr. Owens.

"Would you like a rematch?" he asked the soulless man.

Mr. Owens came to a stop, glancing over his shoulder at Solon.

"Mr. Martel." Andrew stared at Grayson. "You *are* here."

CHAPTER 15

"**W**HAT?" SHE TRIED TO PULL away from Solon, but he wouldn't let her go.

Grayson glanced at her before lifting his gaze to the man who held her. "Release her, Solon. You have what you want."

"Do I?"

The policemen were rounding up the crew. One took the leather tube from Zach and dropped it to the deck. But they did allow Jimmy and Benji to help Eli up.

"Briar?" Eli called, his voice a little slurred.

"Please go." She nodded at Jimmy and Benji to assist him.

Once they had Eli on his feet, they were herded across the gangplank toward the waiting wagon.

She turned back to find Grayson watching her. "You're Mr. Martel?" she demanded. "The ferromancer?"

"Ferromancer?" Andrew spoke up. "Of course not. He just stole their technology and adapted it to his own use. Mr. Solon alerted me to that. Fortunately, I hadn't finalized the investment." Was that what Andrew and Solon had been discussing in Waverly?

Grayson gave him a dark frown.

Andrew's words sank in, and Briar's stomach turned over. Mr. Martel—Grayson—wasn't a ferromancer. Uncle Liam had even confirmed it. The plans contained no ferromancy. Aside from hiding who he was, Grayson had been telling her the truth.

"Let her go, Solon," Grayson repeated. "I won't resist."

"Of course you won't." Solon raised his gloved hand that still held the silver necklace. A shimmer, and he suddenly held Lock in his fist.

"Holy hell," Andrew muttered.

Lock squeaked, and one delicate wing bent under Solon's grip.

"No, don't," Briar pleaded, reaching a hand toward Lock.

Grayson gasped and dropped to his knees, though no one had touched him.

"What mess have you gotten yourself into, Grayson?" Solon asked.

Grayson glared in return, a trickle of blood running from one nostril.

Briar stared at the crimson droplet, suddenly understanding. Grayson had told her that Lock had been created from a piece of Mr. Martel's soul. His soul.

"Mr. Solon?" Andrew cut in. "It seems you have your man. May I take my cousin?"

"You see?" Grayson said to Solon. "She's not what you think."

"She carries your construct."

Grayson shrugged. "She thought it was cute. I let her carry it to remain on her boat and out of your sight."

Briar frowned. Was this another role he was playing? Or had he been playing her all along?

Solon chuckled. "Brilliant, as always. I would never have considered it. Fortunately, my new associate"—he gestured at Andrew—"learned that his stolen boat had been seen carrying a man of your description."

Grayson pushed himself to his feet, a muscle in his jaw flexing. Was he in some kind of pain?

Lock gave an angry whirr of indignation, but he had stopped struggling.

"What are you doing in the country, Leon?" Grayson asked Solon, apparently using his given name.

"It is the land of opportunity, is it not? You've clearly made the most of it."

"As best I could with the limitations you place on me."

"You can't blame this on me. This is entirely your doing."

Briar assumed Solon was accusing Grayson of stealing and using ferro-technology to get ahead in the world.

Grayson neither agreed with nor denied Solon's claim. He merely regarded the man with that cold stare of his, not even glancing at Briar, though Solon still held her. And, come to think of it, she'd had enough of the manhandling.

She rammed her elbow into Solon's stomach, taking him by surprise. He doubled over with a grunt, and she twisted out of his hold. She turned toward the gangplank, intending to make a run for it, but came face to face with Mr. Owens.

He grinned at her.

"What are you grinning at you whoreson of a potato peeler."

"Bridget Ellen," Andrew admonished her. "Must you be so crude?"

She spun to face him and had the satisfaction of watching him step back. "Don't tempt me, Andrew. I've laid you out on this deck before, and I would love to do it again."

"Enough," Solon cut in.

"Told you," Grayson said in the silence. "She's just one of those loud-mouthed canal people. Besides," Grayson continued before she could give him a demonstration, "do you really think I would allow myself to be yoked like that?"

Briar was about to give him an earful, but hesitated. What the hell was he talking about?

Solon studied Grayson for a moment. "Revert," he said.

Briar frowned, not following that.

Solon clenched his fist, and suddenly, he was holding the silver lock Briar had first seen on Mr. Martel's trunk. Solon tucked the lock in his pocket.

"Come along then," Solon said to Grayson, then gestured at the gangplank. "I believe you have a meeting with destiny."

"Mr. Solon?" Andrew prompted, his tone meek and placating. The tone he often used with someone of higher social rank.

"I have business to attend to," Solon answered, sparing Andrew a brief glance. "As I believe you do. I shall call on you at your hotel when I finish."

"Yes, sir," Andrew quickly agreed.

"What are you licking his boots for?" Briar asked her cousin.

Andrew's face turned red, but he was spared a response by Grayson starting toward the gangplank, Solon right on his heels. Neither glanced in her direction.

Mr. Owens stepped back when Grayson drew near, then fell in line behind Solon as the trio left the boat.

"Officer!" Andrew called, waving for one of the blue-coated policemen to join him. "The woman is to be incarcerated with the others."

"You're going to jail me for running my own boat?" she demanded.

"You stole the boat, Bridget."

"Won't my incarceration shame you?"

"Everyone knows what a disgrace you are to the family, and how hard I worked to reform you. I will be commended for the effort, even though it was clearly a losing battle."

"You're a pompous ass, Andrew Rose. I'm glad my uncle didn't have to experience the shame of seeing what you've become."

Andrew slapped her. Hard.

The blow was so unexpected that she stumbled to the side. Andrew never lost his composure, and he hadn't tried to hit her since they were teens.

"Take her away." Andrew's tone was as cool as Solon's.

She considered a few more responses, but decided not to bother. Her breath was wasted on Andrew and always had been.

The officer escorted her from the boat to the wagon where the rest of her crew had been taken. A second officer had a rusty set of shackles waiting for her, but they were too large for her wrists. The officer finally gave up and ordered her into the dark wagon.

"Captain," Jimmy came to his feet, the shackles clanking on his wrists.

Before the door was closed, she saw that they had all been cuffed. Even Benji. Then the door closed, shutting out most of the light.

"I'm so sorry," she said, mortified that it had come to this. "I had no idea that Andrew would respond in such a way. I would never have involved all of you if I'd even suspected."

"Who would have helped man the boat if we hadn't come?" Jimmy asked.

"I wouldn't have taken the boat," she clarified.

"This is our livelihood, too," Jimmy insisted.

"There are plenty of other boats you could sign on to."

"As far as I'm concerned there's only one boat for me," Eli's deep voice rumbled out of the darkness.

"Aye, same here," Jimmy said.

"Us, too," Benji surprised her by answering.

She dropped onto the bench beside Eli, overcome by their words.

"That cousin of yours is a black-hearted bastard," Jimmy said. "No offense, Captain."

"None taken." She smiled at his fervent tone. "I wouldn't have phrased it so nicely."

The wagon lurched forward, and she heard Benji's soft gasp.

"Now listen to me," she said over the rattle of the wheels across the dock boards. "I intend to claim that none of you knew that I had taken the boat without my cousin's permission."

"But captain," Jimmy began.

"No. I won't have you going to jail for this. You have a wife who depends on you. And if you're thinking anything along these lines, Zach, then you need to think of Benji. Eli, you—"

"I don't have anyone, Miss Briar. I won't leave you alone in some jail with a bunch of convicts."

"But, Eli—"

"That's final, Captain. I don't mean to be disrespectful, but I won't budge in this."

She sighed, well aware that he never backed down when he had his mind made up.

"What of Mr. Grayson?" Jimmy asked. "Won't he testify that we kidnapped him?"

"Mr. Martel, you mean," she corrected him, still annoyed at Grayson's deception. But she couldn't sustain that anger as she thought of the meek manner in which he left with Solon.

"I don't think we have to worry about any repercussions there," she said. "I suspect Mr. Martel is in a worse predicament than we are."

"But I thought you said Mr. Martel is a ferromancer."

"I was wrong," she admitted. "My friend, Mr. Adams, found no ferromancy in those plans, then Andrew confirmed that Mr. Martel was just an engineer who had adapted some ferro-technology to mundane use—and pissed off a ferromancer in the process."

"Oh." Jimmy's tone said it all.

"What's that ferromancer going to do to Mr. Grayson—I mean, Martel?" Benji asked.

"I don't know," Briar lied. She had a sick feeling that Grayson was going to come away with more scars—and a few less organs.

THEY WERE GIVEN A LARGE cell in the downtown jail while they waited to be taken before a judge, Briar assumed. This jail, located on the top floor of the courthouse, served as a holding cell for those awaiting trial. The single, narrow window in their cell provided a way to track the sun as it crossed the sky. As the day faded, her anxiety grew.

She found herself frequently touching her pocket where Lock hid. It was a painful reminder of his absence. She had truly come to care for the little dragon, and felt his loss deeply.

As for Grayson, she still couldn't decide what his true motivation—or even his character—had been. Maybe he did have ulterior motives for everything he did, but he had always come to her defense and had taken care of her when she was injured.

And try as she might, she couldn't forget that kiss.

"You're going to wear a path in the floor, Captain," Jimmy called out to her from where he sat on one of the bottom bunks.

She had been pacing along the iron bars that lined one wall of their cell, and made herself stop.

"I'm sorry," she said. "I'm probably driving you all crazy, but I don't do well when I'm forced to stand still."

Jimmy chuckled. "We know that, Captain. Aren't we always the first boat out in the spring?"

"I'm fortunate I haven't drowned us by attempting to navigate the spring floods."

"We're better than that, Captain."

"True." She walked over to join Eli at the window. He hadn't said much since they'd been locked up.

"You doing all right?" she asked, laying a hand on his arm.

"I'll be fine, Miss Briar."

"Next time, listen to me. That was the same man who found me in Chillicothe. He's soulless."

"Soulless?" Jimmy asked. "What the hell does that mean?"

"As I understand it, ferromancers can take part of your soul to power their technology."

"It's true?" Jimmy asked, his voice dropping to a whisper. "They really can lock your soul in iron?"

"I don't know if they can take it all, but I know they can take pieces. They cut out your organs and replace them with metal ones."

"But the soulless man seemed to work for that Solon guy," Jimmy said. "Willingly."

"I'm just telling you what I know."

"Maybe he already swapped out his brain," Benji said, his tone awed.

"That would make more sense than working for him willingly," she agreed.

"Do you think that's what he intends to do to Mr. Grayson?" Jimmy asked, reverting to the name they knew him by. "Is he going to take his organs—and his soul?"

She slumped against the wall beside the window. "I don't know." She glanced at Zach, catching the knowing look in his eyes. He had seen Grayson's scar.

"I know he works for the railroad and all," Jimmy said, "but no man should have such a thing done."

"No, he shouldn't," she whispered.

A door opened from somewhere down the hall and footsteps approached. A moment later, a guard stepped into view on the other side of the bars.

"You're all free to go," he said, slipping the key in the lock. "Except the girl."

"What?" Eli demanded, his voice the loudest, though the others made similar exclamations.

Briar sighed. It seemed Andrew had come to his senses, mostly. "Gentlemen, please," she said, once the exclamations had died out. "We've discussed this."

"Yes, we did," Eli agreed. "I'm not leaving you here alone."

"You are. Go back to the boat and wait. I'm sure Andrew will drop the charges against me in the morning. He'll want us to return the boat to Portsmouth. He's just doing this to me to make a point."

Eli's frown turned uncertain as he thought about it.

"Don't make it worse," she told him. "We'll play along with

Andrew. Maybe, once this matter is settled, I'll just buy some other boat."

"I don't like this, Captain."

"Neither do I, but I don't have much choice. Now please..." She gestured at the open door.

Eli finally relented and the rest of the crew followed suit. She hoped they'd leave quietly, but Eli stopped to eye the guard.

"You'd best not let anything happen to her, understand?"

"Are you threatening me, sir?" the guard demanded, though he had to tip his head back to look up at Eli.

"No, he's not," Briar quickly added. "He's just asking you to look after my welfare, which I'm sure a gentleman such as yourself would readily do anyway."

"I'm a law-abiding citizen," the guard answered, perhaps as a subtle dig at their incarceration.

"As are we all," she added. "My cousin tends to be temperamental, and completely overreacted when I took the family boat without his leave. You can ask anyone along that canal that I've lived on that boat since I was three, and I've served as its captain the last two years."

"It's not me you need to convince," the guard answered before turning to her crew. "If you're leaving, let's go. I've got supper waiting."

The crew relented, and after a few farewells, they walked off down the hall.

Briar released a breath, glad they'd left without a fuss. She walked over and took a seat on the nearest bunk. This was going to be a long night.

BRIAR WOKE, NOT CERTAIN WHY. It could have been the scratchy blanket she lay on, the fleas, or perhaps the total lack of anything resembling a mattress between her and the rope-bed frame. With her worries for Grayson and of her own uncertain future, she was surprised she'd dozed off at all.

Something cold and hard poked her in the cheek, and she recoiled with a gasp.

A little head leaned in, the moonlight catching on silver scales.

"Lock," she whispered on an exhale.

He blinked his gem-like eyes.

"What are you doing here? Did Grayson send you?"

She didn't realize Lock held something in his jaws until he dropped it on her chest. It was a small scrap of white fabric, perhaps torn from a shirt. Unrolling it, she was surprised to find a written message.

Sitting up, she climbed from the bunk and walked to the window where the moonlight enabled her to see the words. She immediately recognized Grayson's elegant hand. It was the same as the writing on the locomotive plans. But the rust-colored ink suggested it wasn't ink at all.

Miss Rose,

I'm giving you Lock. Love him, and he will be forever yours. Fear not, soon Solon will be unable to sense him.

Forgive me,
Grayson Martel

Lock landed on her shoulder.

"What does this mean?" she whispered to him. "Why won't Solon be able to sense you?"

Lock moaned, an utterly forlorn sound, and rubbed his cheek against hers.

"Do you know where Grayson is?" she asked. "Can you take me to him?"

The little dragon perked up, his tail swishing in eagerness.

"Good. But first I need to get out of here." She turned back toward the door. "Can you help?"

Lock sprang into the air and, flapping his delicate wings, flew across the room to land on the bars of her cell with a soft clink of metal on metal. Apparently, Solon hadn't damaged him when he'd squeezed him earlier, which surprised her. Of course with Lock's ability to change forms, perhaps he could repair damage as well.

Climbing around to the other side of the door, Lock disappeared from view as he crawled to where the door lock was housed. A clank sounded a moment later, and the door swung open an inch or two.

Lock climbed up to a cross bar and gave her an expectant look.

Smiling, Briar hurried across the room. She pulled the door open, going slowly in case a hinge squeaked, and looked out into the hall. There was no one around.

Lock hopped down onto her shoulder as she left her cell. She gently closed the door behind her, making her escape a little less obvious.

Her cell had been the last in line and only a few feet from the stairwell door. She tested the knob and found it locked.

"Can you help with this one, too?" she whispered to Lock.

He hopped down to the knob, his nails tinking softly against the metal knob. He stretched out his tail and slipped it into the keyhole. An instant later, a snap sounded.

A flap of his wings, and Lock returned to her shoulder.

"I should call you Lockpick," she whispered, opening the door. She stepped into the stairwell and closed the door behind her.

Lock jumped to the newel post on the flight going up.

"Are you suggesting I go up? What if there isn't a way down?"

Lock spread his wings.

"That works for you, but I can't fly."

He cocked his head, and she had the impression that he found that odd.

A door closed below them, echoing up the stairs.

"I guess that decides it," she whispered. "Come on." She hurried up the stairs, and Lock leapt to her shoulder as she passed. She'd have to take her chances on the roof.

After climbing the single flight of stairs, she stopped before a door at the top. Like the other, it was locked, but the little dragon went to work on it without being asked. A moment later, she stepped out onto the roof.

"Where to now?" she asked.

Locked jumped into the air and, spreading his wings, flew to one side. He landed on the low stone wall surrounding the roof.

Briar walked over, expecting a ladder or something. Instead, there was a five-story drop to the cobblestones below.

"You remember that I can't fly, right?"

Lock answered with his typical whirr of hidden mechanisms, then morphed into a silver sphere. A thin silver rope emerged from one side and slipped over the edge while a second, shorter rope ending in a grappling hook emerged from the other. The hook slipped over the lip of the stone wall and caught there. The sphere finished morphing into a coil of silver rope that continued to slip over the side until it had all run out.

Briar eyed the small hook and the incredibly thin rope. "You expect me to climb down that?"

A ripple ran through the rope, clinking softly against the stone. A metal rope. Crazy. How would she even be able to grip it?

She stepped forward and more out of curiosity than planning to use it, gripped the rope. It was surprisingly supple and not slick at all.

Before she could do more than feel it, the rope coiled around her wrist, making several loops around her forearm.

"Uh, Lock. I—"

A sound came from behind the shed-like structure that housed the stairwell door.

"This door was locked," a male voice said. Guards checking the doors? Had they discovered the unlocked door to her cell floor, or maybe her empty cell?

Out of alternatives, she took a seat on the stone wall and swung her legs over.

"Check around," another voice carried to her. "Frank will make us come back up and do it if we don't."

Briar pulled in a breath and, gripping the rope in both hands, slipped over the edge.

The coil around her forearm tightened, but not to the point of cutting off circulation. Suspended over the alley five stories below, she clung to the rope with increasingly sweaty hands.

She tried to twist around to get her feet on the wall with the intention of walking herself down, and noticed that she was slowly descending. For a heart-pounding moment, she thought the much too small hook was slipping, then she felt movement around her wrist and forearm. She was sliding down the rope in a slow controlled motion.

She loosened her grip with the other hand, allowing the rope to slide a little faster, though the descent remained slow. Normally, she wouldn't complain, but if the guards were inspecting the roof, they were bound to notice the rope.

"Can you go a little faster?" she whispered.

Her speed of decent increased, but it wasn't exactly fast. She looked up, watching the edge of the roof and listening for a shout.

Glancing down, she judged herself to be about two stories above the ground. Perhaps another ten feet and she could—

"Lock, stop."

She jerked to a stop. A man had just entered the alley below her. She couldn't tell for certain in the low light, but he might be wearing the uniform of a prison guard.

A decorative ledge encircled the building just above the second floor. She set her feet on it and reached over to grip the edge of the nearest window. She was in plain sight, but high above the man's head. If she didn't move, she didn't think he'd notice her.

Her heart thumped in her ears as she watched him stroll along. Hopefully, he made this trip often and had grown complacent.

"Hey, what's that?" the voice carried down from above. Fortunately, the distance was too great for the man below to notice.

Suddenly, the loop encircling her wrist loosened, then retracted all together. It rose in the air, shooting up and out of sight.

"Lock!" she whispered, pressing back against the side of the building. The ledge she stood on was so narrow that her toes hung over the edge.

The man below her continued on, oblivious to everything.

"I swear I saw a rope, or something," the voice above her was clearer now. The speaker must be closer to the edge.

She didn't dare look up for fear of losing her balance. Would she be visible if the guy looked over the edge?

Something gripped her shoulder, and she almost screamed before she heard the concerned coo near her ear.

"Lock," she breathed.

"I don't see anything," the other man said above her, the words barely audible with the distance.

"I tell you, it was something." This voice was louder with the speaker's excitement. "Let's go downstairs."

"Lock, we've got to hurry."

The weight vanished from her shoulder, though she didn't look up to see where he had gone. A good minute ticked past.

Suddenly, a thin silver rope dropped in front of her. She gripped it with one hand and once again, it coiled around her wrist and forearm.

Taking a deep breath, she stepped off the ledge.

Her descent was agonizingly slow, and she expected the guards to come rushing around the corner at any moment.

She watched the cobbled ground grow closer. Twelve feet. Ten. Closing in on eight—

A door slammed.

"Lock, drop me!"

The rope vanished from her wrist, and even expecting it, she gasped.

She tried to relax into the fall, planning to bend her knees and let her momentum drop her into a squat. She hit sooner and harder then she expected and landed on her butt with a bone-jarring thump.

She didn't get to dwell on the painful landing as running feet headed her way.

Pushing off the ground, she broke into a sprint before she was fully on her feet. Slipping and stumbling, she managed to regain her balance before ending up face down. That would be an embarrassing end to this mad adventure.

Somehow, she reached the end of the alley before anyone saw her. Slowing to a fast walk, she rounded the corner and came face to face with Eli.

"Eli!" She stared up at him. "What are you—"

Eli gripped her arm and urged her to a quick walk beside him. "A guard patrols this area." He gave her a frown. "I assume they didn't just let you leave."

"Well, no…" She lengthened her stride to keep up with him.

"That isn't going to look good on you, Miss Briar."

They turned the corner into a dimly lit street.

"I know," she answered. "But—"

Eli released her with a gasp and swatted at something on the back of his shoulder.

"Eli?"

"Something bit me." He continued to struggle to reach whatever it was.

Briar caught a glimpse of something of a silver wing. "Lock, don't. He's my friend."

Eli turned away, revealing a few rips in his shirt, but no dragon. "Lock?" Briar called.

A familiar weight settled on her shoulder, accompanied by a questioning coo.

She reached up to rub Lock's chin. "There you are."

Eli spun to face her, his eyes going wide.

"Eli, this is Lock." She continued rubbing the little dragon beneath his chin. "Lock, this is my friend, Eli."

"What *is* that?" Eli demanded.

"Ferromancers call them constructs. They're created from a piece of a captured soul."

Eli stared at her.

This time, she gripped his arm and pulled him after her. "Come on." They couldn't stand around here.

"Lock was made from a piece of Grayson's soul," she continued after they were moving again. "I suspect Solon did the capturing."

"Dear God," Eli whispered. "That's how you learned about all of this."

"Yes." She met his gaze. "Lock knows where Grayson is."

"You're going after him."

"Yes, I am."

Eli sighed. "And nothing I say will deter you."

"Grayson stole some ferro-technology. Solon is pissed. I think he plans to make Grayson soulless." She turned back to the little dragon. "Show me where Grayson is?"

Lock scampered down her waistcoat and dropped into her pocket.

Not sure what to make of his actions, she reached in after him. She expected to pull out the silver pocket watch; instead, she held a silver compass. The needle swung to her right, then held steady.

"That's ingenious, Lock."

"Did he just change into a... compass?" Eli asked, staring at the silver instrument she held.

"Yes, he's showing us what direction to go."

"Us?" Eli asked.

She looked up. "I know you don't like Grayson, but I also know that you wouldn't stand by while Solon cuts out more of his organs."

Eli swallowed, the graphic description getting to him. "You're right, Miss Briar. I can't stand by and let you do this alone."

That wasn't the answer she expected, but it would have to do.

CHAPTER 16

BRIAR CROUCHED BEHIND A BOXCAR, eyeing the huge building that housed a foundry. Smoke billowed from a smokestack, but she saw no one around this end of the building. The night watchman had already walked through the area, though she could still see his lantern in the distance.

Leaning around the side of the boxcar, Briar eyed the wide doorway over the train tracks that led into the building. An orange glow illuminated a distant point, but her view was blocked by several large pieces of equipment.

"The guard's gone," Eli whispered.

She glanced over and noted that she could no longer see the guard's lantern. She turned to the little metal dragon sitting on her shoulder. "Grayson's in there?"

Lock moaned, snuggling closer to the side of her neck. Was he worried for Grayson or afraid of Solon? Probably both. She could certainly sympathize.

Taking a deep breath, she rose to her feet, and stepping around the boxcar, she and Eli followed the tracks into the building.

Eli released a soft whistle. "This place is huge."

"And hot," she added in the same low tone.

Though no one was working in this end of the foundry, the building still held the heat. Thick chains hung from large overhead cranes perhaps used to load or unload the boxcars. Having only the most rudimentary understanding of how a foundry operated, she could only speculate on the use of the objects around them.

They crossed the cavernous room, keeping to the edges or behind larger pieces of equipment. As they moved closer to the orange glow, the low rumble of male voices became words.

"A little more, Mr. Owens."

Briar gripped Eli's wrist, pulling him to a stop. She recognized Solon's accented voice. Lock had led her to the right place.

"Do as I ask, Grayson," Solon continued, a hint of exasperation in his cool tone. "This will be most unpleasant otherwise."

Grayson didn't answer.

Briar rubbed her palms against her thighs, not certain if it was the heat within the building or her nerves that made her sweat.

She crept forward, leading Eli toward a gap between pieces of machinery that she hoped would offer a good view. She just prayed it was only Solon and his soulless henchman. Once she got a good look at the odds, she could decide how to go about freeing Grayson.

Dropping to a knee, she peered around the edge of the machine.

She spotted Grayson immediately. He'd been stripped to the waist and bound to a concrete vat-like structure that held the molds.

The orange glow came from the enormous crucible full of molten iron. Mr. Owens operated the lever that controlled it. Currently, he was pouring the liquid metal into one end of the mold Grayson was strapped to.

Briar pressed a hand to her mouth as the molten iron crawled along the trough toward Grayson.

"Cooperate!" Solon was angry now. "I will kill you, Grayson. You are worthless to me—to all of us—otherwise."

A muscle flexed in Grayson's jaw, but he remained silent, gazing up into the rafters above him. The glowing orange metal crept closer.

Eli quietly picked up a long metal pole. "If I engage that soulless man—"

She caught his sleeve. "Wait," she whispered, then turned to the little dragon that still sat on her shoulder. "Lock, can you help

172

Ferromancer

Grayson?" If Lock cut Grayson's bonds, he could roll free and escape. If they could make a run for it, maybe they wouldn't have to face Solon or his soulless henchman.

"Mr. Owens," Solon command. "Empty the ladle." The ladle? Was that the official name for the crucible-like container?

With a maniacal grin, Owens reached for the lever.

"Lock, go to him now!" she whispered.

The little dragon left her shoulder and leapt into the air. Orange light caught on the sleek scales and delicate wings, glinting as brightly as the molten metal.

Grayson's head whipped around, his eyes widening when he saw Lock.

Folding his wings, Lock dropped into a graceful dive and landed on Grayson's bare chest.

"No!" Grayson cried, staring at the construct with something close to horror. Did he fear Solon would capture Lock again?

Lock's wings drooped and he lowered his head, taking Grayson's word as a reprimand or perhaps a command.

Mr. Owens grabbed the lever and pulled.

Briar shoved herself to her feet. "Lock, do it!"

Solon spun to face her and she glimpsed his surprise.

She was aware that Eli had stepped out behind her, metal pole in hand, but her attention was focused on the liquid metal now pouring from the upended ladle.

She expected Lock to sever Grayson's bonds, freeing him to roll off the platform. Instead, Lock spread his legs on Grayson's chest and dug in his claws.

Grayson cried out. Had the metal reached him? Certainly, a stick from Lock's delicate claws wouldn't elicit such a response.

Eli shouted, raising his pole, and ran at Solon.

Looking unimpressed, Solon lifted his silver hand, and the pole Eli held suddenly twisted in his hands like a large metal snake.

173

Eli stumbled to a stop as the pole curled around his upper body, pinning his arms to his sides.

Another gesture from Solon, and a heavy chain dropped from the crane above them, its metal hook catching the bent pole that now encircled Eli's upper body and lifting him off the ground.

Briar gasped as he was hoisted a good ten feet into the air, but another cry from Grayson pulled her attention back to him. The liquid metal had filled one end of the mold and rolled toward him, the heavy flow spilling over the sides of the mold into the vat below.

"Lock, free him!" she shouted. Why did the little dragon hesitate?

In a shimmer of silver and reflected orange, Lock began to morph into...

Briar frowned as he puddled on Grayson's chest, mimicking the molten iron. Except Lock became liquid silver, flowing across Grayson's skin, coating his chest, then his shoulders and down his legs. Was he just forming a barrier to protect him? Why hadn't Lock cut Grayson free?

An oddly metallic roar sounded directly behind her.

Briar jumped and spun to face whatever it was. She thought perhaps a piece of machinery had kicked on. Instead, a shape stepped out of the shadows.

A roar had been an accurate description for the sound it made, because she found herself staring at a metal lion.

Having been around Lock, she immediately recognized it as a construct. It was a mechanical marvel with its sculptured silver body plates and mane of small, overlapping triangles. It moved with the smooth powerful stride of the actual animal, making it seem more like a living being rather than a machine. Yet there was something crude and unrefined about it. She couldn't define what, but it wasn't in the same class as Lock.

"Leave her be, Solon," Grayson said, his voice oddly deeper and more... metallic.

Briar turned, keeping the lion in sight as she glanced over at Grayson. Her mouth dropped open.

He now stood beside the mold vat where he'd been tied, most of his body covered in what appeared to be silver armor. Lock?

The armor completely covered his torso and shoulders, a large part of his upper arms and the back of his forearms, most of his thighs, and the front of his shins. The brilliant silver metal was molded perfectly to his body, defining each muscle in an eye-catching display. Oddly, there wasn't a single strap to hold the armor in place. It was almost as if it was his actual skin.

"She isn't part of this," Grayson added, turning to face Solon. The strange quality of his voice she attributed to the helmet he wore. It wasn't as fitted as the rest of his armor. A slitted visor covered his face. From the crest of his helmet, down his neck, and along his spine was a series of plates shaped like slender dorsal fins. They reminded her of Lock's raised scales on the same part of his body, though Grayson's looked sharper.

"Not part of this?" Solon demanded. "She just commanded your construct. Actually, she overrode a command from you."

"I gave him to her."

"Him?" Solon frowned, glancing from her to Grayson. "What game are you playing, Drake?"

"Don't call me that." Grayson's strange voice was low and dangerous.

"The process has already begun."

With something like a roar, Grayson sprang at him, startling Briar with the suddenness of the move.

"To me!" Solon shouted.

The lion that had been watching her spun and leapt across the space that separated it from Solon. It was on him in two bounds. At the last moment, just before impact, it morphed like Lock had a moment ago. It became a liquid, flowing over Solon's body. The process was much quicker, and in the blink of an eye, Solon was covered in similar silver armor—except his covered his entire body.

The lion's mane was part of the armor, flowing down from the helmet to Solon's shoulders. Otherwise, Solon's helmet was contoured to his face, leaving his mouth and chin uncovered.

Grayson collided with Solon in the next instant, their armor hitting with the clank of metal on metal. The impact knocked them apart, but Grayson came right back, throwing a punch at Solon's exposed chin.

In a move so fast it was a blur, Solon caught Grayson's fist in his armored hand.

Briar flinched at the sound of Grayson's unprotected hand smashing into Solon's gauntlet.

"Don't be a fool," Solon said. His voice had a similar tone to Grayson's, though nothing covered his mouth.

Solon closed his hand around Grayson's fist, iron claws emerging from the ends of his metal encased fingers. The gauntlet was identical to the hand that was already made of metal.

"She's an innocent." Grayson sounded like he was speaking through clenched teeth. "If she is ferra, she doesn't know it."

Briar frowned. Ferra?

Solon looked over at her, and she noticed that the whites no longer showed in his eyes. Either they had darkened to the same gray of his irises or the iris now stretched from lid to lid. His eyes looked like those of an animal.

A chill crawled up her spine. He looked so alien, yet there was still something human about the way he studied her.

She took a step back.

"Leave her be!" Eli shouted down at them, wiggling on the hook that held him like a large fish.

Solon didn't even glance at him.

"She's mine, Leon," Grayson said.

Any other situation, and she'd have a few words to say to

that. But in this case, she knew Grayson was trying to draw away Solon's attention.

"Yours?" Solon smiled, his dark eyes returning to Grayson. "Then prove it. Fight me for her."

He released Grayson's fist with a shove, and Grayson stumbled back several steps before regaining his balance.

"Mr. Owens," Solon continued. "Please hold the prize while I give the young dragon a lesson."

Owens laughed and started toward her.

She turned to run and took two strides before he caught her by her braid.

She cried out at the pain of being jerked to a stop by her hair. She reached back and gripped the braid close to her scalp in an effort to relieve the pain.

"Do something, Grayson," Eli shouted down at them, surprising Briar with the request. She wouldn't have thought Eli would ask Grayson for anything.

Grayson didn't acknowledge him, his attention on Mr. Owens. "Get your hands off her, you soulless vermin, or next time, I'll remove your head instead of your heart."

Briar blinked her watering eyes. Grayson's visor covered his features, but there was something in his cold tone that chilled her as deeply as Solon's gaze. What had Solon done to him? He seemed changed.

"That'll do," Solon cut in. "My toy will hold yours until this is decided."

"Listen, metal ass," she spoke up. "I'm no one's toy. Got it?"

Solon studied her a moment before turning to Grayson. "She lacks the manners, but she certainly has the ferra condescension down."

"Did you take a ferromancer for a lover, girl?" Mr. Owens whispered, close to her ear.

"What? No." Why would he think—

"As hot as he is for you, I think you lie. Not that I blame him." He reached around from behind and gave her breast a hard squeeze.

Briar cried out as much from surprise as pain.

"I warned you." Grayson held out a hand to his side, then flicked his fingers.

Briar didn't understand the meaning of his gesture. Suddenly, a slender metal pole was streaking toward them. It missed her by a fraction of an inch and slammed into Owens's chest. The force lifted him from his feet, and the pole rammed into the side of the building, hitting hard enough to drive it into a thick wooden support timber. The impaled Mr. Owens dangled a good foot off the ground.

"Briar, run," Grayson said.

She just stared at him, her mouth too dry to speak and her muscles unresponsive.

"Now, now," Solon chided. "This isn't over." He made a gesture very similar to Grayson's.

She flinched and looked around for a pole flying her way. Then she heard a rattle on the floor near her feet. A coil of chain had unwound and now slithered toward her.

The sight finally broke her paralysis, and she turned to take Grayson's advice. Suddenly, the chain shot out and wrapped around her ankle. As it crossed over itself, the links fused, forming a permanent loop.

"Now where were we?" Solon asked, paying no heed to Mr. Owens's struggles.

"Here," Grayson answered. He held out his hand, palm toward Solon and curled his fingers.

Solon gasped, and with a frantic flick of the wrist, sent an iron bar from a nearby pile flying at Grayson.

Grayson stopped whatever he was doing and raised both hands. The bar seemed to slow, but it still smashed into him with enough force to send him flying.

"Do you remember nothing I taught you?" Solon asked as Grayson climbed slowly to his feet. "You cannot stand against a ferromancer of the final casting, Drake. And you certainly can't reduct a soul."

"Then why were you afraid?" Grayson had regained his feet.

"Because dragons are as unpredictable as they are rare."

Briar's heart pounded a hollow beat in her ears as she watched the two men face off once more. Men, no. Ferromancers. She had been right all along. Mr. Martel, Grayson, was a ferromancer.

"I won't be your rallying figure, Leon, whatever comes of this. And certainly not if you're going to use an innocent against me." Grayson waved a hand in her direction, though he continued walking toward Solon.

"So if I let her go, you'll embrace your true nature and join us?"

Grayson stopped in front of him, but didn't immediately respond.

"Hey," Briar spoke into the silence, and both men turned their heads to look at her. "I don't understand a fraction of what you just said, but I won't be anyone's bargaining chip. Do we understand each other?"

"You know," Solon said to Grayson, "the first thing I'd recast is that tongue."

Without warning, Grayson lunged forward and pressed his hand to the center of Solon's chest. The armor rippled, the wave radiating from around Grayson's hand.

Solon cried out and threw both arms wide.

A clang came from the ceiling and Briar looked up. The beam of an overhead crane came loose at one end and swung downward—fortunately, not the crane Eli hung from.

"Grayson!" she shouted.

He released Solon, who staggered away, and turned to face this new threat. He got an arm up, but whatever his ability, he didn't get a chance to use it.

The beam hit him square in the chest and sent him flying.

Briar flinched at the crunch of impact—then she saw where he would land.

"No!" she screamed, hearing Solon echo her.

Grayson landed in the vat of molten iron, sending a splash of the glowing liquid into the air. It settled with a thick plop an instant later.

If he had tried to scream, it never escaped his throat.

CHAPTER 17

BRIAR PRESSED BOTH HANDS TO her mouth, trying to hold in the whimper that wanted to escape. Grayson had lied to her, about a lot of things. Perhaps he'd had a good reason. Whatever he was, he certainly didn't deserve to die like that.

She noticed another sound and realized that Solon was cursing, his armored hands curled at his sides.

Abruptly, he stopped and smacked a hand to his chest. The armor split along the center of his chest as if it were a shirt being opened. The metal rolled back over his shoulders, around his ribs, and up his arms and legs, disappearing behind him. An instant later, a silver sphere dropped to the ground behind him, then morphed into the lion.

Solon gave his waistcoat a tug, then straightened his coat. Finally, he turned to face her.

Briar wanted to shrink back into the shadows under the force of that angry stare, but she stood her ground.

A clank sounded overhead: Eli, still trying to get free.

"What did you do to him?" Solon demanded.

"Me? You're the one who launched him into—" Her voice cut out so she waved a hand at the vat that was now Grayson's tomb. She couldn't decide if she wanted to cry or scream.

"You bent him to your will ferra witch."

"I met him five days ago, and about half that time he spent tied to the stable wall."

Solon frowned. "Why?"

"I was going to prove that the railroad had hired a ferromancer. I was trying to save the canals." Her voice rose and sounded a bit hysterical to her own ears. She took a breath and tried to regain control. "What's a ferra?"

"Not what, who."

"All right. Who?" She lifted her brows, waiting for him to answer.

He sighed. "They are the female half of my race. More descriptively, a pack of smothering, self-righteous shrews."

Ferromancers were their own race? And there were females?

Solon captured her wrist in the grip of his iron hand.

"What are you doing?" she asked.

A flick of the fingers of his other hand, and the chain fell away from her ankles.

"You commanded a construct," he said.

"So?"

Solon just smiled.

"She's got a great ass, master," Owens said from his place on the wall.

"Shut your mouth, scum," Eli shouted at him.

"The big man has a point," Solon said. "Don't be crude, Mr. Owens. Besides, I can observe these things for myself."

"Sorry, master. A little help?" Owens gestured at the pole through his chest.

With a sigh and another finger flick, the iron pole came free from the wall and Owens dropped to the ground. He pulled the pole from his chest, then examined the slightly bloody hole in his clothes.

Solon turned away, attempting to pull her with him.

Briar dug in her heels. "I'm not going anywhere with you."

"Perhaps you don't realize, but you really have no choice."

"Why take me?"

He stopped and faced her, leaning in so that his eyes—human

once more—were on level with her own. "Because you just cost me the opportunity of a lifetime."

"Grayson," she whispered.

"He had a talent that only comes along once in a millennium. He had the potential to change the world."

And he hadn't wanted to, she realized, remembering all his talk about being free. Free to make his own choices. And she had unwittingly taken that from him, yet he'd died trying to free her.

A tear slipped down her cheek, and her hand drifted to her pocket for comfort. Her pocket was empty. "Oh, Lock," she whispered. Coming here, she'd damned him, too.

Solon glared at her, then turned, pulling her after him with an iron grip she couldn't defeat. Eli renewed his struggles overhead.

"At least let Eli go," she said, stumbling along after Solon. Even if Eli managed to get himself off that hook, he would likely break a leg falling that far.

A reverberating crack echoed around the room. If she couldn't still see Eli above them, she would have believed her fears had come true.

Solon stopped. A frown creased his brow, and the iron lion beside him growled softly.

Another crack, this one louder than the last, was followed by a heavy thump.

Solon spun toward the sound, pulling her with him.

She was trying to locate the source of the sound when the concrete vat exploded.

Solon released her to throw an arm up, smacking away a large chunk of concrete that had flown their way. Fortunately, she had been standing a little behind him, but she still dropped to her haunches, throwing her arms over her head.

It sounded as if someone had upended a wheelbarrow of rocks on the concrete floor as the broken chunks of the vat settled.

"Jesus," Owens whispered.

"Holy hell," Eli muttered.

Solon started to laugh.

Briar lifted her head and abruptly fell on her butt. Lock's name rose to her lips until she realized that what she saw was much bigger than Lock.

He knelt in the remains of the vat, his head bowed. Horns just like Lock's sprouted from his head, and the raised plates along his spine were tipped in gold. Taking an audible breath, he rose to his feet, a man.

"Grayson," she whispered.

He lifted his head to display a helmet more like Solon's with the open lower face and sculptured lines.

She pulled in a breath as his eyes met hers. His eyes were the same blue-gray they'd always been, but like Solon, the whites were no longer visible. An animal's eyes.

"To me," Solon muttered.

His lion tensed to spring.

Grayson lifted a hand, now encased in a bright silver gauntlet. "I wouldn't."

He curled his fingers, and the lion made a soft whine.

"Very well." Solon raised his hands, palms out.

Grayson didn't lower his arm. "I'm going to let you live, Leon, but test me again and you won't like the results."

Solon fisted his iron hand, pressed it to his heart, then bowed at the waist. When he straightened, he was smiling. With a nod, he turned and walked away, his lion pacing beside him.

Mr. Owens glanced between them, then scurried after Solon.

Briar watched them go. "That's it?" she asked. "Hell, I at least hoped to knee him."

When Grayson didn't answer, she turned to face him. She expected a smile at her crudeness, but he was still staring after Solon.

"Grayson?"

He made no move.

"You still in there?" She took a step closer, reaching out a hand.

A clatter sounded behind her and she turned with a gasp, expecting that Solon had launched a new attack. Instead, the crane holding Eli had released, lowering him to the floor. The moment his feet touched, the bent metal pole that held his upper body unwound and fell away.

Briar turned back to Grayson. "Did you—"

Without warning, he fell to his knees. His eyes closed and he swayed.

She stepped forward and caught him against her, noting the odd warmth of his armor.

"Grayson?" She touched his cheek and found it like ice. "My God, you're freezing."

"Briar?" he mumbled her name.

"Yes, I'm here." He had practically collapsed against her, and damn, he was heavy. She helped him lie down, though he had to lie on his side due to the metal plates along his back.

"Briar, I'm ready to tell you who I am."

She smiled, about to tell him that wasn't necessary, but when he turned his head to gaze up at her with those alien eyes, she didn't. "Who are you?" she whispered.

"I'm Grayson Martel." He took a breath. "Ferromancer."

"Nice to finally meet you, Mr. Martel. Now, how do we get this armor off?" He'd be easier to move without it, and they definitely needed to move.

"It's not armor," he muttered.

She waited, but he didn't elaborate. "Grayson?"

"Call him to you," he answered.

"Lock?" She paused, but when Grayson said nothing, she continued. "Lock, come here."

The armor that wasn't armor rolled back off Grayson's skin, collecting into a silver sphere on the floor beside him. A moment, and the ball morphed into the familiar dragon. Well, not entirely familiar. He was a little bigger and gold now accented his scales.

"Lock," she whispered.

A whirr of happiness, and he sprang up on her shoulder.

She brushed him under his chin and turned back to Grayson. Without the armor, he was once again clad in only his pants. The scar down the center of his chest was a livid red against his extremely pale skin.

"Grayson?" She reached out and touched his shoulder. God, he was so cold. "Are you still with me?"

Nothing.

She rose up on her knees, intending to push him over onto his back and gasped. Along his spine, the plates were still visible. They weren't part of his armor; they protruded from his skin as if each vertebra had grown a silver dorsal fin. Each fin-shaped plate was perhaps an inch long at the base and tapered to a wicked-looking point. Blood oozed from the base of each one where it must have torn through his skin.

"Lock, did you forget something?" she asked.

He moaned and rubbed against the side of her neck. She took that as a no.

"Dear God, what happened to him?" Eli whispered from above her. She hadn't heard him walk over.

Not wanting to look, but unable to deny her curiosity, she lifted one of Grayson's eyelids. The eye had rolled back, but she could see enough of his iris to verify that his eyes were human once more.

Leaning back, she rested her hands on her thighs. "He's out cold." She looked up at Eli. He was frowning at Grayson. "We can't leave him here." Not with those metal fins growing out of his back. "Can you carry him?"

He didn't answer.

"Eli?"

"He's a ferromancer."

"Yes." She was still coming to terms with that herself.

Eli turned his frown on her. "Did you know?"

"Of course not." She pushed herself to her feet. "Did you? Is that why you've disliked him all along?" She very much doubted that Eli knew, but at least it would be some explanation for his dislike.

"No. I just..." Eli turned his frown on Grayson once more. "I never trusted him. I knew he wasn't telling us everything."

"We took him captive. He hardly had a reason to be honest with us."

Eli maintained his silence.

"Are you going to help me with him or not?" she asked.

Eli's shoulders slumped. "I can't carry him through the streets with those spikes sticking out of his back."

"True." She rubbed her chin to hide her smile. Eli would help her. "I wonder what Solon did with his coat."

Lock jumped from her shoulder and flew across the foundry.

"Lock?" she called in a loud whisper, afraid to raise her voice. Solon may not be out of earshot.

Lock didn't fly far before landing on the other side of the busted vat. He returned a moment later, carrying Grayson's black coat in his talons.

"Thank you," she said as Lock dropped the coat into her hands. She lifted her gaze to Eli's. "Can you still manage with those metal fins? They look sharp."

He sighed, clearly not pleased. "As long as he don't have nothing down his front."

"He doesn't." She stepped to the side, giving Eli plenty of room.

Eli dropped to a knee beside him and, gripping one arm, pulled Grayson into a seated position. The scar on his chest was glaringly obvious. She saw the way Eli frowned when he glanced at it, but he said nothing. Oddly, it bothered her that Eli had seen it. Perhaps because she knew how much it bothered Grayson to have it viewed.

Eli gripped Grayson's other arm, pulling him closer. "His skin is cold."

"I know." She crossed her arms. "I intend to put him in the cook's bunk and fire up the stove."

Eli looked up.

"Don't give me that. The poor man is like that because he came to my defense. He almost died. He still might." She blinked, and a warm tear rolled down her cheek, surprising her.

Eli watched her scrub the tear from her face. "All right, Miss Briar." With an ease she envied, he pulled Grayson over his shoulder and rose to his feet. She had to roll up on her toes to drape the coat over him.

"For a little guy, he's heavy," Eli commented.

"He's not that little." She'd wager that Grayson was at least six feet tall. "Everyone is small to you, Eli."

"I meant thin," Eli corrected.

She wouldn't call Grayson thin, either. Perhaps lean would be a better description.

"Do you reckon it's the metal?" Eli asked, lowering his voice.

The notion made her a little queasy. "I don't know." She turned back the way they had come. "I'll walk ahead and make sure that guard isn't around."

Lock made a sound of inquiry.

Briar turned her head to study him. "You can check for us?" she surmised. "Those silver scales are eye-catching, especially now with the gold."

Lock stood a little taller, his next sound assertive, and maybe a touch indignant.

"All right," she relented. "Don't get caught."

With something very close to a huff, Lock sprang into the air and flew off toward the train door they'd used to enter the building.

Briar glanced over to find Eli watching her. "What?" she asked.

"You understand him."

She shrugged. "I've been around him more, and his body language is very expressive."

"You can't have known him for more than five days, and he's made of metal. There's no body to read."

"Just wait until you get to know him better."

"Uh-huh." Eli headed for the door, Grayson's unmoving form draped over his shoulder.

Briar frowned after him, not sure how to take his comment, but at least he was helping her. At the moment, that was all she could ask for.

CHAPTER 18

THEY MADE THEIR WAY THROUGH the streets, sticking to the back alleys where they could. Fortunately, this area was populated by factories, which were currently closed for the evening, so there were few people about.

Eli walked quickly, and Briar was forced to lengthen her stride. She was almost jogging by the time they reached the docks.

Since boatmen lived on their boats and often made overnight hauls, the docks weren't as deserted as the streets around the factory district. She had a moment of anxiety when she found a different boat in the berth where she'd been docked, then Eli spied her boat at the far end of the pier.

A lantern glowed on the deck of the aft cargo hold, and as they approached, she saw that the crew was gathered around the card table. The gangplank was down, so they had no trouble slipping aboard.

"Is this how you celebrate your first night without a captain?" she asked.

Jimmy came to his feet first, overturning the card table in his haste. Zach managed to capture the bottle of whiskey before it hit the deck, while Benji stared at them with wide eyes.

"Captain!" Jimmy cried. "What are you doing here? Did they let you go?"

"Not exactly."

"How did you get Mr. Grayson back?" Benji asked. "Is he hurt?"

Briar looked up, meeting Eli's gaze. "We got him away from that ferromancer, but he's not well." She pulled the coat off Grayson.

"Dear God," Benji said, staring at Grayson's back. "Are those spikes?"

Zach stared in wide-eyed horror as well.

"That ferromancer did a number on him," Eli surprised her by answering.

"Sweet Jesus," Jimmy whispered. "How did the ferromancer do *that*?"

Briar bit her lip. She didn't want to lie to them, but she didn't think Grayson would want her spilling his secrets.

"Did he make him soulless like that other feller?" Jimmy continued. "You said that one had all his innards replaced with metal."

"No, Mr. Grayson isn't soulless, but he's in a bad way," she answered. "Eli's going to put him in the cook's bunk, and I'm going to light the stove. He's chilled through."

Jimmy nodded, his eyes as wide as Zach's had been.

"Would you get us underway?" she asked him.

"The boat's not to be moved unless Andrew gives us leave." Jimmy didn't look happy about that.

She hesitated. If they helped her take the boat, they wouldn't be able to claim ignorance next time they were caught. "I can't ask any of you to break the law, but I don't know what to do with Mr. Grayson."

Zach patted his own chest and gave her a firm nod.

"You'll help?" she asked.

Zach dipped his chin in agreement.

"What about Benji? If you help me—"

"I want to help, too," Benji spoke up. "You've been very good to us and so has Mr. Grayson. It wouldn't be right to abandon you both in your hour of need."

Zach clapped Benji on the shoulder and nodded again.

"You're not leaving me behind," Jimmy said. "And if that damn ferromancer hurt our cook, we need to help get him healed. We're a crew."

She smiled at the way he'd claimed Grayson, though it wasn't a career choice Grayson had made. She looked up at Eli.

"I'll put him in the cook's bunk," Eli answered.

"Thank you." She gripped his forearm. "Thank you all."

"Go tend him," Jimmy said. "We'll get ready to shove off."

She agreed and followed Eli to her cabin. He lowered Grayson to the bunk with surprising care. Well, maybe the care was so he didn't cut himself. Once he had Grayson lying on his side, he straightened.

"He'll probably shred the blankets." Eli frowned at Grayson's unconscious form. "Mattress, too, if he rolls over."

"So be it." She grabbed the blanket off the end of the bed and pulled it over him.

"You didn't tell the crew he's a ferromancer."

She straightened. "I don't feel it's my secret to tell."

Eli studied her a moment, then walked to the stove. To her surprise, he began to prepare it for lighting.

"Thank you, Eli."

He glanced back at her. "I don't like you getting mixed up in this, Miss Briar."

"Too late for that."

He grunted, but said nothing else. She turned her attention to gathering her meager doctoring supplies, though she wasn't certain what she could do for Grayson. She didn't even know what was truly wrong with him.

She was filling the teakettle to heat some water when Eli turned away from the lit stove.

"Guess I'd better get to the tiller." He headed for the door.

Briar watched him go, wanting to offer some word of reassurance, but she had no idea what that might be.

Eli opened the door and abruptly came to a stop. "Miss Briar?" he called to her, though he didn't face her.

Unease crawled down her spine at Eli's hesitant tone. "What is it?" She walked to the door and Eli stepped aside, allowing her to exit the cabin and join him in the cargo hold.

She stumbled to a stop.

"Stealing my boat again, Bridget?" Andrew asked.

Briar stared at her cousin. "What are you doing here?" Had the jail informed him that she had escaped?

"I hired a boy to watch the boat. He was to alert me at the first sign of anyone making preparations to leave."

Damn. She glanced toward the dock, but didn't see a police wagon this time. Zach and Benji stood with a pair of the mules, though neither was hitching the team. They were both watching the boat.

"You're supposed to be in jail," Andrew reminded her.

Fisting her hands, she took a step closer. "How dare you lock me up for taking my own boat."

"We've been over this. You'll be returning to that jail cell and as a repeat offender, I doubt you'll get out any time soon."

"She's not going anywhere," Eli said.

"Aye, that's the truth," Jimmy said from the roof of her cabin.

Andrew lifted his gaze to look at her crewmen. The lantern light caught in his eyes, making his pupils contract.

Briar gasped as she noticed that his eyes were no longer green. His irises were steel gray and appeared to be made of fine, overlapping layers of metal that slid over each other as his pupils shrank.

"Andrew," she whispered. "What has Solon done to you?" Had all of this been Solon's idea? She had known Andrew would be angry about the boat, but arresting her had been so over the top.

"Done to me?" Andrew abruptly grinned, a manic glee in his metallic eyes. "He's given me immortality."

Briar stared at him.

Andrew barked a short laugh. "You look envious, Bridget."

"I look horrified. You *let* him make you soulless."

"The process is not yet complete, but it will be once I sell the boat."

"Huh?" Yes, he had lost his mind.

"The money, Bridget. All my funds are tied up in investments. The only asset I can make liquid is the boat."

"You're paying him to make you soulless. Well, that's not so bad then." She rolled her eyes.

"I'm *paying* for this huge international gala he's planning." Andrew stood a little straighter, clearly proud of the fact.

"Solon's throwing a party?"

"It's none of your concern. You'll be rotting in jail."

"No she won't," a new voice said.

Andrew spun away from her, clearing her view of the gangplank. She blinked in surprise as Uncle Liam stepped onto her boat. Something glinted in his hand, and she saw that he held a small pistol like none she'd ever seen. Though the shiny silver metal was suspiciously familiar.

"What's happened to you, Andrew?" Liam asked.

Andrew's manic grin didn't falter. "I've been given immortality." He spread his hands, offering himself as an illustration.

"Oh no, lad. I'm afraid you've been deceived. You are simply another man's toy."

Briar frowned at Liam's word choice. Solon had called Owens his toy.

Andrew dropped his arms and glared at Liam. "No, it is you who've been deceived. I will show you." Without warning, he sprang at Liam.

Briar gasped, well aware of the strength and speed of the soulless. She was about to shout a warning when Liam fired.

A bolt of red light shot from the muzzle of the little pistol, though it didn't make a sound. The light hit Andrew square in the chest. He jerked to a stop and threw his arms wide. His body convulsed, though he didn't move or fall. He threw back his head, and like the time Grayson had attacked Owens in that alley, silver light erupted from Andrew's mouth and eyes. An instant later, he collapsed on the deck with a hollow thump.

"What the hell?" Eli whispered.

"Is he... dead?" Briar asked.

"No more dead than he was," Liam answered. He walked past Andrew's prone form without a glance. "Where's the ferromancer, Briar?"

"What?"

"I know that was his construct around your throat today. Is he holding you captive?"

Briar blinked, suddenly understanding Liam's strong reaction when he noticed her necklace earlier.

"It's quite the reverse," a familiar, though winded voice answered. Briar spun to find Grayson clinging to the frame of her cabin door.

"Step over here by me, Briar." Liam had the gun trained on Grayson.

"What are you doing?" she demanded.

"I might have retired, but that doesn't mean I wouldn't recognize a bloody ferromancer. A fully cast ferromancer standing in the doorway of my goddaughter's cabin." Liam's voice rose at the end. "If you've touched her..."

"I haven't done you, or her, any wrong," Grayson whispered. "But I know my words are lies to your ears. Finish what you've come here to do. In the end, you'll be doing the world a favor."

"What the hell are you two talking about?" Briar demanded. "Do you know each other?"

Grayson's eyes met hers, his tone soft when he answered. "He's Scourge."

CHAPTER 19

BRIAR TURNED TO STARE AT the man she'd known pretty much her entire life. "Is that true?" she asked Liam.

"Briar, please, step over here by me." Liam didn't take his gun off Grayson. "I won't let him hold you captive any longer."

"No, he's telling the truth. I kidnapped him, stole his plans, and sent them to you for inspection."

"He's Martel?" Liam asked.

"Yes." She had been unaware of that fact when she retrieved the plans earlier today, or was that now yesterday. God, what a long day—and night.

"As unlikely as it sounds, that's the truth of it." Grayson's knuckles were white where he clung to the door. Briar wondered why Liam continued to hold a gun on a man who looked ready to collapse. "I have no design on you or yours, sir," Grayson added.

"He's telling the truth, Uncle Liam," Briar added.

"Liam… Adams?" Grayson must have remembered Briar mentioning his name.

"McAdams," Liam clarified.

"What—" Briar didn't get to finish.

"Bloody hell," Grayson muttered. "Fitting." His eyes rolled back, and he released the doorframe. He slumped to the deck with a soft thump.

"What did you do?" Briar demanded of Liam.

"Nothing." He lowered the gun.

She gave him a frown, then hurried to Grayson. He lay on his side, half in and half out of her cabin doorway. She gripped his cold shoulder and gave him a gentle shake. "Grayson?"

It seemed he had passed out again.

"Dear God," Liam said from above her. He was staring at Grayson's back. "The missing drake."

Briar glanced up. "Drake?" She remembered Solon calling him that.

"It means dragon," Liam answered. "Ferromancers are named for the form their construct takes."

Grayson had called Solon *Leon*. She had a strong suspicion that meant lion.

"He must have used the name Martel to hide what he is," Liam added.

Did he? Or was Grayson honoring the old watchmaker he had admired?

Liam shifted a little closer, his gun still trained on Grayson.

Briar glared up at him. "Would you please put that gun away? He's not even conscious." She turned back to Grayson. "Eli, could you help me get him back into the cook's bunk?"

Eli spared Liam a worried glance, but came forward to do as she asked.

"No, Briar," Liam spoke up. "You don't understand what you're dealing with."

She looked up and was shocked to see that he still held his gun. "Uncle Liam?" Was he really going to shoot Grayson?

Someone was crossing the gangplank. Briar glanced over, expecting Benji or Zach, and was shocked to see Agatha step onto her boat. It wasn't so shocking that she was here, but what she was wearing. Agatha was dressed much like Briar in trousers and man's style coat—though both fit as if they had been made for her.

"Put away the gun, Liam," she said. "The young man is hardly a threat."

"He's a drake, Aggie," Liam argued, though he did slip the gun beneath his coat.

"A drake who doesn't look like his final casting is going to take." Agatha's gaze met Briar's, her expression sad.

Briar rose to her feet, seeing an ally in Agatha. "Another ferromancer forced this on him by throwing him in a vat of molten iron. Is there anything we can do for him?"

Agatha gripped her shoulder, her expression still sad. "No, Briar, there's not. He'll either pull through on his own or he won't." She took a breath and released it. "I know you don't want to hear this, but it will be better if he doesn't survive this."

Briar couldn't believe kind-hearted Agatha—who would catch and release a spider rather than smash it—would say such a thing. "Well, I'm not giving up on him." She turned away. "Eli?"

Eli still looked worried, but he gave her a nod and carefully picked Grayson up.

Briar looked up to find Jimmy standing on the deck above her. She hated that he'd had to learn that Grayson was a ferromancer this way. By his wide eyes, she could see that he was stunned.

"Jimmy, are you still with me?"

"Of course, Captain," he responded immediately.

"Would you please dump my cousin on the dock, then prepare to cast off?"

Jimmy nodded, then hopped down from the deck above them. He eyed Andrew. "Is he dead or not?"

"He's soulless," she answered. "I'm guessing dead is better."

Jimmy swallowed, then reached down to pull him upright. Zach hurried across the gangplank, then bent to give Jimmy a hand.

"Thank you, Zach," she said to him.

Zach just nodded and continued with the task.

Briar turned back to Liam and Agatha. "I'm leaving. Are you going to try to stop me?"

"No," Agatha said.

"We're going with you," Liam added.

Briar frowned. Did he intend to stick around in case Grayson did survive? "You're really part of the Scourge?" she asked.

"In a past life," Liam answered. "One I thought I had left behind."

This was so surreal. He had always seemed so harmless. Her kindly godfather who spent rainy afternoons making crazy contraptions with her in his workshop.

Briar took a breath. "If you're staying, give me the pistol. Otherwise, I must ask you to leave." She held out her hand.

Liam glanced at Agatha, and at her nod, pulled the pistol from beneath his coat. But he didn't immediately hand it to her. Instead, he turned the small gun on its side. "See this switch?" He pointed to the tiny lever just above the trigger.

"Yes?"

"When it's pushed forward, as it is now, the gun cannot fire."

"All right."

"Always keep it in this position when it's in your pocket."

It was almost funny that he was instructing her about the weapon he intended to use to shoot her friend. God, she was so tired. "I understand." She accepted the weapon from him.

Flicking the switch he'd shown her, she turned and held the weapon on him.

"Briar?" Liam's eyes widened.

"I'm sorry," she whispered. "I know you're just sticking around to see if Grayson survives, but I'm not going to let you kill him. He deserves a chance at life, just like any man."

"He's not a man."

"Please. Just go."

"You don't understand," Liam continued.

"Probably not, but is that my fault or yours?"

Liam sighed. "If you're doing this because you're angry at me—"

"I'm doing this because it's the right thing to do."

"You haven't seen what I've seen, Briar. You have no idea what a fully cast ferromancer is capable of doing."

She shrugged. "Guess I'll find out."

"Briar—"

"Let her be, Liam." Agatha laid a hand on his arm. "We'll go, Briar, but know that we're only trying to protect you. This never ends well, my child."

"I have to try," she whispered.

"I know." Agatha slipped her arm in Liam's.

"Use the gun if you have to," Liam said. With those chilling words, they left the boat.

THEY MADE IT OUT OF Columbus without incident. Just another boat among many, making their way along the canal.

Briar trusted her crew to get them out of town and traverse the dark waterway. She remained in her over-warm cabin, trying to help Grayson.

Retrieving a bowl of water and a cloth, she sat down on the edge of the bed and began to carefully clean the wounds around the metal fins protruding from his upper back. One finger brushed the inner curve of one, and she gasped as it sliced her knuckle with ease. Grayson groaned.

"Grayson?" She gripped his cold shoulder.

"Scourge," he breathed, a note of alarm in his soft voice.

"He's gone," she said. "I didn't know. He never told me."

Grayson didn't respond.

"Hey, you still with me?" She gave his shoulder a small shake, but it seemed he'd slipped into unconsciousness once more.

She took a moment to dab her bleeding knuckle with her rag, then went back to trying to help him. He was going to survive this; there wasn't any other option.

EXHAUSTED, BRIAR COLLAPSED ON HER own bunk some time in the early morning hours, but remained dressed with her curtain open should he wake and call out during the night.

The light was just brightening the curtains on the cabin windows when she woke. A brief moment of confusion, and she remembered the events of the day before with painful clarity.

Hurrying back into the main part of the cabin, she stumbled to a stop. Zach sat on the side of Grayson's bed, blotting his forehead with a cloth. But Zach sprang to his feet when he saw her.

"You're fine." She walked to the bunk. "How is he? Did he wake any?"

Zach shook his head.

She sighed and touched Grayson's forehead. His skin was still ice cold, but the edges of his dark hair were wet with sweat.

Grayson groaned, and his hand fisted against the sheets.

"He acts like he's in pain." She looked up at Zach and he nodded.

She turned back to Grayson, feeling worthless with her inability to help him.

A knock at the door made her look up to see Jimmy standing on the threshold.

"How's the human pin cushion?" Jimmy asked.

She smiled at his attempt at humor, but her smile didn't last. "Not good." She walked over to him. "Are you upset that I didn't mention that he was a ferromancer? I only found out myself after Solon took him, but I wanted Grayson to be the one to tell."

"It's all right, Captain. It's good of you to keep a man's secret like that. None of the crew blames you."

"Thank you."

Jimmy cleared his throat. "I thought I'd give breakfast a go. I watched Grayson make the last couple of meals."

"Until he recovers, you're the best we got," she said, trying for an encouraging tone. If Grayson did recover, she doubted a ferromancer would want to remain cook on a canal boat.

BREAKFAST TURNED OUT BETTER THAN she expected—which meant it was edible. Jimmy's cooking talent exceeded hers, but he was still a long way from matching Grayson's skills at the stove.

They took breakfast on the deck as usual, calling Benji in from the towpath for the meal. Zach had remained at Grayson's side, seeming to have appointed himself his nursemaid. And judging by the silence at the breakfast table, the rest of the crew was equally concerned. Even Eli was subdued.

"Do you think we should seek out a doctor?" she asked, breaking the silence.

"Can a doctor help him?" Jimmy asked. "His ain't a common ailment. At least, not in these parts."

She returned her fork to her plate, her appetite gone. She pressed a hand to her pocket where Lock hid. With the constant company in her cabin, she hadn't been able to comfort him.

A thump came from below them in her cabin.

"What was—" Jimmy didn't get to finish as the lower door into the cargo hold banged open.

They all sprang to their feet, hurrying to the edge to look down into the cargo hold.

Zach emerged from the cabin, helping an apparently conscious Grayson. Zach had pulled Grayson's arm around his shoulders, while wrapping his other arm around Grayson's back. A bloodstain marred Zach's sleeve where a metal fin had gotten him, but he didn't move his arm.

The two men stumbled to the side of the boat, and Briar's joy of seeing Grayson up was dashed when he fell to his knees and vomited over the side. Zach gripped his shoulder, perhaps in comfort or simply to keep him from falling overboard.

Briar jumped down into the cargo hold, aware of the rest of the crew following, and hurried to where Grayson hung over the side of the boat.

No longer beneath a blanket in a dimly lit room, she got her first good look at him. His skin was so pale it was almost translucent, and the fins protruding from the vertebrae of his upper back were no longer the only metal visible. The skin had split over his shoulder blades, revealing blood streaked metal instead of bone beneath.

The vomiting subsided to dry heaves, and Grayson collapsed against the deck, pulling up his knees as if in pain.

She knelt beside him, noting the blood on his lips. "Grayson?" She gripped his shoulder. His skin was still ice cold.

He didn't respond, but the hand gripping the edge of the deck tightened. A glitter drew her eye, and she watched as the dark veins in the wood turned silver. The board was turning to metal.

"Grayson, don't," she said, alarmed. She started to reach out and grip his wrist, but hesitated.

His eye lids fluttered as if he tried to respond, then he pulled his knees tighter to his stomach, whimpering in pain.

"Miss Briar?" Eli's voice was soft and uncertain.

Grayson cried out and a stream of blood ran from one nostril.

"Whatever's happening," Jimmy said, softly, "I don't think he's going to make it."

With nowhere else to turn, Briar pulled the silver pocket watch from her pocket. "Lock?" She waited, but nothing happened.

"These people are my friends, Lock. We can trust them. Please, can you help me save Grayson?"

"Miss Briar, what are you—" Jimmy gasped as the watch transformed into the little dragon.

"Sweet Jesus," Benji muttered.

Lock looked up at her, his gem-like eyes full of sadness.

"He's dying, isn't he?" she whispered.

Lock moaned.

"Is there anything you can do? Anything we can do?"

He studied her a moment, then leapt into the air. In a flurry of silver wings, he flew back to her cabin.

"Captain, what's going on?" Jimmy asked.

She gripped Grayson's shoulder as he continued to writhe in pain, oblivious to his surroundings. "Solon, the other ferromancer, forced this on him. He's going through something called a final casting."

"Like when metal is poured into a mold at a foundry?" Jimmy asked.

"I suspect it's very much like that." Her voice dropped to a whisper. "I think it's killing him."

A glint of metal drew her attention. Lock was flying back, holding her fiddle case in his talons. He dropped it in her hands, then landed on her shoulder.

"Is that an automaton?" Benji asked, his tone more awed than alarmed.

"Yes." She turned to see Lock. "You think I should play for him like I did before?"

Lock cooed and rubbed his cheek against hers.

"That'll help?" Eli sounded skeptical.

"It helped after Grayson stopped that soulless man in Chillicothe." She opened the case and took out her fiddle and bow.

"Is that where you learned he was a ferromancer?" Benji asked, he looked more intrigued than upset with her secret.

"No, I didn't find out until Solon did this to him." She got to her feet.

Grayson cried out again, drawing his legs tighter to his chest.

She tucked the fiddle under her chin and took a deep breath. She didn't see how this would help, but she was willing to try anything.

A hand touched her leg, and she looked down to find Zach looking up at her. He placed his hand over his heart, then pointed at her.

"Play from the heart," she whispered. "Or as Grayson told me, from the soul."

Zach nodded.

She wondered at this connection Zach seemed to have with Grayson. She remembered seeing them together on the towpath. Had Grayson opened up to him? Certainly, he wouldn't have told Zach the truth.

Zach gave her leg a squeeze of encouragement, then withdrew his hand.

"Here goes," she whispered.

Lock snuggled closer to the side of her neck opposite the fiddle.

She took another breath and drew the bow across the stings. She ran through a couple of scales, thinking about how badly she wanted to help Grayson, to encourage his body to accept this new form and heal. Certainly, others of his race had done it and survived. Solon had wanted this too much to lose him to death.

Briar didn't know when she stopped playing scales and launched into a heartfelt tune of hope and healing. She played until her fingers were raw, then played past it. A little discomfort wouldn't distract her. She poured her determination into her music, willing Grayson to beat this thing with the same stubborn fortitude.

"It's working, Captain," Jimmy said, his voice little more than a whisper.

She opened her eyes and looked down. To her shock, Grayson's skin was no longer pale and translucent, but regaining a healthy ruddy glow in the warm morning sun. His tight ball of pain had relaxed, and though he seemed to be looking at nothing in particular, his eyes were open.

She continued to play, encouraging him and sending him strength. The tune grew more lively and upbeat as her hope welled.

With Zach's help, Grayson sat up. He fisted his hands against his thighs, and one by one, the metal fins began to retreat into his body. Oval-shaped, silver orifices remained over each vertebra like a line of oblong silver rivets down his back.

As her song continued, the exposed metal to either side of his spine morphed and grew until a series of overlapping silver plates was molded over his shoulder blades.

Finally, his hands relaxed against his thighs, and he bowed his head, allowing his damp hair to fall across his forehead.

She pulled the bow from the strings, and the last note echoed across the calm waters of the canal.

Lock gave a little squeal of delight and leapt from her shoulder to his.

"Grayson?" she prompted in the silence.

He got up on one knee, but hesitated before pushing himself to his feet.

Zach offered him a hand.

Grayson looked up, and after holding Zach's gaze for a moment, allowed him to pull him to his feet.

She expected Grayson to be weak, but he seemed steady on his feet.

He looked down, then ran a hand over his chest as if noticing for the first time that he was shirtless.

Zach pulled off his own shirt and offered it to him.

Briar stood rooted to the spot, feeling like a voyeur in this incredibly private moment, but unable to look away. She'd never seen Zach without a shirt—which was unusual on a cramped boat in the middle of summer. But seeing him now, she understood why.

She'd noticed the scars on his neck, but she now saw that they covered his right shoulder, chest, and stomach before disappearing beneath his waistband. How he had survived burns like that was a wonder.

Grayson studied Zach and his offered shirt, then, without a word, reached out and gripped his scarred shoulder.

A shimmer of light danced across Zach's skin as if he'd been dusted with a fine layer of glittering sand.

Briar's mouth dropped open as Zach's scars gradually faded, though his skin retained that faintly glittery property.

Grayson's hand slid over from Zach's shoulder. With his palm resting against the side of Zach's neck, he pressed his thumb to the front of Zach's throat.

Briar frowned, watching the silent exchange. She could tell by the way the rest of the crew had begun to shift their weight that they were also growing uncomfortable, wondering what Grayson was doing to Zach.

Grayson finally took his hand from Zach's neck. But with the support gone, Grayson swayed on his feet.

Zach caught his shoulder steadying him. Zach's Adam's apple bobbed with an exaggerated swallow. "Perhaps you shouldn't have done that," Zach whispered.

Briar pressed a hand to her mouth, shocked to hear Zach speak for the first time.

"Perhaps," Grayson agreed with him, his tone cool and devoid of emotion. "You will find that your new voice will give you a new ability, but I believe you possess the temperament to use it wisely." Grayson gripped Zach's shoulder, and without another word to anyone, walked off toward the bow of the ship, Lock still perched on his shoulder. The metal in Grayson's back glinted in the sun.

With a sob, Benji came forward and wrapped his brother in hug.

"It's all right, Ben," Zach whispered, hugging Benji in turn and rubbing a hand over his blond hair.

"Dear Lord," Jimmy found his own voice. "He healed you?" he asked Zach, but didn't wait for an answer. "I didn't know ferromancers could heal."

"Was it healing?" Eli asked. "His skin glitters."

Benji pulled back, scrubbing a hand across his eyes. "Eli's right.

It's like that board Grayson touched." He gestured at the board on the edge of the boat. The metal in it glinted in the sun.

"I don't think Zach is complaining," Jimmy said.

"It's like he infused metal in his skin," Eli said, eyeing Zach's scarless skin. "Did he do the same for his throat?"

"That's what ferromancers do," Jimmy said. "They work with metal, right?"

"They can also make a man soulless," Eli said.

Briar sighed. "He wouldn't do that, and besides, this is between him and Zach." She returned the fiddle to its case. "Zach can give him a good cussing later."

Zach smiled. "I'll refrain." His voice was still little more than a whisper, but perhaps it would get stronger with use. Even if it didn't, it was still amazing.

She smiled in turn, and patting Zach on his faintly glittering shoulder, turned and carried her fiddle back to her cabin.

Setting the instrument on the table, she eyed the rumpled cook's bunk with its bloodstained and ripped blankets. She knelt and pulled out Martel's trunk—no, Grayson's trunk. The clothes inside were his. But she only glanced at them. Her eyes were drawn to the leather tube. Someone had returned the plans to Grayson's trunk. Zach?

Picking up the tube and a white shirt, she took a deep breath and left the cabin.

Grayson still sat on the rail at the bow, not paying much attention to them. Fortunately, there were no other boats nearby at the moment.

She walked to the bow and stopped beside him. "We're not the only boat out here." She offered him his shirt.

He eyed it a moment, then took it from her. "Thank you." Lock hopped down while Grayson pulled the shirt over his head and let it drop into place, then he turned his attention back to the canal. Lock returned to his shoulder and rubbed his cheek against Grayson's.

She sat down beside them, setting the leather tube at her feet. "Are you all right?"

"I am well." He fell silent once more.

"I'm going to take that to mean that you are physically past the point of danger. How are you otherwise?"

He turned his face away. "You shouldn't have come for me."

"You were just going to let him kill you? That seems cowardly."

He finally faced her, a frown shadowing his eyes. "You don't know what you've done."

"And I never will if you don't explain."

He took a deep breath and slowly released it.

When he didn't speak, she ventured on. "Solon was trying to force a change on you that you didn't want. Why didn't you want it?"

"Why?" he demanded. "Can't you guess? I wanted to remain human—or something like."

"You still look human to me."

He gave her a frown.

"Minus a few metal bits," she added.

He huffed and turned his attention back to the canal. "The metal bits are not the concern. As time passes, as I use more of my abilities, I will gradually lose my humanity. I'm talking about what makes us human: empathy, compassion, the innate drive to be part of the social order."

"I don't do so well with the social thing, either. Ask anyone who knows me."

"This isn't a joke," he said with heat, though his gaze was cold when it met hers. "I'm going to become a monster."

"Because you're a ferromancer."

"Yes." His voice softened, and she got the sense that he still didn't like confessing that.

"So, that's it?" she asked, growing annoyed with his pessimism. "You're just going to give up and accept it?"

"After a ferromancer's final casting, there's nothing to be done."

"Always? No exceptions? No one's ever tried to beat this thing?"

He hesitated. "Not in the last fifty years. I'm sure you've heard the stories out of Europe."

"Stories, yes. You hesitated. What happened before these recent problems?"

"It's just a myth. A tale of hope whispered among the damned."

"That's borderline poetic."

He gave her another frown before looking away. "The ferra keep us in the dark."

"The ferra. Solon said they're the female half of your race. Can they do... the things you can do?" She had yet to develop a full of understanding of just what a ferromancer could do, so she kept it vague.

"The active power only manifests in the male."

"Curious." She thought back over her conversation with Solon. "Why did Solon think I was one of them?"

"You can command a construct and—" he stopped.

"And?"

"And it's not a common ability."

She lifted a brow. "So I can do some things other people can't. I'm pretty good on the fiddle, too."

His forehead wrinkled.

"And what's up with that? Why does my playing seem to help you?"

"I speculate it's your connection to my construct." He took a breath. "To Lock."

Lock sat up and made something like a little roar.

Grayson slumped. "And so it begins."

"So what begins?"

He shook his head and got to his feet.

She caught his wrist. "Would you please stop being so cryptic?"

"Were you able to get the plans? You'll give them back to me and we're done?"

It surprised her how much it hurt to hear him say that. After everything they'd been through...

She could only see one reason. "You think I'm ferra, too."

He held her gaze, saying nothing.

"I've lived on this boat since I was three years old. I don't know anything about any of this—except what you and Solon have told me."

"That doesn't mean it's not in your ancestry," he replied, his tone soft.

She was stunned. "You think I have some kind of ability to control you? You think that I would?"

A bitter smile curled his mouth. "You already command a crew of men."

She shoved herself to her feet. "Not against their will!" She made herself continue in a softer voice. "I realize that you hardly know me, but that goes against every fiber of my being. I've worked too hard to hang on to my freedom. I would never take it from another—even a self-described monster."

He studied her. "Then you'll give me the plans?"

She reached down and picked up the tube, then offered it to him. "Uncle Liam said that the technology is influenced by ferromancy, but that the plans contain none. He said the designer was a mechanical genius."

"He did?" Grayson looked surprised, and perhaps, pleased.

"That was before he knew what you are, of course. What I don't understand is why *you* would design something like that."

"The challenge. To make what is impossible to the mundane, possible." For the first time, his tone warmed and a glint of enthusiasm lit his eyes.

"But didn't you make Lock?"

211

He glanced at the little dragon on his shoulder. "Yes, but he's one hundred percent ferromantic."

She marveled at the way he went on and on about the locomotive, yet he shrugged off something as miraculous as Lock. "They're both beautiful."

"But it's the locomotive's function that is the marvel." The enthusiasm in Grayson's tone grew more pronounced. "I hope to get a patent. That's why I wanted the plans back. I'm surprised you returned them. If I sell them to the railroad, the need for the canals will decrease even more."

"Those plans are the creative children of your soul. I would never take that from you."

He studied her for a moment. "Technically, so is Lock, and you see how that turned out."

Lock lifted his head to look at her with soulful eyes.

"Lock is a hell of a lot cuter than those plans." She braced a hand against Grayson's chest and reached up to tickle Lock under his chin. When she leaned back, Grayson was watching her.

Without comment, he took Lock from his shoulder and transferred him to hers.

"He's yours," he whispered.

"I can't—"

He pressed his thumb to her lips, silencing her. "I can't become a full-fledged monster without all of my soul." A sad smile, and he turned away. "The ferra taught me that."

She watched him walk away, not sure what to make of any of this.

CHAPTER 20

THEY DOCKED IN LOCKBOURNE a little over an hour later. The gangplank was already down when Grayson emerged from her cabin, carrying his trunk. Briar stood on the aft deck above him. Perhaps she could just stand here and wave farewell.

The silver watch shifted in her pocket as if Lock had heard her thoughts. Who knew? Maybe he picked up on her emotions or something.

She slipped a finger in her pocket, brushing the warm metal surface. "You're right," she whispered. "I'm being a coward."

Grayson turned and looked up at her, though she knew there was no way he could have heard her. She flashed back to him and Lock playing chess, or any of their other interactions. Could the two of them communicate at a distance? She found the notion disturbing.

Walking to the hatch, she descended the ladder into her cabin, then stepped out through the door into the cargo hold. Grayson glanced over as she joined him.

"You and Lock can communicate," she said, keeping her voice low.

"Not in words."

"Because you don't need words when he's part of your soul."

Grayson grunted, but didn't argue.

She frowned. "I don't think you should leave him behind."

"He'll be more sad if I take him. He loves you."

Lock stirred in her pocket once more, and she had the sense that he wasn't happy with Grayson's revelation.

She slipped her fingers into her pocket again. "Yes, he over-shared," she said to Lock. "But it's all right. I love you, too, Lock."

She glanced up at Grayson, expecting amusement, but he wasn't smiling. He looked intrigued, as if he hadn't expected her to understand Lock so well. But she didn't get to question him about it as Eli and Jimmy joined them.

"So long, ferromancer," Eli said.

"Don't you mean good riddance?" Grayson asked.

"I was being polite."

Grayson smiled, then turned to Jimmy.

To Briar's surprise, Jimmy offered him a hand. "Thanks again for fixing my father's watch."

"Thank you for letting me," Grayson answered. "I was about to go mad isolated on a wooden vessel on the water."

Jimmy looked puzzled by the comment, but Briar remembered Grayson telling her that a ferromancer wouldn't be comfortable on her boat. Maybe that was another reason he was leaving.

A carriage rattled past on the street that bordered the docks. "Have you the funds for your journey?" she asked Grayson. He would be traveling by carriage to Newark where he would catch a train to who knew where.

"I do." He reached inside his coat and pulled out an envelope. "I also need to settle my bill for my passage."

"I kidnapped you."

"Semantics." He offered her the envelope. "Take the envelope, Miss Rose. Most of that came from your cousin."

"Well, in that case…" She took the envelope from him, then glanced up in surprise when she felt how thick it was. With some trepidation, she looked inside. Stunned by what she found, she began to count the bills. "I can't take this," she said when she finished. "Even if it did belong to Andrew."

"Why not?" Grayson asked. "I personally find it amusing that you'll be using his money to buy this boat from him."

"There's two thousand dollars here." She got straight to the point.

Jimmy's mouth dropped open.

"Which I understand is what a boat like this costs," Grayson said. Had he been asking around?

"The boat might already be mine."

Grayson lifted a brow.

"Andrew is soulless."

"What?" Grayson must not have noticed Andrew lying on the deck when he confronted Liam last night.

"Although he still wants to sell the boat. He intends to use the money to throw some big international gala for Solon. Any idea what that's all about?"

"No." Grayson turned his head, frowning. She realized he was looking north, back toward Columbus. "I don't guess it matters." He picked up his trunk and started across the gangplank.

"Grayson, wait." She hurried after him. "I can't take this money."

"Then toss it in the canal," he said over his shoulder.

She huffed and continued after him. They rounded the end of an empty wagon and Grayson finally stopped. She took a breath for another argument, then she noticed Zach and Benji standing a few feet away. They were talking with a man in a blue coat. A policeman.

Briar gripped Grayson's arm, and he quietly set down the trunk.

"Ah, I see now," the policeman said, his head turned toward the boat. "The *Briny Rose*. Odd name."

"I believe the previous owner was once a sailor at sea," Zach answered. His voice was stronger now, but it had an odd metallic resonance Briar hadn't noticed before.

"Makes sense," the policeman agreed. "Sorry to trouble you."

"No trouble," Zach agreed with an easy smile.

With a tip of his hat, the policeman turned and walked off.

"That was amazing," Benji said as soon as he and Zach were alone.

Zach turned away and seeing her and Grayson, his cheeks turned pink.

"What just happened?" she asked. "Was that policeman looking for me?"

"Yes," Zach answered.

"But Zach told a fib and he *believed* it," Benji said. "He thought the boat was called the *Briny Rose*."

"Zach?" she prompted.

"It's on account of what Mr. Martel did for me." Zach waved a hand at Grayson.

"He can magic people into believing what he says," Benji clarified.

Grayson looked amused by the comment, but remained silent.

"I would never use it for ill," Zach said quickly. "And never on you, Captain."

"I believe you, Zach." She patted his shoulder, and hoped her smile didn't look as forced as it felt. "I'm going to walk Mr. Martel to the carriage station." And try to give him his money back.

"Have a safe trip," Benji said. He still stared at Grayson with something close to wonder.

"I will, Ben." Grayson laid a hand on his shoulder. "Take care of your brother?"

"Of course, sir."

Grayson turned to Zach who watched the exchange with a small smile. "Don't get any ideas. It won't work on me."

Zach smiled, but as was his habit, remained silent.

Grayson offered his hand and Zach took it.

"Thank you," Zach said.

"No problem," Grayson answered. "As I told Jimmy, I enjoy fixing things."

Zach just smiled.

Briar cleared her throat. "If you two would get the fresh team hitched, we can get underway when I get back."

"Where are we headed?" Benji asked.

"North." She didn't elaborate.

She'd never captained a boat on the northern stretch of the Ohio & Erie, though she had traveled it a few times with her uncle. She'd often considered a northern run, just for a change of scenery, but for some reason had never left her home stretch. Now it seemed she may not be going back.

Perhaps it was her penance for the wrong she had done. That seemed ironic since that wrong had been done in an effort to save the canal. In her attempt to preserve what she loved, she had lost it—or would soon. Were wanted posters up in the canal office yet?

Leaving Benji and Zach to their tasks, she fell in beside Grayson as they walked into Lockbourne. When she glanced up, she found him smiling.

"When you healed Zach, you told him he would have an ability. Is that what you meant?"

"It's the nature of soul iron," Grayson answered with a shrug— or the best he could manage while carrying his trunk.

"What's soul iron?"

"The alloy I told you about. We make it."

She realized he spoke of the shiny silver metal that all ferromancer devices seemed to be made from. "That's how you fixed the rudder," she remembered.

He grinned. "I cheated."

"And that's what Solon noticed." When he'd stopped in the middle of the street and climbed from his carriage to look around. "Good thing we didn't meet any other ferromancers while my boat was sporting soul iron."

"Solon felt me adapting it. That's what drew his attention. Most ferromancers are territorial. My use of soul iron would have kept them away—unlike the Scourge. Although, it's the constructs they go after."

She looked up. "What?" She laid a hand over the pocket where Lock hid. "Why go after the constructs?"

"I've told you. A ferromancer's construct holds a piece of his soul."

"You said Lock was Mr. Martel's heart. Your... heart."

He glanced over, his eyes once again cool.

"Oh Jesus, your scar. You were being literal."

"Cut something out of a ferromancer, and he'll instinctively replace it with soul iron. It's how the ferra keep us in line."

Briar stared at Grayson in horror, unable to believe what he was telling her. "I think I'm going to vomit."

"Literally or figuratively?"

She frowned at his levity. "So if the Scourge get Lock..." If Liam got Lock.

"There'll be one less evil ferromancer in the world."

"You're not funny. How will I know them?"

"You won't. Only a ferromancer can sense the Scourge—as they would recognize the ferromancer. But it should please you to know that constructs are otherwise indestructible."

At least there was that. They turned down Main Street, and Briar could see the carriage station at the far end.

"But how would the Scourge recognize..." She thought about all that he'd told her. "What exactly are the Scourge? You make them sound magical. I thought they were just vigilantes who hunted ferromancers?"

"Technically, they're the ferra's police force and executioners."

"But are they magical?"

"They are the antithesis of ferromancy. They don't have an active magic, but they can dissolve soul iron."

She swallowed, remembering how Liam had held the medallion that was Lock in his palm. "So how do the Scourge fit into the family tree? I assume there's some connection."

"There is, and it was how it was determined that ferromancers— be they male, or the female ferra—and humans were different races. If we stay within our own races, our offspring are like their parents.

Cross the two races, and you get the variant that make up the Scourge. Think of them as mules—just don't call them that to their faces. They get pissed."

"Mules are sterile."

"Yes, and they carry a huge chip on their shoulders about it."

She stared at him.

Grayson lifted a brow in question. "What?"

"It's a lot to take in," she admitted. "It's like there's a whole other world I knew nothing about."

"Maybe next time, you'll think twice before kidnapping a ferromancer."

"Ha ha." She thought back to that first night. "How did I manage that?"

"You isolated me in a world without modern technology and bound me in something other than iron."

"Dumb luck," she admitted, letting his slight dig at the canal's lack of technology go. "What about Lock? You could have used him to get free."

"You had already taken him from me."

She frowned. "You still think I'm ferra."

"You're not Scourge. I'd feel it."

"I don't actually remember my father, but he wasn't a ferromancer."

"And your mother?"

"Died when I was a few months old."

"Don't take this the wrong way, but what if you weren't your father's natural daughter?"

"I guess it's possible, but you've seen my cousin. People often mistake us for brother and sister."

Grayson shrugged. "I'm just telling you how things work according to what I've been taught."

They had arrived at the carriage station. They walked inside, but found the small room empty. There must not be any carriages departing soon.

Grayson set his trunk beside an empty bench. "I'll go purchase my ticket." He headed for the ticket window.

Briar watched him walk away, her mind awash with all he had told her. It was odd, but she had never sought out any details about her parents. Between Uncle Charlie, and Agatha and Liam, she had a wonderful childhood. She'd always felt a bit like she was betraying them by asking about her parents.

Could she really be something other than human? The notion stood her whole sense of place in the world on its ear.

Grayson tapped on the ticket window. "Hello?" he called.

Briar left him to figure out where the attendant was, and pulled the silver watch from her pocket. Cradling it in her palm, she watched the light catch in the grooves that created the image of Lock on the cover's surface. She really should give Lock back to Grayson. How could she even consider keeping him? Brushing her thumb across the warm metal, she blinked her suddenly blurry eyes.

"Briar!" Grayson shouted.

She lifted her head, but before she could turn toward him, a hand seized her wrist. Instinctively, she fisted her hand around Lock.

"I see the drake survived," a voice said from behind her. Briar had no trouble recognizing Liam's familiar Scottish brogue. She had been so preoccupied that she hadn't heard him walk up behind her.

Grayson had started toward them, but stopped as Liam's hand slid down to cover hers. A panicked surge of static electricity tingled across her palm.

"Briar," Grayson said, the same panicked tone in his voice.

Heart in her throat, Briar lunged backward. The move seemed to take Liam by surprise, and she was able to land an elbow in his ribs.

He grunted, and the hand holding hers loosened.

Briar spun toward him and, trying not to think about what

she did, brought her knee up. Liam moved a lot faster than she expected. His palm smacked against her knee, blocking her before she could connect. The blow knocked her off balance, and she stumbled back. Liam followed, reaching for her.

"To me," Grayson shouted.

A burst of static, and Lock was now the little dragon. He twisted out of her hand and began winging his way toward Grayson.

"No!" Briar shouted. "Stop!"

Lock changed his course and landed on the bench instead.

"No armor," she said to the little dragon, though her eyes held Grayson's. She turned to face Liam. "Both of you, stop this."

Lock snapped his jaws at Liam.

"That goes for you, too," she told the little dragon.

Liam stared at her with wide eyes. "You can command a construct? Is that how you're controlling the drake?"

"His name is Grayson Martel. And I don't make him do anything."

Liam's eyes narrowed. "How is he up and about today? Judging by the look of him last night, I wouldn't have expected him to survive his casting."

"She's a soul singer," Grayson answered before she could.

Liam's mouth dropped open.

"What's a soul singer?" she asked Grayson.

"The violin thing."

"It has a name? You never mentioned that." She frowned at him. Why did he constantly hold back information from her?

Grayson gave her a shrug.

Liam found his voice. "She's a soul singer?"

"Through the violin, of all things." Grayson eyed Liam, though Briar would categorize it more a look of curiosity than animosity. She wondered if he'd ever come face to face with a member of the Scourge before.

"That's unusual?" she asked.

"I've never heard of such a manifestation," Grayson answered, "but it's a ferra talent."

She turned back to find Liam's brow wrinkled in something between concern and wonder. "You knew my parents," she said to him. "By any chance, was my mother ferra? Am I my father's natural daughter?"

Liam seemed to recover himself and turned his frown on her. "Your mother was not ferra, and you are David Rose's natural daughter."

She turned back to Grayson and spread her hands.

Grayson studied her a moment before turning back to Liam. "She's not Scourge; I would feel it. Yet you say she's not ferra. How—"

"None of this is any concern of yours, Drake."

"Not my concern?" Grayson demanded. "She took my construct, named him, and made him hers."

"Him?" Liam asked. Apparently, he was aware of the ferromancer aversion to using gender-specific pronouns with constructs.

Grayson sighed, the fight seeming to go out of him.

"If she had the ability, how would she even know how to use it?" Liam asked him.

"I've wondered that myself. It could simply be because he loves her."

Liam frowned, studying Grayson. Abruptly, he sighed and his shoulders slumped, making him look so much older. "Maybe Aggie's right." He bowed his head.

"Right? About what?" She took a step toward him.

He sprang forward without warning, snatching Lock from the back of the bench. He'd moved so fast that Briar hadn't even seen it coming. Had his momentary melancholy been a ruse to get her to lower her guard?

Lock struggled, trying to get free from Liam's fist.

"No! Don't!" She held out a hand.

Lock shrieked, and Grayson dropped to his knees.

Ferromancer

Briar choked on a sob. "Please don't hurt him."

Liam stood watching her, as if considering her words. "I'll spare him," he said, his tone soft, "on one condition."

"Name it," Briar whispered.

Liam held her gaze, his expression full of sorrow. "It breaks my heart to lay this on you, but I see no other recourse."

Briar frowned, not understanding.

"The drake will be your responsibility," Liam said.

"Of course," she quickly agreed.

"No, it's not that simple. All his misdeeds, the atrocities he will instigate, the horrors he will inflict—they will be yours."

"He wouldn't—"

"Silence!" Liam snapped. "This is my world. It is a world I wished to shield you from, but in keeping you ignorant, I left you vulnerable. The fault is mine, yet you will be the one to pay for my failure."

"Enough with the cryptic doom and gloom. Spell out what you want from me. I will do it. Then we will prove you wrong." She lifted her chin daring him to say otherwise.

The briefest of smiles touched Liam's face. Out of the corner of her eye, she saw Grayson lift his head to look at her. She wondered what he was thinking.

"You will make the drake yours. Irrevocably. He will do nothing without your leave."

"What?" she whispered. Her gaze drifted back to Grayson where he knelt a few feet away. He had bowed his head, a white-knuckled grip on each thigh. Was he in pain or was he anticipating what was to come?

"You make it sound as if I'll be taking away his free will." Her heart thumped in her ears.

Liam held her gaze. "That is the only way it can be."

When she didn't respond, Liam's hand tightened and Lock shrieked again. Grayson groaned.

"I'll never forgive you for this," she whispered to Liam.

"You would hate me more if I had simply killed him. This way, you will understand why this must be done."

Lock moaned in Liam's fist.

She couldn't stand to see Lock in pain—or perhaps it was simply fear, if he didn't feel pain. "Tell me what to do," she said.

"You have not fully taken his construct. You must complete the binding."

She remembered Grayson's comment when he carried her away from her failed fight with Hester. He had told her that he wasn't hers to command *yet*. Was this what he was referring to?

"How do I complete the binding?" she whispered.

"With the ferromancer's blood upon your tongue, you name the construct and claim it as your own."

"His blood? On my tongue?" The notion nauseated her.

"The body houses the soul, collecting in the organs and the blood. You will be speaking to the construct with the soul that created it. It will obey."

"I already named him, and he does as I ask."

Liam held her gaze, and she knew that look. He would not relent. He reached in his pocket and pulled out a folding knife, then offered it to her.

Taking the knife, she opened the blade. The snap as it locked in place echoed in the empty room.

"Hold out your hand, Drake," Liam commanded.

Grayson wordlessly complied, though he kept his head bowed.

Briar walked over to him and cupped the back of his offered hand with her unsteady one. "I'm sorry," she whispered.

Grayson didn't respond.

She laid the blade against his fingertip and, gently as she could, nicked it. Bright red blood immediately welled along the minor wound.

Swallowing her revulsion, Briar leaned over and touched her

tongue to his bleeding finger. Holding her breath, she kept her tongue away from the roof of her mouth in an effort not to taste it. She turned to face Liam.

He held out Lock to her. The little dragon had stopped struggling and now looked up at her with forlorn eyes. Was he just anxious over his capture or dreading what was to come?

Briar took a deep breath through her nose and for the first time became aware of the metallic taste that filled her mouth. A knot rose in her throat, but she couldn't swallow it back down.

"Lock," she whispered, the taste of blood now overwhelming her senses. "You are mine."

The little dragon looked up at her, his soulful eyes innocent, his coo questioning. He didn't understand.

She doubled over with a sob, then gripped her knees as she retched. It wasn't so much the taste of blood that made her want to vomit. Though she swallowed repeatedly, nothing would eliminate the taste of betrayal in her mouth.

A hand settled on her back. "Briar?" It was Grayson.

She bit back a sob and straightened. She couldn't face him, so she faced Liam instead.

"Give him back," she said between clenched teeth, lifting the open knife she still held.

Liam held her gaze for one long moment, then opened his hand. Lock sprang across the space between them. He landed on Briar's shoulder, then pressed against the side of her neck. A burst of static, and she felt him settle around her throat. She lifted her hand and felt a multi-strand choker encircling her neck. A small oval hung from the lowest chain. She could feel a carved image on its surface and knew it was the depiction of a dragon.

"We're leaving," she told Liam, her fury made it hard to speak. "Are you going to try to stop us?"

"No," he answered, his tone subdued.

Steeling her courage, she turned and looked up at Grayson. His gray-blue eyes met hers, but she couldn't read what she saw reflected there. Sadness? Resignation? At least he didn't appear angry—until he lifted his gaze to Liam. Then he frowned.

"You know what she is," Grayson said, his tone devoid of all human warmth.

"There's the ferromancer." Liam looked smug.

"Let's go." She pressed a hand to Grayson's chest, fearing he might do something. Or that Liam would.

Without speaking, he turned and picked up his trunk. She took a breath and started for the door.

"Briar," Liam called to her.

She stopped and looked back.

"I've loved you as my own. I would never lead you astray."

She held his gaze, deciding it was better not to speak.

"Don't forget about the gun I gave you," Liam said. "He'll devolve quickly."

"I have more faith in him than that."

"He's a drake."

"He's right," Grayson said, his words soft.

She turned to face him, annoyed by how easily he admitted defeat. "At some point, you need to stop listening to what other people say you are, and be the person you want to be."

A slight smile curled Grayson's mouth. "Like a mouthy canal boat captain?"

"Exactly." Casting Liam once last glance, she led Grayson from the room.

CHAPTER 21

BRIAR SAT ON THE BOW rail and watched the unfamiliar banks slide past her boat. A week ago, setting out on a journey on the northern stretch of the canal would have excited her. Now, it just made her feel more alone. It seemed she had lost everyone and everything that meant anything to her: her boat, at least legally; Liam and Agatha; and even if he was an ass, Andrew, who was her last blood relation.

"Miss Briar?" Eli stepped up behind her.

All right. She hadn't lost everyone. She still had her crew.

"Dinner's ready. Shall we bring the boat in for the night?" he asked. Grayson had resumed to his duties as cook without any prompting from her. She hadn't said a word to him since returning to the boat.

She got to her feet. "Yes, let's bring the boat in."

Eli nodded, but didn't turn away. "Won't you talk to me, Miss Briar? What happened with you and Mr. Martel back in Lockbourne? All he'll say is that you had some kind of confrontation with your Mr. Adams."

"Yes," she whispered. "But I can't talk about that right now."

"Why not, Miss Briar? Whatever happened, I'm not going to judge you. I know these magical folks had your back to the wall."

"Please, Eli." How could she ever tell him what she'd been forced to do? He would lose all respect for her. She pushed past him and retreated to her cabin.

Closing the door behind her, she leaned against it. The windows were open, letting in the evening air, but it was still too warm with the lit stove. The scent of beans and Johnny cakes hung heavy in the air, reminding her that Grayson had been here, doing what was expected of him as a member of her crew even though he wasn't.

She walked to her alcove and dropped onto her bunk. Covering her face with her hands, she let the tears come. Everything she had done had been for naught. She had made herself and her crew into outlaws, she had stumbled into a war among the magical, and worst of all, she had taken away Grayson's freedom, the very thing she had sworn she would never do.

A questioning coo preceded the brush of a warm metal cheek against hers. She hadn't felt Lock change from the necklace to the dragon.

"Oh, Lock," she whispered. "None of this worked out as it should."

Lock curled closer to her neck, his vocalizations—if she could call them that—sounding more concerned.

She smiled through the tears. At least he seemed to hold none of it against her. She sniffed, trying to regain control enough to comfort him.

"Briar?" Grayson stood in the opening to her little alcove.

She gasped and came to her feet. Lock, still sitting on her shoulder, made a happy sound when he saw Grayson.

Grayson glanced at Lock, dipping his head slightly before his eyes returned to hers.

"He called you here," she concluded.

"Your distress alarmed him."

Her distress. "I'm fine." She pushed past him to escape to the less confining main room.

Lock gave her a questioning coo, then rubbed his cheek against hers. He knew she was lying. But really, what did he expect summoning Grayson would accomplish?

"I'm not upset with you," Grayson said.

She rubbed at her cheeks, trying to scrub away the tears. "Well, you should be. I screwed up everything."

"Not through bad intentions."

So he agreed that she'd made a mess of everything. She faced him. "We can dock in Newark. You can catch a train there."

"And have your Lock crying out to me each time you feel melancholy? He can't communicate in a way that I will know whether you stubbed your toe or if you were dying."

"Then I'll tell him to leave you alone."

"It doesn't work like that. He's part of me."

She spread her hands. "I don't know how to make this right."

"I have a solution."

"Go on."

"I have a… friend who can help. She lives in Cleveland."

"She?" Not a ferromancer than. "I assume you're not friends with some Scourge lady."

"Esme is ferra."

Briar stared at him. "I thought you avoided them."

"She's an exile. Actually, I helped her escape to this country."

"What did she do?"

"Let's just say she got a little over zealous in completing the task given her."

Briar lifted her brows, but he didn't offer an explanation. "How can she help?"

He took a breath and released it. "She can teach you how to separate Lock from me."

Briar straightened. "But you said he's part of you. Part of your soul. How could—" She stopped, realizing she knew the answer. "You'd become soulless."

"It takes multiple amputations to achieve that."

She stared at him. "You would amputate part of yourself to be free of me?"

"It's nothing against you personally," he said quickly. "I mean, I barely know you. How could I even judge?"

Logically, she saw his point, but her heart didn't operate on logic.

"We've discussed this," he continued. "You know what my freedom means to me. You were willing to return the plans. Why not do this?"

"Because..." Because it sounded like something a monster like Solon would do? Because she didn't want to be part of that monster's world?

Because she didn't want him to leave?

The last thought stopped her. No, that was silly.

"Miss Rose?" Grayson cut into her musings.

"Very well. I'll meet with her."

His shoulders relaxed. "Thank you."

She frowned, bothered by his clear relief.

"I will, of course, cook for you and your crew. How soon will we be in Cleveland?"

Cleveland, where Esme lived. Well, Briar *was* headed north. "I'm not running at night, but I don't intend to pick up any cargo." It was too risky now that she was wanted. "Three days."

Grayson nodded. "That sounds good. I'll set up for dinner."

"I'll be right up."

He held her gaze for a moment, as if he wanted to say more, then simply turned and left the cabin.

Briar dropped onto the bench beside her table. A moment later, Lock hopped down from her shoulder, his tiny metal claws clicking against the tabletop. He stared up at her with those soulful eyes.

She reached out and rubbed him beneath his chin. "I love you, Lock."

He cooed, rubbing against her finger.

"I don't want to lose you," she admitted. "But..." She fell silent, not sure what she wanted to say.

She rubbed her breastbone, annoyed by how much Grayson's confession hurt. Then, too, it would hurt if anyone told her they were willing to amputate part of themselves to be free of her. It didn't mean she had any particular feelings for Grayson.

She pushed herself to her feet. Besides, he was a ferromancer. A ferromancer who wanted to work for the railroad. It would be best to end her acquaintance with the Gray Dragon.

She considered the moniker she had just created. Like his own kind, she had reduced him to a thing. But it would be easier to separate herself from an object rather than a friend.

"And I will finally be free of the ferromancer world."

Lock's whirr of agreement sounded doubtful.

Briar saw his point. "You don't believe that, do you?" She took a breath and released it. "Let's get up top and get some dinner. We have a lot of miles to cover in three days."

Lock sprang up onto her shoulder and, a moment later, became the necklace, the metal warm and oddly soothing against her throat. Could she be free of the ferromancer world? Or was she in too deep?

AFTERWORD

THANK YOU FOR READING *FERROMANCER*. I hope you enjoyed it. If you liked it well enough to leave a review; that would be great! There's more to come in The Iron Souls Series. If you want me to notify you when I have a new release, all you need to do is subscribe to my newsletter at http://beccaandre.com. As an added bonus, you'll also receive an alternate POV scene from one of my novels when you sign up.

Looking for more to read? Check out my Final Formula Series. Filled with action, magic, humor, and romance, this unique urban fantasy tells the story of amnestic alchemist and her quest to recover her lost past. The first book, *The Final Formula*, is free everywhere my books are sold.

Discover the Final Formula
http://beccaandre.com/books/

Lake Erie

Cleveland

Newark

Columbus

Lockbourne

Circleville

Chillicothe

Ohio River

Waverly

Portsmouth

Ohio River

The Ohio & Erie Canal

GLOSSARY

FOR THOSE WHO DID NOT grow up with the remnants of an abandoned canal in their neighborhood (the old timers still called the road into town *the towpath* when I was little), the concept of mule-pulled boats may be something completely foreign. To help clarify this world, I wanted to include a glossary of common canal terms.

The terminology used aboard a canal boat can be confusing, especially for those with some maritime knowledge. Since most canal boatmen did not come from a nautical background, their word choice was often quite different from their seafaring counterparts. Sometimes a boatman might use a nautical term, but apply it to something completely different. For example, a deadeye on a canal boat was not the same as a deadeye on a sailing vessel.

Another interesting feature was how the terminology changed whether inside or outside the boat's cabin. For example, the upper level of the boat (the roof of each cabin) was called a deck while inside the cabin it was simply the floor. A wall was a wall, not a bulkhead, yet a boatman would often call the little corner containing his bunk, his stateroom. It was this delightful mix that gave the canal system a language of its own.

Aqueduct – A bridge-like structure that carried the canal and towpath across a waterway or other obstacle.

Balance Beam – The long, wooden beams that form the top of a lock's miter gates. The length of the beams helped balance the weight of the gate and made it easier to manually open.

Boatman – A person who owned or worked aboard a canal boat. The term could refer to a man or a woman (yes, in those days, women called themselves boat*men*).

Bow – The front end of a canal boat.

Bow Cabin (Bunkhouse) – The cabin in the front of the boat where the non-family members of the crew slept.

Bowsman – A canal boat worker who secured the bowline around a snubbing post when the boat was entering a lock. This stopped the boat and kept it from slamming into the miter gates at the far end.

Bridge Plank – A wooden plank used to walk the mule team from the stable to towpath and vice versa. It was stored aboard the boat when not in use.

Catwalk – A walkway connecting the decks (or roofs) of the cabins on a three-cabin freighter. It made it easier to get around the boat when the cargo areas were full.

Deadeye – An iron bar or eyelet mounted to the roof of the bow cabin and used to secure the towline.

Doubling – The ability to use a lock as found. The water level did not need to be adjusted before steering the boat into the lock chamber.

Driver – The crewman who controlled the mule team on the towpath.

Dry Dock – A chamber built beside the canal and used for boat maintenance. Once the boat was floated in, the water could be drained, exposing the hull for repair work.

Fit a Lock – The process of preparing a lock for the boat. If the water in the lock wasn't on the same level as the boat, the water would need to be raised or lowered.

Freighter – A canal boat used to carry freight.

Guard Lock – A lock that connected the canal to the pooled water above a dam. A guard lock raised the boat to the level of the pooled water and guarded the canal below the lock from high water.

Hatch – A trapdoor in the roof of a cabin that allowed access to the cabin by means of a ladder. Hatches were used when the cargo holds were full.

Headway – A command shouted by the captain to indicated that the boat had sufficient speed to enter a lock. The towline would be detached and boat allowed to coast forward on its own.

Heelpath – The bank of the canal opposite the towpath.

Level – A section of canal between locks.

Light Boat – A canal boat with no cargo.

Lines – Ropes. The common lines on a canal boat were the towline, bow line, and stern line.

Lock – A chamber closed on each end by miter gates. Most locks on the Ohio & Erie were made of stone.

Lock Chamber – The space between the gates within a lock.

Locking Through – The process of taking a boat through a lock.

Miter Gates – The large wooden gates at either end of a lock chamber.

Paddle – A small "door" in the lower section of a miter gate that allowed water to flow in or out of the lock chamber. The door was controlled by the "paddle gear" at the top of the gate.

Rudder – A flat board hung vertically at the back of the boat and used to steer the vessel.

Snubbing Post – A heavy post embedded in the ground beside each lock. The bow line was wrapped several times around the snubbing post to bring a boat to a stop upon entering the lock chamber.

Stable Cabin – The center cabin on a three-cabin freighter that housed the mules.

Steersman – A canal boat crew member who steered the boat via a tiller mounted near the back of the boat.

Stern – The rear part of a canal boat.

Stern Cabin (Aft Cabin) – The cabin in the back of the boat. Typically where the captain and his or her family lived.

Tandem Hitching – An arrangement of towing animals hitched one behind the other.

Tiller – A horizontal handle attached to the rudder post. The tiller was used to control the rudder in order to steer the boat.

Tiller Deck – A small rail-enclosed deck behind the stern deck where the tiller was installed.

Towline – A braided rope up to 200 feet long used to hitch the mule team to the canal boat.

Towpath – The path on one side of the canal where the mule team and driver walked.

Transom – The stern end of the boat where a boat's name was painted.

ACKNOWLEDGEMENTS

It's time again to thank all folks who help me make my stories better. I'd to thank:

Lindsay Buroker, Kendra Highley, Kelly Crawley, Cindy Wilkinson, Genevieve Turcotte, and Walt Scrivens for taking the time to help me make this book the best it can be.

Shelley Holloway for her editing awesomeness.

Glendon Haddix and the team at Streetlight Graphics for the amazing cover art and formatting. (Check out my gorgeous website. They did that, too!)

And you, kind reader, for letting me entertain you. I really appreciate the reviews, comments, and emails. Thank you!

ABOUT THE AUTHOR

BECCA ANDRE LIVES IN SOUTHERN Ohio with her husband, two children, and an elderly Jack Russell Terrier. A love of science and math (yes, she's weird like that), led to a career as a chemist where she blows things up far more infrequently than you'd expect. Other interests include: chocolate, hard rock, and slaying things on the Xbox.

For more on her books, upcoming releases, and random ramblings, stop by http://beccaandre.com

Twitter: https://twitter.com/AddledAlchemist
Facebook: https://www.facebook.com/AuthorBeccaAndre

25120060R00148

Made in the USA
Columbia, SC
29 August 2018